DEADLY PAIRING

Books by Randy Shamlian

Murder in the Kitchen *series*
Deadly Recipe
Deadly Essence
Deadly Pairing

For more information
visit: www.SpeakingVolumes.us

DEADLY PAIRING

Randy Shamlian

SPEAKING VOLUMES, LLC
NAPLES, FLORIDA
2023

Deadly Pairing

ISBN 978-1-64540-846-8

Once upon a midnight dreary, while I pondered, weak and weary,

Over many a quaint and curious volume of forgotten lore—

    While I nodded, nearly napping, suddenly there came a tapping,

As of some gently rapping, rapping at my chamber door.

" 'Tis some visitor," I muttered, "tapping at my chamber door—

    Only this and nothing more."

—1st verse of "The Raven"

by Edgar Allan Poe

Deadly

    adjective

    - likely to cause death

       (plus)

Pairing

  synonyms

 - collaboration, partnership

               —Collins Dictionary

       (and/or)

Pairing

  in culinary

 - to match wines with foods

Chapter One

Doctor Bollinger, a reasonably handsome man with a PhD in clinical psychology, entered an exam room holding a chart and the results of a blood test. He stepped towards Marty, gave a glance at the woman sitting on an exam table wearing a pink medical gown and said, "Ms. Remy, why aren't you taking your clozapine on a regular basis? You know I'm legally bound to report the results to your husband's lawyer?"

"He's my ex-husband," she replied. "Give me your hand, Doctor," she requested. He complied. Marty then slipped his hand underneath her panties and pressed it against her vagina. "You feel that?" she said as the doctor's eyes grew wide. "Really get a good feel of that. You ever heard of noble rot?"

"No," the doctor said. His heart rate began to rise as he enjoyed the warmth of her moist pussy. *God, she's gorgeous*, he silently muttered as Marty slowly let go of his hand while he stared into her sparkling cobalt-blue eyes.

"The Italians call it *Muffa Nobile*. Well, in winemaking, it's when the grapes start to raisin on the vine. It's how my pussy gets when I'm on those pills. I get to the point where I can't even feel a thing down there. It's starting to shrivel up like a prune."

"Trust me, Ms. Remy. It's not," he said confidently and then handed her a pill. "Now, let me see you swallow this." He gave her a small bottle of water to chase down the pill. She reluctantly but obligingly complied. "Okay, open up your mouth so I can take a look. Lift your tongue?" the doctor commanded while absorbing the intoxicating tangerine essence that Marty always exuded. Why did he let himself fall for her trickery? Perhaps he was able to cop a feel of absolute beauty, without feeling the guilt, although he knew he was stretching the rules a bit. It was a game—and so is life.

"Doctor? I have a question for you," Marty said out of the blue.

"Yes?"

"Why is it that I have to go through a physical exam every time I am here?" Marty asked.

"A healthy mind starts with a healthy body. A balanced stasis. Besides, in your case, giving blood is a requirement each time you visit. We don't want you in your street clothes," he responded. Marty got a sense that he probably wanted her in no clothes at all. "So, are you having any other issues besides your anatomical problem, currently? No delusions of any sort?" the doctor asked.

"Like seeing ghosts from the past?" Marty quipped. "No, not lately." Marty lied a bit. She had been seeing people that she knew who for all practical purposes were dead. And not just seeing them but having full-on conversations with them. *Why stir the pot?* Why give "them" more ammunition against her? It was difficult enough to have to comply with John's demands, let alone have to answer for her mental state. *Keep the status quo.*

"I'm happy to hear that," the doctor said with some condescension as he checked Marty's lymph nodes on her neck and then under her armpits. Marty got a quick read on the inadvertent sigh from the doctor.

"Is there a problem?" Marty asked.

"None at all," the doctor whispered.

"So, are we good? Can I get dressed?"

"Only if you promise to take your prescribed medication. But yes, you may," Doctor Bollinger replied. As he was about to leave the exam room, he turned back towards Marty and asked, "How about we meet for a drink later?"

She paused. She'd known that sooner or later this would happen. How long could she play this favor game without consequences, like having to give up the goods because she was bound by the courts to be on psychotropics or lose any chance of seeing Jackie, her son, on a regular basis? It was hard enough that he was in Hawaii, and she had to travel every month to see him. Chaperoned, at that.

"I think both of us can benefit from this symbiotic relationship we have. It's been several months. Long enough to have built some trust between us," the doctor proffered.

"All's well and good. But what would your wife say?" Marty posed the question to prompt guilt, thinking the doctor might reconsider so she wouldn't have to be obligated.

"Mrs. Bollinger and I have an understanding. We can do as we please, as long as it doesn't affect our marriage."

"What if you get to the point that you can't live without me?" Marty asked because she knew how possessive a partner could get. This had happened in her past relationships.

"I know a great place. We can have some nice wine. Some good seafood. A walk along the beach," Doctor Bollinger said, trying to sound enticing.

"And a roll in the sand?" Marty said as she got up off the exam table and slid out of her gown in front of the doctor. He stepped closer toward Marty and attempted to kiss on her lips while caressing her bare behind. She quickly stepped away and said, "Relationships have to develop in time, like a good wine. Don't you agree, Doctor?"

The doctor humbly smiled and said, "I'll pick you up at seven." And then left the room.

Marty got dressed and left the office. As soon as she was outside, she stepped towards a bush, stuck her fingers down her throat and vomited.

An Asian woman with a French accent appeared out of nowhere and asked inquisitively, "Are you okay, Marty?"

Marty looked up at the woman, whom she knew immediately. "Yes, Sookie, I'm fine."

"I worry about you," Sookie said with genuine concern.

"So do I. I'm talking to a dead person," Marty said coyly as she prepared to enter her car. "Are you coming with me?"

"Where else am I going to go?" Sookie replied.

"Maybe you can go visit Lorraine."

Sookie began to cry. "I miss her so much. You know I can't. She's in prison."

"And I'm not?" Marty asked as she drove away.

"You like that doctor?"

"He's handsome. But he wants one thing. Sex," Marty complained.

"That's so bad?"

"It's not so good when I have no desire."

"That didn't stop you with Lorraine," Sookie said sulkily.

"Lorraine took advantage of me. Don't you remember? You both abducted me," Marty said with a bit of anger. "Why don't you just leave?"

"I'm sorry, Marty. I wasn't the one who seduced you," Sookie pleaded.

"No, but all that you, Lorraine, and that nutcase, Baron, did to me fucked me up. Especially Lorraine. She turned me into an opium addict. I wouldn't be here, in this situation, if it weren't for you three."

"How can I make it up to you?" Sookie asked.

"Make me better. But I don't think you can do that," Marty cried.

"I'm so sorry, my little kitten," Sookie said as she caressed Marty's shoulder and then began to fondle her breast.

"What the fuck are you doing!" Marty yelled at Sookie.

"I, I thought you needed some affection," Sookie apologetically said.

"Get out of the car, now!" Marty screamed.

Later that evening, Marty and Doctor Bollinger sat a table for two at the Ravenous Feline restaurant, overlooking the Palisades and the Pacific Ocean. It was a hotspot for seafood and meats, locally grown produce, regional wines, cocktails, and micro-brews. They even boasted their own smokehouse. The modern décor of the restaurant included a polished stainless-steel bar and tables and a huge bounty of iced seafood from Alaskan king crab legs, Maine lobsters, Pacific sea urchins to a bevy of shrimp, blue crabs, fresh clams, oysters, and mussels for all the patrons to admire and drool over.

Marty took the privilege of ordering the first bottle of wine—a 2013 Alma Tass Pinot Blanc to start the evening while they shared a small bucket of steamed oysters, shrimp, and mussels, and a toasted baguette to soak up the juices. The mineral nose and acid edginess of the wine, with its peach and apple notes, paired well with the shellfish and put a smile on Marty's face. She had begun the evening with a solemn demeanor. But Doctor Bollinger had the perfect solution in his pocket if things didn't go off so well with Marty. Her change of disposition pleased him.

The doctor raised his glass of wine and said, "Nice selection."

"It's one of my favorites. From Santa Barbara, you know," she said.

"We're so lucky to have such good wine in our backyard," the doctor responded.

"It's the new Napa of Southern California. That's why I moved here to open my business," Marty said.

"What's the name of your business, again?" the doctor asked.

"Remy Wine and Spirits. We also have a charcuterie and cheese shop connected to the store," Marty replied.

"Sounds like a substantial undertaking," the doctor said.

"I learned to appreciate good wine and good food, especially with my French grandparents. It's the reason why I chose the name 'Remy.' Besides wanting to distance myself from the past," Marty said, though she didn't want to stir up that conversation. The doctor knew better than to open a can of worms—digging up the sordid details of murder, presumed murder, and speculation.

"I'll have to come visit you there sometime," the doctor said, steering the conversation back to the moment at hand. "So, I brought some little pills that are designed to help you with your condition." He cleared his throat. "They're actually in the clinical trial phase, but I was able to get my hands on some." He paused for a second while he fished in his coat pocket for the vial of pills.

Marty was intrigued. "Please, tell me more. What are they called?"

"Amoros. They're a form of Viagra for women. They can be taken with the medication you are on with no contraindications," the doctor said. "They promote greater blood flow to the genital area—to increase sexual sensation."

"I like the sound of that," Marty said. But what she didn't realize was that—although there were no indications of this in the trials—the pills would exacerbate her burgeoning schizophrenia, especially if she didn't take the clozapine on a regular basis, which she hadn't for many weeks. Thanks in part to Doctor Bollinger, who seemed to have obvious ulterior motives.

The doctor got very serious. "Now, Marty. It's very important that if you take these pills, not to say anything to anyone. I could lose my license. Also, I need to see you weekly. Maybe even more often to check on your condition if you choose to take these pills. Do you understand?" The doctor peered into her eyes as he asked the question.

"Yes, I do," she said and put out her hand. The doctor opened the vial and dropped one of the orangish-red oval pills into her hand. Marty popped it in her mouth, chased it with the Pinot Blanc and gave a big grin.

As the evening progressed to their surf and turf entrees of Lobster Chimichurri and Red Chile Teres Major, which they shared, Marty's sexual arousal became very apparent. Her vagina awoke for the first time in many, many months, as if it were the first day of spring and the daffodils were in full bloom. The doctor noticed Marty's ear-to-ear smile grow larger, which made his penis grow large. He called to their server for the bill, paid it promptly and hurriedly left with Marty on his arm. Marty whispered in his ear, "The pill is working."

"I know," he replied as they rushed outside where they locked lips and bodies together. They shared one long wet kiss, jumped into the doctor's car and sped away from the restaurant's parking lot. Marty rubbed the doctor's penis with one hand and stimulated her clitoris with the other. Her vagina was vibrating and drenched with moisture.

"Oh my God, I'm so fucking horny," she belted out and proceeded to unzip the doctor's pants, pull out his manhood and suck him off like she never had any other man while the doctor rubbed her breasts and vagina. The doctor moaned and groaned until he climaxed. But Marty wanted more. She was able to pull down his pants far enough and suck on the good doctor's testicles with so much fervor that he had to pull to the side of the road. He maneuvered Marty so her crotch was in his face and her head on the car floor in front of him and performed cunnilingus on her. His face was soaking wet from her fluids as he licked her clitoris. She came several times—moaning at each climax.

"Let's get to a hotel," the doctor pleaded as he huffed with excitement.

Marty and the doctor entered their hotel room, flipped on the light and pulled off each other's clothes as they maneuvered towards the bed. They immediately engaged in sexual intercourse. The doctor thrust himself vigorously against Marty's firm, lush body. The two were heightened sexually as their groans sounded and their hips moved in unison for well over an hour until the doctor finally rolled off her in exhaustion. Marty, sweating profusely, got up out of bed, blew out a sigh, drew the curtains and opened the sliding glass door to a balcony that overlooked the ocean. She took in the fresh sea air, brushed back her hair and then rushed back onto the bed where she mounted the doctor in the sixty-nine position. They indulged themselves in each other's genitalia. This continued for thirty minutes or more until she noticed Sookie by the sliding glass door, peeking into the room.

Sookie waved at Marty. Marty mouthed at Sookie, "Go away."

"You two were fucking like rabbits," Sookie said in disbelief. "And I thought Lorraine was a horny woman."

Marty waved at Sookie to leave. And then Chef Didier Gaston popped his head into the room from the balcony. "Hi, Marty," he called out. "Remember me? I was your cousin's lover."

"Oh no, not you!" Sookie yelled out at Didier.

"Of all the gin joints. The *lesbienne,*" Didier moaned. And then Sookie and Didier began to argue in French. They pushed and shouted at one another.

Oh no, Marty commiserated with herself as she stopped performing on the doctor.

"Everything okay?" the doctor asked.

"Everything is fine. I just need to talk to my assistant," she said and got out of bed, grabbed her cell phone and stepped onto the balcony, closing the sliding glass door behind her. In a whisper she commanded while speaking into her phone, "You two need to get the hell out of here."

"Aren't you happy to see me?" Didier asked.

"No, Didier, I am not," Marty whispered. "Now, take Sookie and leave. I'm trying to enjoy myself."

"I see that, Marty. You are one sexy woman. It's too bad we weren't lovers. We would have made beautiful music together," Didier crooned.

Marty rolled her eyes and looked over her shoulder at the doctor who rose from the bed and headed toward the bathroom. Marty quickly hauled off and punched Didier in the nose.

In pain, Didier palmed his bleeding nostrils. "What the fuck did you do that for?" he cried.

"That's because you're being a *cachon*. I don't know what my cousin ever saw in you," Marty snapped.

"I don't know how you two are cousins. She's so sweet and you are a nasty bitch. That's twice you've broken my nose. The first time I couldn't smell the gas. And you know what happened to me?" Didier said while holding his head back to slow the flow of blood.

"You deserved it," Sookie called out.

Marty looked inside the room. The doctor was coming out of the bathroom. She pleaded, "Go, you two. Go wherever you have to go." And then Marty stepped into the room, closing the sliding door behind her.

"Get a hold of her?" the doctor asked. In the back of his mind, he sensed that something strange was going on inside Marty's head. To abruptly stop in the middle of the intense sex they were having didn't seem quite normal, even if it were a last-minute thought, unless it were a life or death matter.

Marty nodded and then pushed the doctor down on the bed, attacking him with her tongue, trying to forget Sookie and Didier. She knew it was some manifestation in her mind. First Sookie and now Didier. But where was it coming from?

Chapter Two

When Marty first arrived at Alala Holistic in Hawaii after her abduction ordeal, she was in a catatonic state. Her reality consisted of a hallucination of Dominika, her one-time lover, a dominatrix she had met in San Francisco as a senior in high school. Marty had a deep-rooted sense of this woman since it was her first sexual encounter with a person of the same gender. She fell instantly and madly in love. But, tragically, Marty murdered the woman in a jealous rage, executing her while she lay unconscious in a bath after Marty shoved her against the bath wall. The truth about Marty killing Dominika and several others had been suppressed when she was in a car accident, which had resulted in her having some head trauma.

Whether it was a ruse, since she was a person of interest in the murders of several of the chefs who were connected to the TV show she worked on as an assistant to John, her former husband, or not, she continued to suppress the memory of murdering Dominika. Her abduction by Lorraine Lacroix, who had a domineering effect upon Marty, in some deep pyscho-sexual way, flushed out Dominika in her brain as a real entity. Perhaps it was Marty's sense of guilt for murdering the woman she once had hot desire for; nonetheless, the impact on Marty of being held captive, largely as a sex slave, where Marty gave into Lorraine's every whim, further traumatized Marty and shook the core of her psychological being. And it didn't help her emotional state when Lorraine seduced Marty into indulging herself with smoking opium. Marty, who was normally strong enough to resist temptation, fell into Lorraine's trap. For Lorraine had ulterior motives and knew every trick in the book.

Psychologically, Marty was so deep in the rabbit hole that Dr. Mya Lau had to spend an inordinate amount of time with her in relation to her other patients. Although her condition could not normalize with the more holistic approach Alala Holistic and Dr. Lau espoused, the doctor did help Marty come to terms with her schizophrenia. In one of their sessions together, Dr. Lau was able to ascertain some bits of vague memory Marty had of Dominika. She asked, "Marty, when you went back to Dominika's apartment, tell me what happened?"

"I watched her place from across the street. I first saw a man leave by a cab. And then I waited a little more," Marty said.

"How were you feeling at the time?" Dr. Lau asked.

"I was very excited. I had fallen in love with this woman, and I couldn't wait to see her," Marty somberly spoke.

"What happened next?"

"I saw a woman rush out of the apartment. She looked worried. And then she quickly disappeared up the street," Marty said. But Marty had conflated the story. It was herself who had rushed out of the apartment and ran up the street after she had murdered Dominika. "I crossed the street and rang her buzzer. I waited. Rang it again and then decided to find another entrance."

"Why were you so adamant?" the doctor asked.

"Not only did I have to see her again, I felt something was not right. Especially with the woman who rushed out of the apartment," Marty said. "Should I continue?" Doctor Lau nodded with keen interest. "Well, I went around back and started to climb the fire escape. Her bedroom window was open and so I climbed in. I stopped and called out for Dominika. And then I saw her in the bathtub. I ran in there because she was underwater. I screamed out to her..."

Dr. Lau interrupted her, "Were the lights on?" She knew the basic circumstances of the incident. Specifically, Dominika was electrocuted by a stimulating device while she was in the bathtub. Presumably, the woman who left the apartment in a hurry was Dominika's former lover, who was convicted and tried for the murder and sent to prison. *So, shouldn't the circuit breakers have blown if taxed by a situation like that?* the doctor pondered. But she wasn't there to be a detective. She was there to assist Marty in getting mentally, physically and emotionally well.

"As far as I remember, she had candles lit in the rooms," Marty cleverly responded.

"What happened then?"

Tears ran from Marty's eyes as she stared at Dominika who was in Dr. Lau's office opposite her. She slowly said, "I checked for her pulse. There was none. And then I got scared and ran down the stairs. I tripped, and I think I tumbled down most of them." Marty then cried out to Dominika, "I'm sorry, Dominika."

Doctor Lau took notice. "Marty, were you apologizing to Dominika?"

"Yes," Marty said somberly.

"Why? Because you couldn't help her at that point when she was already dead?" Doctor Lau asked, knowing that if Marty had killed Dominika, acknowledging the fact could only make Marty's condition worse, because she would publicly have to bear that guilt, which she wasn't strong enough for, and because what was done was done. Better to suppress the emotion than have her go to prison for something that happened over a dozen years ago and that would ultimately destroy her soul. Besides, Marty was in her own psychological prison. That was the doctor's logic. In any case, she was obliged to notify the authorities if she discovered evidence that Marty had committed a federal crime. *Besides, Marty didn't admit to murdering Dominika.*

"Yes."

"Marty, before we stop. Because I know this has been challenging for you, I need you to understand that even though you see Dominika in the room, know that she is deceased. And even though she looks real to you, she is just a figment of your imagination. Interacting with her, albeit you would be speaking with yourself, will only make Dominika more real in your mind. It's all about playing a trick. The more you ignore Dominika, the less you will see of her. Does that sound reasonable?" Dr. Lau proffered.

Marty stared at Dominika with heartfelt emotion. It's hard to deny something or someone when it's staring you in the face. "I'll try," Marty said reluctantly.

"I need you to truly make every effort to try. This is all about healing and getting back to living your life with your husband and Jackie. They want you to be better. There are also people in your businesses who want to see you better." John had power of attorney over Marty's affairs and already was prepared to sell both The Pearl Perfumery and the restaurant she owned if Marty's condition didn't improve. It had been several months since Marty had entered Alala, and it had been taxing on John on several levels.

John ultimately sold both businesses and took Marty out of Alala. His patience had worn thin. He placed her in Maui Treatment Center, a more traditional clinic where she was immediately put on an anti-psychotic drug treatment therapy. Marty was displeased at having to leave Alala, but her condition did improve dramatically. Dominika slowly disappeared from her life, although Marty was not quite the same energetic and vibrant person she once had been. She was not a fan of synthetics, especially energy-sucking ones like the psychotropics she was prescribed daily. But that changed over time as Marty used some trickery of her own, slipping the pills underneath her tongue and smiling like the cat that swallowed the cream. When the aides continued with their rounds, she spit the pills into a potted aloe plant and then stuffed them down into the dirt. As holistic as the plants were, they succumbed to an untimely demise only to be replaced several times by John on his visits.

As Marty became more cogent and livelier over several months time, John gave Marty some unfortunate news. He presented her with divorce papers, an action that was okayed by her doctor at the treatment center, even though she was still not quite mentally well. It came as no great surprise to Marty, who had sensed John's caring but lack of affection ever since Alala. Several caveats came with the divorce papers. One— John would have full custody of Jackie. Two—visitation with Jackie would be at John's residence and would be chaperoned by someone of John's choosing. Three—visitation with Jackie would be once a month for two days, consecutively. Four—Marty would have to pay for all her own medical and psychological needs, past, present, and future. Five (and the most damning)—Marty would have to receive treatment and be tested every two weeks for proper levels of psychotropic drugs by an approved psychiatric care center. Failure to do so would result in losing all visitation rights to Jackie.

Marty knew she had no real recourse, even though she had nearly ten million dollars in the bank. She could have fought him, but she was beholden to John. He held her future in his hand. At the stroke of a pen, he could have made her a prisoner of psychiatric care for the rest of her life. He was still legally her husband. And she was still deemed mentally unfit by her doctor. If she complied, at least, she could share in Jackie's life when she got better. She could see him grow up. Share whatever love she could with him. Or, be a mother in absentia. When Jackie turned of legal age, would he want any part of her? She couldn't take that risk. She must acquiesce to John's demands, for life is a compromise, she realized. Besides, John was straight out of Brooklyn, New York, and knew how to get what he wanted.

Marty ultimately signed the papers after she was deemed mentally stable enough by her doctor. She had yet to see Jackie in all the time she had been receiving care at Alala and the Maui Treatment Center. That would come in time. First, she would have to work on being deemed mentally fit and getting released on her recognizance from the current *prison term*, as she called it. That did happen after three more months of treatment. She had decided to stay in Maui, so she could see Jackie, whom she hadn't seen in almost a year since she went on her ill-fated trip to Nice, France. Why she had to go there still plagued her mind. But, deep down, she knew. She had to exorcize the demons of Dominika that were creeping into her thoughts.

Marty was looking especially fit when she had her visit with Jackie. She had a golden tan, had let her raven-black hair grow to shoulder length, went to yoga classes regularly, replaced the ridiculous gold tooth that she had mistakenly gotten in Marseille because of a language barrier, and was dressed in a blue silk summer dress that stunned all who had a chance to see her, even John, who was taken aback. *She still has it, but something is amiss with her mind,* John said to himself. He just hoped that Jackie didn't have that bad something in his brain. Marty was a little nervous. *What if Jackie rejects me? Maybe John poisoned his mind.* But that was the fear any parent has when she sees her child for the first time after a divorce has occurred and considerable time has elapsed. Jackie had grown several inches and filled out. His hair was rusty-red, and his big blue eyes beamed at her when he entered the room with Jacqueline, his nanny. But she was more than a nanny. She was now John's soon-to-be wife. Marty sensed that after observing a large diamond engagement ring on her hand, the way she was formally dressed and the way she looked at John. She knew the look he used to give her.

Jackie was shy at first. Marty met Jacqueline's eyes. She said in her French accent, "Hello, Marty. I'm happy to see you. It's been too long."

"Hello, Jacqueline. I'm happy to see you too," Marty said as they hugged. And then Marty bent down to hug Jackie. Jackie grabbed hold of Jacqueline's leg as he pulled away from Marty.

"Jackie, it's your mommy. Don't you remember me?" Marty pleaded.

"It will take a little time," Jacqueline said.

"He's gotten so big and handsome. You have been with him ever since I was gone?" Marty asked.

"She has. Marty, I want to tell you something. Jacqueline and I are getting married. I hope you approve for Jackie's sake?" John said almost condescendingly. But more to appease Marty's sensibilities.

"Of course, I do," Marty said and smiled at Jacqueline. Although she felt a certain betrayal, how could she fault her? John was still vital, he had his good looks, and he was financially solid, especially after selling his shares in the family pepper business. *She must have provided him comfort when I was locked up in the prison,* she whined to herself. *Yeah, and she slept with him in our bed.*

"Let's go on the patio. The cook prepared us some food," John said and escorted his ex-wife, his new wife-to-be and their son out back.

Lunch consisted of octopus poke, grilled teriyaki mahi-mahi, pineapple, purple potato and Maui onion salad, and iced tea. It was tasty and pleasant. *But where is the wine?* Marty asked herself. *What happened to John? He loved his wine. What is good food without wine to pair it with?* And that was the answer to the question she asked herself—what now since both her businesses had been sold from underneath her? *Thanks, John.* What was she to do? Where were the best vineyards and the best wines close enough to Hawaii that she could hop on a plane and visit

Jackie? Had she lost him for good? He didn't respond to her at all during lunch. But it was her own fault for running off to France. *Maybe he'll warm up to me at some point*, she hoped. So, California. Santa Barbara, to be exact, was the new wine hotspot. And that's where she would live and set up a boutique wine and spirits store where she could sell charcuterie and cheeses. Why not? She had the resources, the vision and most of all the interest in wines to make it successful. Hopefully, John would have no qualms with her plan. He didn't. In fact, he encouraged her. Better she was far enough away that if she had to exorcize her demons, he wouldn't have to deal with it directly. But first, she would change her last name to her maiden name—to Remy. Martina Remy, after her grandfather, Martin Remy, was the legal name she would take to get a fresh start. *But I like Marty Remy better*, she smiled to herself as she said goodbye to John, Jacqueline and Jackie. "I'll see you in a month, okay, Jackie?" Marty said in a child-like voice to Jackie. She blew him a kiss and then curtly smiled at John and Jacqueline as she thought, *The little bitch. While the cat was away.*

Chapter Three

Marty sat at her cluttered desk full of wine and liquor invoices going over the latest inventory sheets. There were several boxes of wines on the floor that needed to be returned. Unopened sample bottles of exotic liquors, as well as bottles of the latest wine releases, stood on shelves. She devoured an avocado, Havarti cheese and sprout sandwich on some gluten-free rice bread as she punched numbers into the computer. She had purchased the sandwich down the street. It was one of those upscale health food places that also offer wine that seemed to be everywhere in Santa Barbara. The sandwich was tasty and healthy enough, regardless of the dryness of the bread. She could have had a sandwich made from her charcuterie, but she wanted a change of pace. And it's always good to check on your competition, she felt.

Marty had the radio on to her favorite public broadcasting station, a show she religiously listened to every Friday afternoon. Even though the narrator seemed lethargic and dusty most of the time, she was amusing and informative. It excited Marty because she had found a new muse to occupy her life—wine. It was something she had grown up with, mostly from the traditions of her French grandparents who lived their lives around it. It was central to their culture. She was tickled, as she was when she had her perfumery, The Pearl. Maybe one day she would have her own vineyard so she could grow her own grapes and create her own vintages. After all, she had a chemistry background. She could easily do it, she thought. But now it was time to listen to her radio show. She turned up the volume.

The show opened to Beethoven's *Bagatelle No. 25 in A Minor* and slowly faded as the narrator came on. "This is Wine Chat with your one and only, Dorothy Lanore, coming to you live from the Cliff House just above the rocky shores overlooking the grand Pacific Ocean," Dorothy said in a drawn-out somber voice with the clatter of china and the hustle of a midday restaurant in the background. "It's such a lovely California day. It makes me feel so spry," she continued. "And I'm no spring chicken," she said, mimicking Mae West. "Speaking of Mae West, I had an opportunity this week to saunter downstate to Santa Barbara and visit Remy Wine and Spirits." Marty quickly stopped what she was doing, put her sandwich down and turned the volume higher.

"Mae West, as some of you may know, said the famous line, 'Is that a gun in your pocket, or are you just glad to see me?' in the 1933 film, *She Done Him Wrong*. Well, let me tell you. I think the proprietor of Remy Wine and Spirits done me wrong," Dorothy Lanore said as Marty's jaw dropped. "Upon entering the store, I was hit with a waft of sausage meat and cheese that were certainly past their prime. I was forced to take a look at where the odd smell was coming from. Right in the middle of the store was this deli case. It looked interesting enough with a variety of cheeses, dried salamis, salumis, and some other prepared products. I sampled some. Okay, maybe I overreacted. After tasting the locally made North Valley prosciutto, I decided to purchase a half pound at $24.99 a pound. And then I decided to purchase a half pound of the San Jacinto Wild Boar Salami at $26.99 a pound. I said to myself, *Why not?* Of course, I needed some cheese to go along with the meats and it was suggested I try the Misty Gardens Chevre at $20.99 a pound. I like cheese, so I ordered a pound. I also ordered a pint of some appetizing olive salad. All well and good. Then, I needed wine to go with the little goodies. Of course," Dorothy Lanore said, emphasizing *Of course*. "And now, it's time to acknowledge our sponsors."

Marty lowered the volume on the radio. She was unsure whether the broadcast was a hit on her, but there was more to come. The final punch. But to that point, it wasn't all that bad. Yet all the innuendo, particularly with the *She Done Me Wrong* bit, troubled Marty. She turned up the radio again. A music interlude opened the next segment. "Hello, my little chickadees. I'm back," Dorothy Lanore said in a spirited voice. This was a woman who truly loved wine, to the point where she consumed three to four bottles a day. Some said she was a bit of a lush. That was quite the understatement. In fact, she encouraged her listeners to send her bottles of wine so she could critique the wine. Not so. She just wanted them for her personal consumption.

"A little reminder, November twelfth through the fifteenth I will be at the Regency Hotel at the Embarcadero in Downtown San Francisco for the California Grand Sommelier Competition where I will be signing my new book, *My View of the World as Seen Through a Wine Glass*. Don't forget that's November twelfth through the fifteenth at the Embarcadero in downtown San Francisco. Be there or you'll miss out on some great fun. And don't forget to send in your favorite wines. You know that's one of my favorite tasks on the show—to sample and critique. And remember, previous episodes of the show can be played on our website on the world wide web at 'w' 'w' "w' dot winechat dot com. That's 'w' 'w' 'w' dot winechat dot com," she said in a drawn-out fashion.

Marty wrote down the information on a piece of paper. She had heard about the California Grand Sommelier Competition before and was interested in participating in the event. It meant lots of studying, training of the palate and trying plenty of wine from all over the world. It was a prestigious accolade if you were one of the top contestants. In fact, it could draw plenty of attention to her store if she did well. But it was a time-consuming, focused process. One that she hoped she could muster up the energy for, given that she was on the damned psychotropics, which played with her mental acuity. She had to manipulate the process somehow. Maybe even connive Doctor Bollinger. Whatever it would take. (This all occurred before her sexual encounter with him, still a week away.)

"Back to my little story of *She Done Me Wrong* at the Remy Wine and Spirits in Santa Barbara," Dorothy Lanore said with tongue in cheek. Marty rolled her eyes in disgust. "I needed some wine. Don't we all? So, I asked one of the sales associates, a young, attractive woman who was quite nice but a little snooty, to recommend several bottles to pair with the meats and cheese I had just gotten from the deli. Well, after ten minutes of one suggestion after another, I settled on one red and one white. They were both from Santa Barbara County. Apropos. But I'm sure she was getting some kickback on the sale. Nepotism, you have to admire it. The red was a Happy Canyon Pinot Noir, and the white was a Santa Ynez Vineyard Chardonnay. It was time to check out. Well, let me tell you. It felt like I was held at gunpoint because the total sale for my little shopping spree came to one hundred fifty-five dollars and twelve cents including tax. My heart began to palpitate at such extravagance.

"But this is not the end of the story. As I got to my car, the marinade from the olive salad somehow seeped through the flimsy paper bag I was given by Remy Wine and Spirits. The two bottles of wine slipped out of the bag straight onto the concrete and broke open. *Mercy,* I cried. I gathered up all the contents as best I could. Stormed back into the store and demanded a refund. The best they offered was a credit to the store for the full amount. *I want to speak with the proprietor*, I said to the sales associate. *She's not here today. Perhaps you can come back tomorrow*, she responded. *Perhaps I'll call the police*, I screamed. *Sorry, ma'am*, she kept saying with a condescending smile. Well, in all my years in dealing with wine merchants, I've never experienced such inexcusable treatment. Ms. Remy Wine and Spirits, you done me wrong. Confess to the *mea culpa*."

Marty turned off the radio, went onto her laptop computer and plugged in 'winechat.com' into the search engine. When the Wine Chat website displayed, Marty scrolled to the photograph of Dorothy Lanore. She began to laugh. Dorothy Lanore was a woman in her late sixties with orange-red hair, wearing hideous blue eye makeup that went up to her forehead. Marty then went toward the storefront and approached Tina, the sales associates she presumed was the one who assisted Dorothy Lanore, based on the description she gave. "Tina, did you have an issue with a customer last Saturday, an older lady with reddish hair?" Marty asked.

"Yes, she came in the store and bought some charcuterie and wine. But before she checked out, she started to sample the wines we had on special and then she began to eat the olives she picked up from the charcuterie. She must have not closed the lid on the salad, and it leaked through the bag and the wine must have slipped out. She wanted a refund on a hundred-and-fifty-dollar purchase. I offered her a credit since she was clearly at fault," Tina said.

"You know who that was?" Marty asked.

"Not really, she used cash."

"That was Dorothy Lanore from Wine Chat, and she just ripped us apart."

"So, that was Lanore the bore? I'm sorry, Marty. I didn't know. Can I make it up to you somehow?" Tina was concerned.

"Don't worry about it," Marty said in frustration, yet attempting to appease Tina, her most trusted associate whom she admired very much.

"She looked like a barfly. I'm really sorry," Tina continued.

"No, you did the right thing," Marty said. "Maybe I'll send the haggard twat some wine."

Tina smirked at Marty's remark. It was the first time since she started working here that she felt that Marty let her hair down and that she had connected with her boss. She had never heard Marty use descriptive language like that. Feeling the connection, she asked, "Marty, would you like to take one of my yoga classes?"

"I'd like to, but I'm going to be busy studying for the California Grand Sommelier Competition," Marty said.

"Oh?" Tina said with a tinge of jealousy. She was one of those persons who have to conquer the world with every breath they take. Not only was she working for Marty, she had yoga classes she taught, she was working on an advanced degree in Viticulture and Enology at Santa Barbara College, and she was quietly developing wines at her family's vinegar orchard. "When did you decide to do that?" Tina asked.

"A few minutes ago," Marty responded, surprising herself. Like Tina, Marty was motivated, if not competitive. "I just need to find the extra time and energy," Marty confessed.

"You know, if you took a few of my yoga classes a week, you would find that energy you're looking for," Tina boasted.

Less than a hundred miles southwest of Marty, Paul Cooz, now a private investigator after retiring as a detective from the Los Feliz Police Department, was on a dirt bike trail in Laurel Canyon. He stopped on his bike underneath a tall shady eucalyptus tree to ponder the comments from Dorothy Lanore of Wine Chat about Remy Wine and Spirits. He leaned his bike up against the tree, pulled some earplugs from his ears and grabbed a water bottle from a saddle strapped to his back. He took a swig and then reflected on coincidence. It was the name "Remy" that flashed through his mind. He knew the name. But how could he forget the connection between Marty Kittering and Remy Pharmaceuticals? He had lost track of Marty shortly after he had confronted her back in Maui when he was on his honeymoon. And that commotion in Europe with the

French chef who accidentally blew himself up. That was several years ago.

Marty had a way of drawing attention to herself, he felt. It was more than just her provocative looks. She had a sex appeal that drew people toward her and made them act capriciously. Or perhaps it was she who acted in a way contrary to social norms? Of course, it was. He had found proof that linked her to the murder of Professor Johnson when he broke into her perfume store. But, why did he walk away from that so suddenly? And, although Raveneitzkya Fukovneyev was convicted of gruesomely barbecuing Chef Bubba Arnet, she might have had the means and opportunity, but she lacked a plausible motive other than trying to discredit her ex-husband and producer of the show Bubba Arnet starred in. The question to this day remained: who took the photos of her and Bubba Arnet in sexual intercourse the night of his murder? Why had that not persuaded the jury in Raveneitzkya's defense? He'd never know.

Cooz replaced the water bottle, put his earplugs in and rode away, deciding that he would take a ride up to Santa Barbara to visit Remy Wine and Spirits out of curiosity. He thought of Evie Ann as he rode past a laurel tree and the wild sex they had on *psilocybin* mushrooms. Oh, how he missed her! The mistakes that one makes in life, like believing she conspired with Marty to kill Chef Matt Cumatos. Not his finest moment. And, of course, his flawed marriage to Janet that ended in divorce only months after their union. He had much more in common with Evie Ann than he had with Janet, who had a tighter body and longer legs, yet lacked any true conviction of love and empathy towards him. Evie Ann had a spirit and an ass unmatched by any other woman he had known. How Evie Ann and Marty had paired up as friends and partners in a restaurant business made him wonder.

Chapter Four

Paul Cooz stepped inside Remy Wine and Spirits and glanced about, like a true detective. When it's in your blood, it's hard to change your ways. He passed Tina and gave her a curt smile. She asked, "Can I help you find something?"

"Yes, I'm having grilled salmon. What do you recommend?" he asked. It was the furthest from the truth, but it did sound good.

"Californian?"

"Certainly," Cooz said.

"Okay, follow me," she commanded and led him towards the white wine section. She pulled a bottle from the shelf. "This is an oak-aged Chardonnay. Works perfectly with grilled salmon. It's buttery. Not as ripe, so it has some lemon and green apple flavors."

"I'm going to serve it with a pineapple and red pepper salsa," Cooz said, knowing that the wine she showed him wasn't quite the right pairing.

She replaced the bottle and grabbed another wine—a Santa Barbara wine she knew well. The vineyard was a neighbor to her family's own vineyard. "This one is very ripe. Has prominent pineapple flavors. I think you'll like it very much," she said.

"Okay. So, ah, are you the owner?" Cooz asked.

"Oh, no. I'm just one of the associates."

"Is the owner here?"

"She's not here today. She's studying for a sommelier competition. Is there something I can help you with?" Tina asked inquisitively.

"To tell you the truth, I'm an old friend of her family. Well, I wasn't quite sure if she was the same Remy. Her name used to be Kittering. Marty Kittering."

"Well, Marty Remy is the owner. Not sure if they're the same person," she said, feeling a little unsure of Cooz's intentions.

"She have dark hair? Sparkling blue eyes?" Cooz asked, sounding too much like a detective.

"Yes. If you would like to leave your name and number, I'll make sure she gets it." Tina felt a bit protective as she directed Cooz towards the cashier.

"I'll stop in some other time. Thank you for your help," Cooz said, softening his approach as he put his hand out to shake. "Paul Cooz."

"Tina St. Clair. Thank you for coming in," she said as she shook his hand and politely smiled.

"My pleasure, Tina," Cooz said while he handed her his credit card.

Marty was doing just what Tina had said she was at home in her condo that overlooked the Pacific Ocean. She was going over the world wine regions and having some difficulty focusing her concentration. She knew it was the effects of the clozapine. What she really needed was a good dose of Amoros. Not only would that clear her head, it would energize her focus, as well as charge up her libido. She sent a text to Dr. Bollinger and asked him to see her at her place—as soon as possible. He responded that he'd be there in a couple of hours. That excited her. But this time she'd try to convince him to leave her with some extra Amoros. How could she do that? Maybe she could explain how it helped her to focus. But what about the sexual side effects? She would have to show her gratitude—she would have to be at her most libidinous so he would be so grateful he couldn't refuse her request. Or maybe she could steal some pills.

Marty went back to reviewing the wine regions. She had a good grasp of the seven regions of France. She grew up with it. Her grandparents were from Provence, and she had visited there many times as a youth. Europe would be a quick study. Most of the rest of the world would be a daunting task—more than 6,000 regions in all. There were not just the regions to learn, there were the subregions and every variety of grape grown in those regions. Let alone getting to know the nuances of each variety and how to recognize those nuances with your olfactory sense—your smell ability. "Oh my, what have I gotten myself into?" she asked herself out loud. But she was used to challenges. And she was a competitor. This was for her own self-worth. So she justified the arduous task that lay in front of her. She took a quick look at her watch and headed for the shower.

As Marty was drying herself off in her bedroom, she heard a gravelly male voice with a distinct southern twang coming from the living room. "Hello, Marty. Are you in there?" he called out.

Marty was startled and held her towel up over her torso as she turned and yelled out, "Who the fuck?"

When the man appeared in the doorway, he cooed, "Ou wee, look at those ham hocks. Marty, it's me, Chef Bubba," he said excitedly.

"Oh, my God, it can't be you?" Marty cried out as she looked at Chef Bubba who was in the condition she last saw him—fully barbe-cued. "Why are you here?" she asked.

"I'm here to help you," he said.

"With what?" Marty grasped at the reality of the situation.

"With your studies. I know wine. Shit!" he boasted.

"I don't need your fucking help!" she yelled.

"Now, is that the way to treat your ol' buddy?" he asked.

"You need to leave. I have company coming over," Marty said.

"Then, how 'bouts I come back later? Just you and me. Like old times," Chef Bubba crooned.

"No," she almost whispered.

"Is that little piglet, Boo, right next to you? Come here little piglet. I wants me some ribs," Chef Bubba said while licking his lips. He stepped into the room towards Boo, who went squealing past Chef Bubba straight into the living room. "I'll catch you later, darlin'," he said and then chased after Boo.

Marty looked up towards the ceiling and moaned, "Why him, O Lord?"

Marty cleaned up nice and pretty. She gave herself a quick trim down below, spritzed her body with her favorite tangerine-scented perfume and even glossed her lips to set the mood. She then dressed in her most exotic cream-colored lingerie. She knew this was all for show. The sex with the good doctor was invigorating, yet mediocre at best. But her mind was set on one thing. Well, two things that were pertinent. Remain in good standing regarding the conditions set forth by John as far as her dosage levels of clozapine, albeit she only took half of what was prescribed. And two, get herself a supply of Amoros. So, the question was, either she got him lathered up, metaphorically speaking, and gave him the best sex he'd ever had and then explained to him her need to have the Amoros beyond their sexual encounters so she could focus better. Or? Give him the best sex he'd ever had and, when he wasn't looking, take a few pills.

Marty opted for the latter. She knew if she tipped her hat, she would expose a vulnerability that Doctor Bollinger could exploit. Besides, he was getting what he wanted and then some, even at some risk of losing his license. But he knew that Marty's desire for sex and mental clarity had lessened his risk of being exposed, lest she lose the opportunity he was providing. As long as he monitored the situation, they both were getting what they wanted. Except Marty wanted a little more. Ergo, she had to give a little more in terms of sensuality and sexual gratification. That was the tradeoff.

A knock came at her door. Marty opened it. Doctor Bollinger was standing there with a smile on his face as he looked at Marty. "So, I guess you're happy to see me?" Marty said and then pursed her lips. He planted a big wet kiss on her mouth while they maneuvered themselves inside, closing the door behind them.

Outside across the street sat Paul Cooz, watching their every move through binoculars. He then observed the curtains of the balcony sliding-glass doors close. He waited a few minutes and then stepped out of his car and walked past Doctor Bollinger's car, took a quick photo with his cell phone of the car's license plate number and walked down the street, slightly out of view of Marty's condo. He made a phone call, went back to his car and waited. Fifteen minutes later, he received a text from a detective of Los Feliz Police Department stating that the car belonged to a Steve Bollinger, PhD. A shrink. Gave his address and a closing message: Good luck!

Inside the condo, Marty and the doctor wasted no time. He gave her an Amoros pill from a vial that he slipped back in his coat pocket and proceeded to undress. Marty went to her knees, caressed his penis and then took his testicles in her mouth. She manipulated her tongue and lips with precision and deftness so that the doctor moaned in delight. Marty happened to look over to her side and saw Sookie in the nude, bent over, with Didier attempting to fuck her from behind. He was riding her as if she were a bucking bronco. Didier quipped, "Yee-haw, Marty!" And then he stuck his tongue out and flicked it up and down, mimicking her own actions. Marty ignored Didier and began to stroke the doctor's penis with her hand until he ejaculated. The doctor fell back on the bed. Marty then straddled him and bounced up and down on his groin. She wanted to make sure he was completely satisfied. He was. He was smiling as he groaned.

A half hour later, they finished their session. The doctor lay exhausted but elated next to her. He slowly got up and went into the bathroom. Marty quickly jumped out of bed, slipped her hands into the doctor's coat pocket, retrieved the Amoros vial, pulled out three pills, shoved them in a dresser drawer and slipped back into bed. The doctor returned from the bathroom and began to dress. "That Amoros is really starting to work. I mean, you were incredible. Wow," the doctor said.

"I guess so. You weren't half bad yourself," she said, ingratiating herself with the doctor.

"Sorry, I have to leave. What about tomorrow?" he asked, wanting more of her.

"I can't. I have a meeting with my realtor, and I'm going to be studying most of the day," she said.

"School work?" the doctor asked, a bit disappointed.

"It's for the California Grand Sommelier Challenge. There's so much to know. How about next week?" Marty suggested.

The doctor kissed her neck and said, "I don't know if I can wait that long." And then proceeded towards the door. Marty followed him and stood by the threshold as he opened the door. He kissed her on the lips and left. Marty looked out towards the street. She realized she was totally nude and caught a shining glimmer across the street from inside a car but could not make out what it was. She closed the door. She stepped towards the balcony doors and peeked through the curtain towards Paul Cooz's car, which was taking off down the road. She saw Cooz and got a twinge of anxiety. She tried to shake it off when she saw Didier and Sookie rolling together on the floor. "Jesus. I thought you two hated each other?" Marty called out to them. Sookie punched Didier in the head and then kneed him in the groin. Didier painfully moaned.

"I hate this asshole. He tried humping me," Sookie cried out.

"You loved it," Didier crooned.

"*Cachon!*" Sookie yelled.

"That's it with you two. If you can't get along, you'll have to leave," Marty chastised.

Didier looked up at Marty and said, "My god, Marty. You look so fucking hot."

"Well, you're not getting any," Marty said and hopped in the shower while thinking about Detective Paul Cooz visiting her in the hospital after her car accident. *That wasn't him,* she said to herself, trying to ease the anxiety welling up in her stomach and chest as her clitoris ached for pleasure. She needed a release. A cold shower would have to do for the moment. And then she remembered Tina's yoga class.

Marty stepped out of the shower, toweled herself off and gave a long look at herself in the mirror. Her breasts were still pert even after giving birth to Jackie. Her stomach was smooth, no real flab. She turned to the side to look at her rear end. Felt no dimples or extra fat, although she had filled out some in her thighs. Out of nowhere, Chef Bubba appeared in the mirror next to her. "You got the finest ham hocks this side of the Mississippi," he said. "Um, um...yes, you do."

"Not now, Chef Bubba. I don't have time to entertain you," Marty said as she began to apply some light makeup.

"Another gentlemen caller?" Chef Bubba inquired.

"No, yoga class, if you must know," she responded.

"You mind if I join in?" Chef Bubba asked.

"You're in no condition for the rigors of such a workout," she said. "You'd fall apart."

"Well, I'll just have to wait till you get home. We have to work on your wine studies," he said and slowly disappeared.

"See you later. Much later," Marty said as she left the bathroom. "What do you know about wine anyway? You're a BBQ chef."

Chapter Five

Tina's yoga class had ended. Most everyone was leaving. A gal put her hands in a prayer motion as she passed Tina who drank from a water bottle. Tina smiled with her eyes and then softly said, "Namaste."

Misty, a tall, athletic woman in her early forties with a golden tan and hair to match, called out in a prominent Australian accent to Tina and whoever was listening, "Who's up for some Yum Yums?"

At that same moment, Tina asked Marty, who was about to leave, "You have a minute?" And then responded to Misty, "I'll meet you guys over there."

"Great," Misty said.

Marty stood by Tina and watched Misty, another woman named Rhonda, and Gallagher, a tall, athletically lean man in his early forties with blond wavy hair, exit the classroom.

"Did you enjoy the class?" Tina asked Marty.

"Yeah, it was really good. I'm glad I came."

"Me too. Marty, a guy came in the store today. He asked for you and said he was a friend of the family. He reminded me of a cop."

"What was his name?" Marty asked, but knew who it was right away—Paul Cooz. *What was he sniffing around for?* she wondered.

"Paul Koontz. If I can remember correctly," Tina said.

"Probably my ex-husband hired somebody to keep an eye on me. If he comes in again, just let me know," Marty said.

"Okay."

But Marty sensed that there was something more to it. And then asked, "You mind if I tag along? I could use some sushi."

"Yeah, sure. These guys are a lot of fun. You'll like them," Tina said. But in the back of her mind, she was curious—maybe concerned about Marty's past. Yet she liked Marty a lot—she admired her in many ways. In fact, she had an attraction toward her. Something that was there from the time she interviewed for the sales associate position. She would find herself thinking about Marty all too often. She was getting excited about the evening and forgot about the Paul Cooz situation.

Yum Yum's Nihon was a hot spot in Santa Barbara, not just for sushi. It was a great gathering place, especially for local wines. The interior floors were made of planked blond wood. The walls were mostly slate tiles. The bar was long, made of polished rough-cut oak. There was just enough recessed lighting and greenery to create an eloquent Japanese atmosphere. But it was the contemporary jazz piped through the restaurant speakers that set the mood for the clientele, along with the attentive service. Misty, Rhonda, and Gallagher were already inside seated at a high table sipping on wine—a Bien Navarro Pinot Blanc from vineyards only twenty miles from where they were sitting when Marty and Tina walked in.

"Girls," Misty called out to Marty and Tina, who proceeded to the table.

"This is my boss and friend, Marty," Tina said to the three at the table.

"Hi Marty, I'm Misty, and this is Rhonda," Misty said as she hand-gestured to the gal. "And this is..." Misty was interrupted.

"...I'm Gallagher, the ex-husband," he said.

"Hi, everyone," Marty said as she waved her hand and made eye contact with the three while she and Tina took a seat. "So, what's everybody drinking tonight?"

"It's a lovely Pinot Blanc," Misty said as she gestured for the server. "Here, try mine?" Misty said to Marty as she handed Marty her glass.

33

Marty swirled the glass, sniffed and said, "Orange skin and pecan wood. That's nice." And then she sipped from the glass. Her eyes grew wide.

"Pith of mandarin and lemon rind. Right? Toasty croissant," Gallagher said with enthusiasm.

"You're good," Marty responded as she handed the glass back to Misty. Misty then held it up to the server and raised two fingers.

"He's really got it going on," Tina said. "Gallagher is the Robert Parker of Santa Barbara."

"Just a little hobby," Gallagher said shyly.

"He's so condescendingly humble." Misty sounded less snide than truthful. "He's going to win that California Grand Sommelier Competition. That's how good he is," Misty said.

"That's great," Marty said as she feigned intimidation with a slight chuckle.

"Marty's also entering the competition," Tina said with some pride.

"Oh?" Misty responded with keen interest. "Maybe you two can challenge each other?" she prompted Gallagher.

"For sure," Gallagher said. "Would you be up for that, Marty?"

"Yes, I need all the help I can get. Running a wine store is one thing. Acquiring the knowledge of a PhD is another," Marty said.

Misty put her arm over Gallagher's shoulder and said, "He's your man, then. But you'll never know as much as he does."

"What is it that you do?" Marty asked him.

"I'm a wine rep for Northern."

"You should stop in my store sometime and we can set something up," Marty suggested.

Gallagher scratched his face nervously and said, "For sure." He felt a little bashful because he found himself attracted to Marty. Marty didn't have the same feeling. She had this sudden twinge in her shoulder, which she rubbed.

Misty instinctively leaned over and began to massage Marty's shoulder. "Force of habit, I'm a massage therapist. That's what happens to old surfers. We don't die, we just become therapists," Misty remarked.

"Oh, thanks. Must be all those new moves tonight," Marty said. "So, you're a surfer, Misty?" Marty asked.

Misty looked over at Tina and then said with a hint of tongue-in-cheek, "I was the women's world champion, twice."

"You have a lot of ocean down under. That's a big playground," Marty responded.

"That's how we met," Gallagher interjected.

"In the ocean?" Marty quipped.

"You could say that. We met in Honeymoon Bay at a surfing event we were both competing in," Gallagher said.

"That's so romantic," Tina said. "I always love that story."

The server came back to the table with the Pinot Blancs and then asked, "Have you decided what you would like to start out with tonight?"

"More wine," Rhonda said smartly. "All this talk of romance has got me thirsty."

"Agreed," Misty said, concurring.

"I think the tempura crab claws would work perfectly with this wine," Marty said as she held up her glass. "Here's to romance."

Tina blushed.

As the evening wound down, everybody got up to leave. Misty asked Marty, "How's that shoulder of yours?"

Marty leaned her head over into her shoulder and replied, "I could use a massage."

"Would you like one now? I have time," Misty asked.

"Yes, I would," Marty replied.

"Follow me, then," Misty said and gave her goodbyes to everyone.

"Nice meeting you two," Marty said to Rhonda and Gallagher. "See you tomorrow, Tina," Marty said and followed Misty.

"Bye, Marty," Tina said, wishing it were she that was leaving with Marty—sharing space with her that evening had excited her.

After a two-block walk, Misty and Marty entered her massage spa. It was after hours, so no one was there. Misty turned on the lights and walked Marty into a private room. "You can undress. There's a towel over there to drape yourself," Misty said and turned on some whale ambient music. Marty slowly undressed. Misty also undressed. Marty looked over at the naked Misty. She was tall, lean and taut, in incredible shape and tanned, except for a five-inch, half-moon shaped chunk missing from the right side of her right calf.

"Oh, my God," Marty called out when she realized what she had just looked at.

"Don't worry, it was only a little shark bite," Misty said as she got dressed in some loose-fitting shorts and a tank top and put her hair in a bun.

"I'm sorry, I didn't mean to stare at you," Marty said apologetically as she lay on the massage table fully naked.

"I'm used to it. But I usually go to the beach later in the day. To avoid the lookie-loos," Misty said as she lotioned her hands and got right into massaging Marty's upper back and neck.

"You got bit by a shark!" Marty said as she tried to absorb the reality.

"You don't realize there are a lot of sharks out there," Misty said.

"Didn't a kayaker get attacked last week?"

"Yeah, right off of More Mesa Beach. He lost his leg," Misty said. "You really have to be careful. And there's my favorite spot, Surf Beach. Two surfers were killed there by Great Whites in the past few years."

"And you still surf there? I'll remember that the next time I go in the water."

"Just make sure you're not on your period," Misty offered a word of advice.

"Umm," Marty murmured.

The massage was invigorating and soothing at the same time. Misty had strong but gentle hands, which got Marty a little excited when Misty began to rub the backs of her thighs. She began to breathe a little heavier. But it was more than just the massage. It was the Amoros. It was Angela Jordan, the deceased actress, sitting in a chair with just a sheer smock on while Stan Kravitz, the deceased producer, performed cunnilingus on her. Marty couldn't believe her eyes. She started to pant.

"Are we all right, Marty?" Misty asked.

"I'm sorry. Can I turn over?" Marty said as she turned over on the table. Marty then squeezed her thighs together. Misty had seen this before when her clients got aroused. But with Marty, it was pretty intense. "Misty, can you do me a favor? Can you rub my vagina? I can't help myself. I'll pay you extra," Marty pleaded.

"Marty, I don't normally do that sort of thing," Misty said.

"Please, Misty? I have a condition that needs attention. Give me your hand, I'll show you what to do," Marty demanded.

"I know what a vagina is," Misty said and then obliged, slowly rubbing the outside of Marty's crotch.

"Oh, Misty, that feels so good," Marty moaned. "Put your fingers inside. Rub my clitoris," Marty begged.

"Marty?" Misty resisted.

"Oh please, please," Marty cried out.

"When was the last time you had sex?" Misty asked.

"Four hours ago," Marty moaned as Misty relented and gave in to rubbing Marty's clitoris.

"You need a vibrator, young lady. And don't ask me to go down on you," Misty said, sounding like a reluctant spouse.

"Oh, Misty. I'll give you three hundred dollars if you do. Five hundred," Marty panted.

"No! This is not some cheap massage parlor in downtown L.A.," Misty said and then abruptly stopped massaging Marty.

Marty continued to rub her clitoris until she came.

"Are you finished now?" Misty asked as she handed Marty a towel.

Marty huffed and then wiped herself down below. "That's really what I needed," Marty said with a sigh of relief.

"Good. I'm glad," Misty said sarcastically.

Marty quickly dressed, gave Misty three one-hundred-dollar bills, smiled and then left the spa.

"Don't worry, Marty, I won't say a word," Misty said to herself and then texted Tina.

Chapter Six

Marty arrived at work where Tina eagerly awaited her. Ever since she had received the text from Misty, Tina had begun to imagine getting together with Marty. She let herself run wild with fantasy. It was part physical attraction, part adoration for her boss. She saw Marty as the successful entrepreneur she herself aspired to become. In large part, it was the mystery behind Marty that intrigued her most. And yet there was an element of fear that accompanied her emotions toward Marty, like watching a thriller knowing something suspenseful was about to happen.

"Hello, Tina. Everything all right?" Marty asked.

"Hi. Everything's good. How was your massage last night with Misty?"

"Great. She knows what she's doing," Marty replied in hopes that the conversation about the massage would be a quick one.

"Yeah, she's talented. Marty, I was thinking maybe you and I could have dinner some time. I'd liked to tell you about what I've been working on," Tina said.

"I'm kind of busy with the competition. We'll see. Something important?" Marty asked.

"No, that's okay. Maybe some time when you're free. It's nothing big," Tina said with an air of disappointment. Tina wanted Marty's approval of her ongoing aspirations with a wine venture she had begun at her family vineyard. She also wanted Marty's personal attention. Working beside her would have to do for the moment. At least she, Marty, was in her presence at work. This made Tina happy, but not completely content. She wanted more of a relationship.

Just then, Dr. Bollinger stepped inside the store and headed straight toward Marty. When she saw him, she raised her eyebrows in dissatisfaction. "We need to talk," he said.

Marty looked over at Tina. She got the message and stepped away. "What is it, Bill? Wanting more gratuitous sex? Or should I say, Doctor? Are you just checking up on me?"

"Marty, we both know you took some of those pills from my vial. You're more than welcome to have them, as long as you're in my presence. I'm sorry, but that's the way it has to be," Dr. Bollinger said.

"So, I'm not entitled to extra-curricular activities?" Marty posed to the doctor. "As if your bedside manner is appropriate?" Marty continued to defend herself.

"I don't have to give you the pills. And you can go back to your old self."

Marty knew this was a duel where both parties would lose if they continued on the same tack. "All right, Doctor. Where and when?" Marty asked with a condescending smile.

"Now, that's more like it. You're much better when you're understanding. It's even flattering," the doctor said. "How about your place?"

"Isn't that getting a little too convenient? No dinner?" Marty asked with disapproval.

"I think your place is best. Wouldn't want to get caught in a compromising situation in public."

"So, let's just keep the compromising situation private, then?" Marty cynically questioned.

"Marty, you know what's at risk. Do I have to say it?" the doctor pressed.

"No, Doctor, you don't. But make it six o'clock and don't be late. I have things to do," Marty said, trying to take control of the situation.

"Maybe I should bring some wine. You can pick it out," Dr. Bollinger said and then left.

Marty pondered how she could get out of the current state of affairs with the doctor. She needed to get her hands on some Amoros, so she could wean the good doctor off her vagina. She was in a no-win situation. There had to be compromise. But the doctor wanted his take no matter what. And it appeared he was going to be relentless. The next week she was due for evaluation with the doctor. He must have other patients who were in conditions worse than hers. She needed a scapegoat so as not to bring attention to herself. But maybe that was too extreme.

If something were to happen to the doctor, such that she had to see another clinician for her mandatory evaluations, she would be back to her old self on the clozapine. She didn't want that. But why was he so receptive to her sexual needs? Perhaps he was involved with other female patients he was exploiting, especially with the physical examination process of the evaluation. That concerned her since she was essentially being evaluated for her psychological condition. If she could trump his current power over her, that would put her more in control of the situation. She would have to get him in a compromising situation—say photographs of him and another patient in the act of intercourse. That would give her ammunition against the doctor.

The following week, Marty had her appointment with the doctor. He was cordial, even professional. He didn't want to antagonize Marty. He knew she was a challenge that he best keep on an even keel. Marty acted as if nothing were wrong and was pleasant, even to the point of being coquettish. The doctor was pleased and had a happy demeanor. He waited for Marty to suggest getting together, which she did. He was finished with his exam of brief questions about her mental well-being. It was routine. Marty was compliant with her court-ordered demands, the doctor wrote in his notes. When he left the exam room, Marty quickly jumped from the exam table, grabbed a micro-sized surveillance device from her pocketbook and looked around the room.

As she was leaving the doctor's office, she noticed a woman in the waiting room. She was slight of build, somewhat attractive, with auburn hair. She had a distant look. Marty exited the office and headed toward her car. She got in, opened a laptop that was in the passenger seat next to her and opened a surveillance app. She hit an icon, and a screen came up displaying the exam room. Marty observed the woman from the waiting room prepare herself for an exam. The doctor came in and went through his routine. Marty could hear everything they were saying. The exam was over, and the woman left without incident.

Several other patients went through, including one male and one female. Time passed, and Marty was getting a bit impatient. Finally, another patient entered the room. It was a woman. Marty knew her. It was Linda Brice, the realtor she had worked with when she purchased the wine store and another building that was currently vacant. Linda was in her forties, a buxom brunette who was well-dressed and kept herself attractive, even though she carried some extra weight. Marty wondered why she was there. Linda undressed and sat on the exam table. The doctor entered the room.

He stepped towards her quickly and planted a kiss on her lips. They began to fondle each other. The doctor unzipped his pants, and she began to perform fellatio on him. Marty was stunned but not surprised. She made sure the surveillance app was recording the whole affair. After Linda performed her act, the doctor reciprocated to her moaning pleasure. Marty had what she needed.

Two days later, Doctor Bollinger showed up at Marty's place. Marty was in a satin negligee. He was excited when he saw her. "Before we get started, I want to show you something," Marty said and pursed her lips.

"New lingerie?" the doctor asked.

Marty picked up a manila envelope, pulled out some photos and handed them to the doctor. He looked at them carefully. There were six in all. He said nonchalantly, "So, you got me." And then asked, "What do you want?"

"We both know what I want. The vial," she commanded with a gesturing hand. "And future supplies of the good stuff," she continued.

"Anything else?" he asked.

"And no more sex," Marty said.

"You're a clever one. I should have known. I knew your background and I knew your capabilities," the doctor said. "So, no more sex?" he asked rhetorically as he handed her the vial of Amoros.

"Nope. But it looks like you're getting enough," Marty said and took the pictures from Dr. Bollinger. "Unless you want to keep them for your own pleasure?" Marty asked as she offered the pictures back.

"No. You win, Marty. Just one word of caution, keep an eye on yourself. Too much indulgence in those pills can lead to emotional instability."

"I know how to take care of myself. Besides, I'm not the only one who should be watching themselves with indulgence. You might want to curb that appetite for your patients."

"Fair enough. But remember, if you go off the wagon, I'm not the only one they'll come after," he said warningly and then left her apartment.

Marty immediately popped, not just one Amoros but two and chased the pills with some Pinot Noir she'd been savoring earlier. It was a fine vintage from Russian River Valley—a Brenny Walsh 2012 that was ripe with blackberry, licorice, and minty grass. One of her favorites. Perhaps she knew she would divide and conquer that evening. She quickly texted Tina for Gallagher's number, thinking that she must have it since they were friends. Tina shot back his number. Marty thanked her with an 'xo' at the end of the text. This stirred Tina since it was the first romantic gesture, albeit only in Tina's mind, that Marty had made to her, as innocent as it was. But Marty was excited over her conquest of the doctor and felt elated. *Things will be brighter*, Marty crooned to herself.

Marty texted Gallagher: How about we meet tonight for a bite and wine chat? Yours truly, Marty. She figured, what the hell. He'd have to do, even if he weren't her type. She missed John's masculinity and handsome looks. But he was a memory.

It didn't take long before Gallagher responded. As she dressed, Didier and Sookie made their presence known. "Where you going, Marty?" Sookie gently asked.

"Hey, guys," Marty said. "Dinner with a friend."

"You look *absultment* gorgeous," Didier said.

"Thank you, Didier. You're finally being a gentleman," Marty replied.

"So, you're planning on having sex tonight. Lucky dude," Didier said.

"Why does it have to be a dude?" Sookie asked, emphasizing 'dude.'

"Lots of it, Didier. Lots. Are you jealous?" Marty teased.

"The French are born jealous," Didier said.

"*Oui*, oh yes," Sookie added.

Marty met Gallagher at a cozy dark place called The Plank along the coast where the fare was decent, but the wine selection was exceptional. With its weathered pine construction, it seemed to her like a place that was a part of the natural habitat of coastal Southern California. It had been around for several decades with little modification, including the menu. Marty was already seated at a booth sipping on a Steele Pinot Noir Santa Barbara County 2013 that had fresh raspberry and cherry notes and plenty of herb, sassafras and cola flavors. She was beginning to feel the effects of the Amoros, which made her vagina lubricate as lusciously as the wine she was drinking.

As Gallagher sat opposite her, rhapsodizing about the wine, Marty couldn't help but think that he looked a lot like Fabio Lanzoni, the cover model of the romance novels of the 80s and 90s her mother used to read. Except his jawline wasn't as pronounced. "Did you catch the dried cherries on your tongue?" he asked.

Marty sipped her wine, gargled slightly and chewed for a second. "I'm not sure. I think there's some cherry," she said vaguely.

"I'm not trying to sound like a schoolteacher, but if you're going to compete in the California Grand Sommelier Competition, to get past through the first round, you'll need to distinctly know the multitude of flavors," Gallagher professed.

"What do you suggest?" Marty asked.

"The other night at Yum Yum's you mentioned the Pinot Blanc we were drinking had notes of orange skin and pecan wood. You were a little off. It actually had notes of lemon skin and walnut wood. You were close, but not exact," Gallagher said. "There are kits you can purchase of a variety of extracts that can help you distinguish specific notes and flavors. I highly recommend you look into it. It would be beneficial to you in the long run. Even if you don't win the competition."

"You're confident of yourself, aren't you?" Marty said and stood up, leaned towards Gallagher and kissed him on the lips as she rubbed her thigh against his.

After a shotgun dinner, Marty and Gallagher drove to the cliffs that overlooked Hummingbird Beach where they wasted no time undressing each other. Marty got down on all fours and began to shimmy and gyrate her rear end in the air, slowly inching her way towards Gallagher. Before he could insert his penis inside Marty's vagina, he had lost his presence of mind. He was so excited; he fell backward over the cliff as Marty kept maneuvering her rear end towards him. Marty was so engrossed with her own arousal that she barely knew what happened. She crawled towards the ledge and vaguely could see the cliffs down below. "Gallagher. Gallagher," she cried out in a whisper.

Behind a tree, twenty yards away from Marty, Tina watched. Her obsession with Marty had reached new heights of stalking her. But what she had just witnessed spooked her beyond belief. She was emotionally paralyzed. She held her hands to her mouth, not knowing what had happened to Gallagher, the friend she had known for ten years. If she interceded, what would Marty say? If she called 911, could she be implicated in something sinister? It was an accident, she rationalized. Hopefully, Marty would do the right thing. Tina took off running.

Marty turned toward Tina, hearing a rustle. Then she called out to Gallagher again. No response. She then made a call for help. She would have to tell the authorities what actually occurred—that it was an acci-dent. *But would they believe her*? "This is terrible," she said out loud.

Sookie and Didier appeared out of nowhere. "What did you do?" Didier asked as he looked over the cliff.

"What happened, Marty?" Sookie asked genuinely.

"I don't know. We were about to have sex and, well, I was so excited that I might have pushed him off the ledge," Marty said in misery.

"Stay calm, Marty," Didier said as he attempted to ease Marty's mind.

"What am I going to do?" she asked. "Think, guys."

"You can't run away," Sookie said.

"I know. Of course, they'll just have to believe me," Marty said as her mind churned.

And that's what she did when the EMT, the local sheriff's department, the local police, and a helicopter arrived. She told them exactly what had happened as she displayed distress and sorrow. When they found Gallagher, he was unconscious in critical condition and was medevaced to the Santa Barbara General Hospital. Marty was escorted back to the local police department where she gave a full account of what had happened. And then she was free to go. Hers was the only account until Gallagher regained consciousness. Unless there was a witness? the police postulated.

Marty was visibly shaken, even after she left the police department. The image of what happened ran through her head. She worried about Gallagher, but she also worried about the noise she had heard. Someone had seen what happened and they decided to run. She heard the footsteps. Even with all that happened, her vagina vibrated out of control. She couldn't go to the hospital. What could she do? Besides, she would have to face Misty, she was sure. That wouldn't be easy.

She needed a drink, and she needed sex—with a stranger that she could ravage and not be accountable to. She needed a one-night stand. She drove to the Santa Barbara Airport and parked herself in one of their bars looking for some traveling out-of-towner to pick her up. It didn't take long before she wound up in a hotel room in a highly charged sexual liaison with a married businessman.

Chapter Seven

Marty woke to the incessant buzzing of her cell phone. She groggily rolled over, picked up the cell phone and with one eye open, checked her text messages. Several were from Tina wondering if she, Marty, was coming into work. There was no mention of Gallagher. Marty looked at the time. It was 10:30ish. "Shit," she whispered. There was another text from Misty. Marty figured that Misty must have gotten her cell phone number from Tina. The message read: *What the fuck happened last night?!!!! Gallagher is in a coma in critical condition. You need to call me immediately.*

There were also several missed calls, all from Misty. There was a voicemail from her as well, just moments before Marty awoke. She listened to the recording: *Marty, this is Misty. You need to get your little ass over to Santa Barbara General. We need to talk about Gallagher and what you did. You need help for your thing. You have a problem.* Marty assumed the police told Misty of the circumstances surrounding the accident.

Marty threw the cell phone on her bed, went into the bathroom and doused her face with cold water. And then gave a cold hard look at herself in the mirror. Her eyes were bloodshot and weary. She turned on the shower and popped an Amoros because she needed some clarity. That's what the pill did for her besides get her libido revved up. But she didn't care about her libido. She needed focus. She slipped into the shower. It was soothing as the warm water pulsated on her head. She stood there for five minutes before she began to lather herself with the soap.

As she began to wash her pussy, she had the urge to masturbate as she reflected on the prior night's encounter with Tom. She didn't get his last name. Nor did she give hers. It didn't matter. The sex was hard and fast. Marty put her finger on her clitoris and flicked it while she let the shower stream flow on her pussy. It started to feel good until she heard Bubba's voice say, "Chitlin', you in there?"

"Not now!" Marty called out. "I'm busy," she moaned.

"We need to get to work. You need some schoolin'," Bubba replied.

"A couple of minutes," she said and then let out a shuddering "oh" as she climaxed.

"You need some help in there?" Bubba asked.

"Not anymore," she sighed.

After the satisfying shower, Marty decided to lay low. She texted Tina stating that she wouldn't be coming into work that day. And then she made herself some scrambled eggs with Havarti cheese and dill, toasted sprouted wheat bread and a kale blackberry smoothie while Bubba reviewed the wine regions of Spain with her. "Spain is the third largest producer of wine in the world," he said. "The largest is?" he asked.

"France," Marty said smartly.

"And the second is?" he continued his questioning.

"Italy."

"Good. You passed kindergarten," Bubba coyly said. "Okay, how many wine regions are there in Spain?"

Marty paused, squinted her eyes and finally said with a question, "Sixty-two?"

"Sixty-nine. Like one of your favorite positions," he said with a smirk.

"Don't get smart. I need to learn this," she said and then sipped her smoothie.

"We're going to review each region, then we'll go over the types of wine in each region. Okay, chitlin', you ready?" Then he asked, "What's the matter, darlin', you upset about something?"

"I need to take care of a matter that happened last night," she said with a frown.

"You mean that thing with the surfer dude?"

"Yes. His name is Gallagher," Marty said. "His ex is angry at me. I'm afraid she's going to cause me trouble," she continued. "I think she was the one who saw me with Gallagher. I bet it was her," Marty whispered.

"Well, you need to nip that in the bud," Bubba said. "I mean, really nip it."

"I know," Marty replied. "But if Misty told the police what happened, how could she have explained why she was there? By coincidence?"

"Unlikely," Bubba remarked.

"If Gallagher dies from his injury, will she confess to seeing us?" Marty pondered.

"All the more reason to take care of business," Bubba said.

"And if she told the police what happened? And we know it was an accident. Right?"

"If you say so."

"Unless Misty said it wasn't. And if that were the case, the police would have arrested me by now."

As Marty and Bubba had their conversation, Misty texted Marty again. The text read: *You bitch!!! Gallagher is still in a coma. I know you tried to kill him.*

"Oh, my God," Marty said and showed Bubba the text.

"You're right, she knows," Bubba said in a doom-laden voice.

"She knows what? She was the one I heard running away," Marty said with angst.

Later that evening Marty drove over to the Santa Barbara General Hospital in one of the mini-delivery vans she used for her store. It was nondescript since it was brand new. She had dressed in disguise as a flower delivery man, complete with a matching blue khaki top and pants, a fake beard, a shaggy wig, and a baseball cap. She stepped towards the ICU reception desk and delivered the flowers. The card on the flowers read: *To Gallagher. Be well. From, your friend.* She didn't know his last name. Marty looked over at the waiting room. She saw Misty there, as well as Tina. They were just sitting there and not saying a thing.

Marty exited the hospital and waited in the van, which was parked fifty feet to the side of the entrance. She figured both Tina and Misty would leave soon since waiting hours would be over. Twenty minutes later, Marty watched Tina and Misty exit the hospital. They stopped for a brief moment in front of the entrance and said a few words, hugged each other and then went to their respective cars. Marty started the van and traced Misty's SUV for several miles up into the hills that over-looked Santa Barbara. Misty pulled up to the driveway, opened the remote garage door and entered the garage. Marty quickly parked the car and exited carrying a billy club. As the garage door began to close, Marty sneaked up to the door and slid underneath.

Misty had already entered the house. Was she a creature of habit who had locked the garage door that presumably led into the kitchen or had she not? Marty waited a while until all was quiet and then tried the door. It was unlocked. Maybe it was an oversight by Misty who was preoccupied with emotions about Gallagher. Marty tiptoed through the kitchen and into a hallway that led towards some back bedrooms. She decided to crawl down the hall. Since Misty was probably in bed, she wouldn't be able to get a look at Marty.

Marty waited till she heard Misty was asleep. Hopefully, she wasn't a light sleeper. Misty tossed and turned. Marty waited. She popped another Amoros, to give her clarity. But Marty's libido kicked in before Misty finally fell asleep. Marty writhed her rear end on the carpet and then crawled into the room towards Misty. Marty stood up, raised the billy club and as she was about to strike Misty in the head, Misty lunged towards Marty, grabbing Marty's wrist that held the billy club and punched Marty in the eye.

Marty fell backward on the floor, losing the billy club. Misty was on top of her. They rolled about. Misty seethed, "You fucking animal. You're not going to get a piece of me." Marty reached for the billy club as Misty had command of the situation. She was strong and had five inches and twenty pounds over Marty. Misty tried kneeing Marty in the crotch as she held back one of Marty's wrists while she was on top of her. Marty finally got hold of the club and struck Misty in the head. It dazed her, and Marty struck again, knocking Misty out.

Marty dragged Misty to the garage where she undressed her and re-dressed her in one of her full body wetsuits. She found some masking tape and taped Misty's mouth shut. Marty then opened the backend of Misty's SUV and inched her inside. She shut the door, found Misty's keys, opened the garage door and backed out.

Marty drove over to the back alley of her other building, got out and opened the back door. She grabbed a long black zipper bag and opened it up outside the back end of the SUV. She pulled Misty out into the bag and zipped it up. She then dragged Misty into the SUV. She locked the door on the way out and drove back to Misty's house.

When she got there, she entered the house through the garage. She went inside to the bedroom, turned on the light, looked around and made the bed. She then took a look at her eye in the mirror. She had a nice cherry. It would probably turn black in a day or two. She went back to the garage and picked up Misty's nightclothes and threw them into the SUV. Marty then grabbed one of Misty's four surfboards and placed it on top of the SUV roof-rack and then placed another one on the roof-rack and secured them. She drove down to Surf Beach and parked the SUV next to her own car, wiped down any of her fingerprints, got into her car and drove away.

Marty drove towards Misty's house. She parked her car eight blocks away, got out and jogged to her minivan. When she arrived at her other building, Misty was writhing in the bag. Marty took a couple of swipes at Misty's head with the billy club and knocked her out again. She then opened a string of six boxes that she taped together on the long end. She cut out the bottom and tops, except for the bottom box's bottom and the top box's top. She then slid Misty's body inside the boxes and sealed it with tape, grabbed a dolly, lifted the string of boxes onto the dolly and carted it to her van.

Marty drove to a marina. It was dark, and no one was around. She carted Misty's boxed body down the lighted plank that led to a boat. Slid open a side door to the deck and maneuvered the dolly onto the boat. She secured the box, hotwired the starter to turn over the engine and wait-ed—but only a few minutes. Time was running short. The sun would soon be up.

Marty hoisted off and headed out of the marina towards Surf Beach in a northwesterly direction. When she arrived at her destination, about two miles due west of Surf Beach, she cut the engines. She then took a five-gallon bucket of bloody fish parts and threw the contents into the water. She unboxed Misty's body and unzipped the bag. Misty was groggy. Marty dragged her body to the side of the boat, pulled off the bag and leaned Misty's body over the side. She then slit Misty's wrist and let the blood drip. It didn't take long till there was activity in the water. Marty shone a flashlight into the water.

Marty recognized several of the thresher sharks with their long tails that were cruising about in a frenetic way, including some makos. She tossed another bucket of bloody fish parts into the water. More sharks arrived—larger ones, even. Marty was a little frightened herself, considering the darkness and the number of sharks that were lurking. It was time. Marty heaved Misty's body into the black water. Marty almost fell in after her as she braced herself on the rail of the boat. She shone the flashlight on the water. The body was slowly descending below the surface as the sharks thrashed about. Maybe twenty in all. Who knew how many more were stalking Misty's body in the depths?

As Marty headed back towards the shoreline, she tossed the boxes and the black bag into the water. She beached the boat along the shore not far from the marina. She wiped down the inside of the boat and doused it with sea water. She then hiked along the beach towards the marina, got into the van and drove eight blocks from her car and jogged to it. She drove back towards the van, got in the van and drove eight blocks closer to her store. She repeated the process until the minivan was parked at her store and she was back at her condo with her own car. The crime went off without incident, though not without an occasional dog barking at her and the presence of a patrolling police car, which made her quickly duck behind hedges as it passed.

The sun was rising in the east—she was famished. And horny. When she stepped inside her condo, Didier asked enthusiastically, "Where've you been, *mon cherie?*"

"Oh, shit, the surfboard!" Marty yelled out. But it was too late. If she drove over to Surf Beach and put the board in the water, someone would see her.

Chapter Eight

Marty was awoken by a continuous knocking at her front door. She got up, stumbled through the living room toward the front door and opened it with squinting eyes. Tina was standing there, and when she saw Marty a wreck, with her bruised eye, she asked with concern, "My God, Marty, what happened to you? I've been trying to reach you for the past several days."

"What time is it?" Marty asked in a haze.

"Never mind what time it is. What day is it?" Tina said like a reprimanding parent.

"I've been busy," Marty responded in a cowed voice.

"This whole thing with Gallagher has been awful. I heard that you two were together when he had slipped off the cliff," Tina quietly said as she stared into Marty's eyes.

"Yeah, I guess we got carried away," Marty said with embarrassment. "How's he doing?"

"He's out of the coma, thank God. But we don't know where Misty is. It's been two days. She's not at home. I'm going to call the police," Tina said. "And then you haven't been around. The store is fine. But I've been worried sick," Tina said and then hugged Marty and kissed her on the neck.

Marty slowly backed away from Tina. "Everything will be okay. I'm sure she's fine. And I'm glad to hear Gallagher is all right. I'll go see him later."

"He would like that. He's so humble. He's actually embarrassed," Tina said. "But what happened to your eye?"

"I woke in the middle of the night, needed something to drink and bumped into an open kitchen cabinet door. Stupid me."

"Looks like it hurts."

"I'm fine," Marty said, anticipating Tina's departure so she could get nourishment after her forty-eight hours of pure debauchery at a private sex club she found on the internet.

"Marty, I was thinking later you and I could take a drive to my family vineyard so I can show what I've been working on?"

"Ya, sure," Marty said, almost at the point of being annoyed.

"Oh, great. I'll come by later, around six, and we can go together. Bye, Marty," Tina said with a smile as she forgot about everything else, even her missing best friend, Misty. She forgot everything except Marty, whom she dreamt about constantly—especially in the nude.

Tina returned at six and when she saw Marty, she couldn't help the flutters in her stomach. Marty was dressed in a *ravishing* taupe sleeveless mini dress, a glitter armband, and silver bracelet. Marty's tangerine essence permeated Tina's olfactory senses and set her aloft with desire.

"Ready to go? I can drive."

"Tina, how about I follow you, okay?" Marty said, sensing Tina's extra affection, thinking that she wasn't ready for whatever it was Tina was after. Best to keep a safe distance.

"Okay," Tina said as Marty closed the door behind her.

It was about an hour and twenty minutes later when Tina and Marty arrived at Tina's family vineyard, St. Clair Vinegar Farm—a forty-acre hilly spread nestled amongst the many vineyards in Santa Barbara County's eastern perimeter.

"Your family owns this?" Marty asked exuberantly.

"This was my playground as a child, and it still is in some ways," Tina said with a smile. "Come on, I'll take you to the fermentation shack." They passed the main A-framed house with its white picket fence, where the lights were off. "That's where my mother and father live."

"They're not home?"

"On a tour in Italy. Second honeymoon."

"Nice," Marty said as they rounded the house towards a long barn that was painted a rustic red.

Tina unlocked the door to the barn and then turned on the lights to the shack, displaying a row of modern stainless tanks on one side of the barn and a row of stacked oak caskets on the other. "Most of the tanks contain balsamic and white balsamic vinegar. This one contains a Chardonnay and that one has Pinot Noir," Tina said as she pointed to each respective tank.

"This is what you wanted to show me? The reason why you've been so excited?"

"Well, yeah. You have to try some," Tina said and grabbed two brown paper cups and a wine thief that was hanging next to several oak barrels. She pulled out the cork of one of the barrel's bunghole, dipped the wine thief inside the barrel and pulled it out. She filled one cup and gave it to Marty. She then poured herself one. "Sorry for the crude presentation," Tina said, beaming with joy.

Marty took a sniff, sipped the Pinot Noir and then gargled it. She proceeded to drink the whole cup of wine, savoring its nuances.

"It's not fully aged yet," Tina said.

"Do I taste figs?"

"Yes."

"And blackberry, rhubarb, some coffee, and cocoa. That's incredible, Tina," Marty said with amazement.

"You taste the cinnamon and licorice?"

Marty nodded. "Not much oak, either. Very nice finish. It's like a Burgundy," Marty complimented Tina.

"But with a Santa Barbara *terroir*," Tina said.

"Yes, very nice. Very, very nice."

Tina was tickled by Marty's comments. "So, now the Chardonnay." Tina poured the straw-colored wine into a cup and handed it to Marty, who filled her nose with a waft of the tangerine and nutmeg-scented liquid. "Tangerine. And you know how I love tangerine," Marty crooned as Tina giggled inside. Marty sipped the wine and chewed it for a couple of seconds before she swallowed. "Pear, apricot and this wash of sea salt crystals at the end," Marty offered up to a beaming Tina who was exuding pride and sexual desire.

"It's obviously un-oaked—to keep it crisp. Also, I did that to contrast with the Pinot to get a full spectrum between the two varietals."

Marty sipped more of the wine. "And a touch of lime, I caught. A dash of vanilla would round it nicely. But what a gorgeous wine anyway."

"We experimented with stressing the vines and then testing the results," Tina said humbly.

"Stressing the vines?" Marty inquired.

"I believe that for grape vines, like people, life is a parade of suffering. And the more suffering, the greater the effect," Tina said.

"It's the struggle that causes our instincts to take control," Marty suggested.

"Like the roots of the vine seeking needed nutrients will ironically send sugar, ergo nutrients, to the grapes, producing a much tastier grape. Sort of like, 'What does not kill you makes you stronger,'" Tina continued.

"No, what does not kill you only gives you more character, or maybe drives you insane," Marty said, realizing one possibility of her own situation. Marty then raised her eyebrows. "You can bottle it now and we can sell it at the store," Marty said, shifting the conversation back to Tina's wine.

Tina began to tear. "Oh, Marty, that's so sweet of you," Tina said, wanting to drift off alone on some romantic island with Marty. "I'm so in love with making wine," Tina said, though she really wanted to say *I'm so in love with you.* "I get so excited," Tina said and ran like a ballerina up the grated steps that led up to a walkway along the side of the barn just above the tanks. Tina waved Marty to come and follow her. "I love this place," Tina said, feeling the elation of the moment standing next to Marty. "So, Marty, why do you like wine so much?" Tina asked, wanting to know more about Marty. She wanted to know everything about her.

"When I was probably seven or eight, we visited my grandparents in Provence and all they did was drink wine. It seemed like all day and night, especially the Bandol Rosé. That's what did it for me. It's all sense memory of special moments in your life," Marty genuinely said.

"Like this. Like now," Tina said and kissed Marty on the lips while she stroked Marty's thigh with her hand.

Marty instinctively pushed Tina away and then put her hand on Tina's neck as if to choke her. "What the hell are you doing?" Marty asked angrily with a possessed look.

Partly embarrassed by the situation and partly angry, Tina yelled out, "I saw you with Gallagher. You pushed him, didn't you?"

Marty began to squeeze Tina's neck more tightly. Tina backed up in fear.

"And you were involved with those chef murders. That was you," Tina seethed.

Marty lunged towards Tina, who stepped back, lost her footing and then tumbled backward down the grated stairs, snapping her neck as she hit the bottom rung. It killed her instantly. "Oh, my God, Tina!" Marty yelled out as she descended the stairs and kneeled down next to Tina. Blood had started to trickle from her nose. "Tina. Please. Tina, wake up," Marty cried. But it was too late.

"Not again, Marty?" Didier asked as he stood over Marty and Tina.

"Leave her alone. It was an accident," Sookie said to Didier. "But she died over a kiss?" Sookie asked Marty.

"Ahh, the Oriental *lesbienne* speaks," Didier said, taunting Sookie.

"Asshole," Sookie responded in anger.

"Would you two shut up!" Marty barked.

"*Elle est mort.* This is not good, Marty," Didier said. "So, is this *troisième* in the past couple of days?" Didier asked.

"No. It's only the second," Marty said like an adolescent who was caught doing something bad. "Help me get her up the steps? I have an idea."

"I can't. I'm not of this *provenance,*" Didier said apologetically.

"Then you help me, Sookie?" Sookie just shrugged her shoulders. "You two are useless," Marty said. She picked up Tina, hoisted her over her shoulder and ascended the grated steps. She lumbered like a weight-lifter doing squats—slow and tense while holding onto the rail.

"You can do it," Didier called out to Marty, who was at the top of the stairs.

Marty placed Tina's body down on the grated walkway next to the first tank. She stepped towards the opening, pried it open and then shimmied Tina towards the opening and pushed her body inside the tank. Marty ran back down the stairs, found a towel and began wiping down any incriminating fingerprints, including the tank lid and the railing. She then collected the paper cups, looked around and exited the fermentation shack, shutting the lights and door behind her.

She got in her car. "Wait for us," Sookie called out and stepped inside the car with Marty. Marty backed up quickly and then heard plastic breaking. She slammed on the brakes.

"Fuck," Marty uttered. She got out of the car with Didier and Sookie following. Marty looked at her taillight that was cracked.

"Get every piece, Marty," Didier said as Marty looked for the broken taillight pieces on the ground.

Marty picked up the pieces and then turned to Didier, who was practically on top of her. "Where're your clothes?" Marty asked Didier, who was surprisingly and suddenly naked.

"Pervert," Sookie said loudly.

Didier stuck his penis between his legs, pursed his lips and spoke effeminately, "You like this better?"

"In the car, now!" Marty yelled. And she drove away.

As Marty drove back into town and hung a left on State Street, Santa Barbara's tony strip of boutiques and plazas, she was pulled over by the local police. Marty looked in her rearview mirror at the police officer who was headed her way. "You two keep it down. I got this under control," she said to Didier and Sookie, who were finally quiet after the ride back from Tina's vineyard where they were at each other's throats. Marty had threatened to throw them both out of the car if they didn't stop arguing.

Marty pulled out her license from her pocketbook, put on a charming smile and hiked her dress up to show some thigh. The police officer said as he stood outside Marty's door, "Thank you for stopping, ma'am. I pulled you over because your right taillight is broken. Can I see your license?"

"I'm sorry about that. I have to get it fixed. It just happened," Marty responded as she handed the officer her license.

He glanced at the license, took at a look at her eyes and then took a whiff by Marty's window. "I smell alcohol. Have you been drinking?"

"I own Remy Wine and Spirits. I was on a last-minute delivery and one of the wine bottles broke. That's probably why you smell wine."

The police officer got a glimpse of Marty's thigh and said, "I recognize the name. I really should ticket you for the taillight. But?"

"You should come by the store sometime. I'll give you a discount."

"How about we meet later for a drink? I get off at ten," the officer proposed. He knew she was a player after the Gallagher Simms' incident—it had been the talk of the Santa Barbara Police Department for several days. Here was his opportunity.

Marty looked over at the officer's bulging hard-on and then peered up at his face. "Sure. I'll meet you at the Plank at ten-thirty, Officer Robbins," Marty said as she glanced at his name tag. The police officer handed her her license, smiled and then went back to his patrol car.

Marty put away her license and drove to her store where she loaded her car with several boxes of specialty wine and delivered them to La Boca Tapas Restaurant. The delivery wasn't until the next day, but best to cover her little ass. *Just in case.* She decided to have something to eat. Tapas was the perfect remedy—Alcachofas: grilled artichokes, Spanish goat cheese with orange zest and mint and black mussels in Romesco fish broth, accompanied with a couple of flutes of finely chilled Anna de Corbu Cava Bruit—a Spanish sparkling wine of a blend of Chardonnay and Parellada grapes with a bouquet of ripe apples, tropical fruit and yeasty bread.

As she finished her meal at the bar, a handsome stranger stepped over to her and offered to buy her a drink. Marty responded, "Yes, you may."

Ten-thirty came and went, and the let-down police officer knew he was stood up. He couldn't help but think of the adage, *A bird in the hand is worth two in the bush.* He should have ticketed her and then asked her out. He then headed straight to the bar.

Chapter Nine

Marty went to visit Gallagher with a potted aloe plant and a box of chocolates. When she entered his room, Gallagher was in a full body cast, and his head was bandaged. Tubes snaked into his body.

"Hi, Gallagher," Marty said in a demure but concerned voice.

He looked up at Marty. He blinked his eyes and whispered, "Hello, Marty."

"I'm so sorry what happened. I just got carried away. And then you had fallen over," Marty pleaded apologetically.

"It was my fault, Marty. Don't worry about it. But have you seen Misty? It's been a couple of days," Gallagher asked.

"No, I haven't," Marty said. "I just wanted to see how you were. If there's anything I can do for you, please just ask. Okay?" Marty tried to console him.

"Maybe you can find out where Misty is for me?" Gallagher asked.

"I can do that."

"Oh, great. And maybe we can see each other when I get better?"

Marty put down the plant and chocolates and said, "You be well. I'll come and see you again." She stroked his hand and left.

On the shore of Surf Beach, a jogger happened to find Misty's body or what was left of it. The remains consisted of her lower torso with a stump of one leg and the other leg with the foot missing. The wetsuit was gone. Seaweed, crabs, and fleas covered the shredded torso. The jogger had vomited at the site of the gruesome sight. It didn't take long before the local authorities and the coroner arrived at the scene. The coroner deemed the death a shark attack and the likely victim Misty Mayer based on the shark bite scar on her calf. This was confirmed by the Santa Barbara police when they found her vehicle in the Surf Beach parking lot and an investigation showed she had been missing for several days.

What the police could not figure out was, why were two of her surfboards found on her vehicle? What was she doing at the time of the incident? Swimming? But even with these unanswered questions, there was no presumption of foul play. Which meant that no further investigation of her death would have been warranted unless they had investigated her phone records and found the angry texts sent to Marty over the Gallagher incident. But none of the detectives looked that closely because it appeared that Misty's death was another shark attack off their shores. And the only other person who was privy to Misty's animosity toward Marty was Tina. And she was gone.

Marty was at the wine store when a Santa Barbara police detective showed up. Marty was called to the front of the store by one of the associates who was covering for Tina.

"Ms. Remy. I'm Detective Brian Janson with the Santa Barbara County Sheriff's Department."

"Yes, what can I do for you?"

"You have a Tina St. Clair who works for you?"

"Yes, but she hasn't been to work in a couple of days. Is she okay?"

"I'm sorry to tell you this, but she was found dead in a fermentation tank at her family home."

"Oh, my God. How'd that happen? Was it an accident? Poor Tina," Marty said as she looked stunned. "Who found her?"

"One of the workers. He was cleaning up and found her floating in the tank. I had a few questions. When was the last time you saw her?" Detective Janson asked.

"It was two days ago. She came to my condo and brought me some paperwork."

"What time was that?" the detective asked.

"Nine or ten in the morning."

"And that was the last time you saw her?"

"Yes. But why do you ask?" Marty questioned the detective.

"It looks like there was a struggle. It seems that she may have been choked based on the markings on her neck. And the bruises on her head and body indicate she had fallen, possibly on the stairs. And, well, we don't think she just slipped, hit her head and fell into the tank. It may be a homicide," he said.

"Who would do that to her?" Marty asked in disbelief.

"Was she involved romantically with anyone?" the detective probed.

"I don't know. I never got that intimate with her."

"Anyone ever threaten her at work?"

"No. She was a model employee. One of my best. I'll miss her. I can't believe it," Marty said as she showed signs of sorrow. And as she did, she saw Angela Jordan in a platinum blond wig and kerchief, black sunglasses, and a tight black satin dress walk by outside the store. Marty watched her curiously and was distracted from the questioning at hand.

"Have you ever been to her family estate?" the detective asked as he watched Marty peer out the store window.

"Uh, no. I haven't."

"Well, it looks like you are busy," the detective said and then handed her his business card. "If you have any pertinent information regarding Tina, please let me know."

"Thank you, Detective," Marty said as he was leaving the store. And then he turned around, stepped back towards Marty and asked, "How did you get that bruise on your eye?"

Marty blankly looked at the detective and then said, "I bumped into my kitchen cabinet in the middle of the night. Silly me."

The detective nodded and left the store. Marty also left the store, had her taillight replaced and her car thoroughly cleaned and detailed. After which she went home and scrubbed the shoes she wore the night Tina died.

When Detective Janson returned to his office, he did a search on Marty. Her aliases came up as Marty Kittering and Marty Kittering-Abruzzo. She had no record. It was clean, but he recalled the name. He remembered the chef murders several years earlier in Los Feliz and her connection. She was implicated but never charged. It was the wife of the producer of the show Marty was connected to; she was the one who had been convicted of the murders, he recollected. That wasn't sufficient evidence to substantiate a warrant for Marty, nor did any of Tina's text or phone messages implicate Marty. Tina herself had been discreet with her inclinations toward Marty. Marty was considered unlikely to have killed Tina yet remained a person of interest.

That is, until the detective called the Santa Barbara Police Department where he found out Marty was involved with the incident concerning Gallagher Simms. And that Simms' ex-wife was found dead of an "apparent" shark attack only that same day. *What's going on?* the detective asked himself. He decided to visit Simms at the hospital where he was distraught over the death of Misty. He was in no condition to speak, as he was sedated.

Outside the hospital, Detective Janson called the Los Feliz Police Department. His objective was to question the lead detective on the chef murder cases, which led him to Paul Cooz. Janson called him at home and left a message. Shortly after, he received a call from Cooz. "Detective Janson," he said when he answered the ring.

"Paul Cooz," Cooz responded. "She finally do something she's going to get nailed for?"

"The body of a woman who was working for her was found dead in a wine fermentation tank," Janson said. "Looks like murder. What do you know of this Marty Remy?"

"Officially or unofficially?" Cooz asked.

"Whatever you have," Janson said.

"She was our prime suspect. You have all day? She has a sordid past."

"I'm here," Janson said.

After a lengthy conversation, Janson decided that all the evidence against Marty Remy in the chef murders was circumstantial. It was during the unofficial and illegal breaking and entering of Marty's perfume store that Cooz found the incriminating evidence against her that convinced Janson she was the likely perpetrator of Tina St. Clair's death. "Why did you do it? The B & E, I mean?" Janson asked.

"I had to know. I didn't know what I would find. And it just fell out of a notebook, as if the hand of God was involved," Cooz said.

"Too bad it wasn't by the book," Janson said. "I doubt that I can get a warrant against this Remy woman. But my gut is telling me it was her. She has a bruised eye. That could have occurred during a fight between her and the St. Clair girl. Maybe the coroner will find something, like Remy's DNA."

"That would help."

"But I have a feeling he won't. Remy is too smart. Your message on your cell phone said you were a private investigator. How about doing some consulting work for us? Look at the crime scene. Dig deeper into Remy's relationship with Tina St. Clair. See if there was something going on between them."

"Janson, I've been waiting for this day ever since Hawaii. I knew I had her, but I had to walk away. I'll do it."

"Good. I could use the help. We're short-staffed," Janson said. "You know, this thing with the surfer and the ex-wife, with the shark attack. I'm trying to wrap my head around that. She was a professional surfer. What was she doing in the water without her surfboard?"

"I believe Marty Remy is capable of most anything—poisoning, barbecuing, death by wild boars. You name it, this woman did all kinds of freaky things. Who's to say she didn't kill this woman, chop her up and throw her into the water where there were sharks," Cooz elaborated about Marty's propensities.

"She's that psychotic?" Jason asked in surprise.

"And then some."

"See if the Santa Barbara Police have anything more on the surfer woman. Maybe we can get access to her cell phone records, text, and voice messages. Push the investigation angle between Remy, Tina St. Clair, and the surfer woman. Maybe they'll oblige," Janson said.

Cooz wasted no time. He drove up to the crime scene the next morning after he went through some personal files that he had kept on Marty. He knew that Marty Remy, aka Marty Kittering-Abruzzo, aka Marty Kittering, was involved with Tina St. Clair's death. It was that gut feeling that all good detectives get when they are hot on the hunt. The key to solving any crime case is having not only enough evidence, but the right evidence. DNA, Marty's DNA, if found at the crime scene or on Tina St. Clair's body or clothing would speak volumes.

If the Santa Barbara County Sheriff's office could have shown that Marty was at the crime scene, then a forensic examination could have been performed on Marty within a reasonable amount of time so that evidence such as Tina's skin underneath Marty's fingernails was not destroyed by a thorough washing. But the murder had occurred two days prior and the likelihood that the DNA still existed was slim to none.

Cooz drove up the gravel driveway that led to the crime scene. He parked his car in front of the fermentation shack where the front doors were taped off. He got out, bent down and picked up some of the gray gravel. He inspected it for a second and then placed the gravel in his pocket. He walked around, getting the lay of the land and then stepped towards a wooden fence that ran in front of the fermentation shack and noticed a portion of the fence was pushed back a little from its vertical position. He inspected the fence more closely, bent down and sifted through some dirt. What he missed was a piece of Marty's rear taillight casing that she had missed as well on the night of Tina's death. The piece of casing was underneath a bush next to the fence.

Presumably, if he had found the broken piece of plastic, then he could have postulated that it was from a mishap as a result of a quick getaway, as in the case of a murder. Tina St. Clair's murder. He then would have inspected Marty's car for a broken taillight or a newly replaced taillight. By this means, he could have placed her at the scene of the crime. If he had a suspicion that Marty had replaced her taillight, he would have investigated further by tracking down all local auto parts stores that sold the specific taillight part and/or tracking down the local BMW dealer who may have replaced Marty's taillight. But since he did not find the broken piece of plastic, the potential lead was nonexistent.

Cooz went inside and stepped through the shack toward the back end. He envisioned Marty choking Tina at the top of the stairs. He opened his file, peered at the photographs of Tina's scarred neck and the injuries to her head, back, and knees as a result of falling on the grated stairs. He imagined Tina falling down the stairs and then Marty picking her up and placing Tina inside the tank. He replayed the vision in his head several times. *Why would she have killed her? Had it been an accident and Marty covered her tracks? Or was it a crime of passion?*

A woman entered the shack and stepped towards Cooz. He extended his hand and said, "I'm Paul Cooz. I'm assisting the Santa Barbara Sheriffs with the investigation of Tina St. Clair's death."

The woman shook his hand and said solemnly, "I'm Nancy St. Clair. Tina's mother."

"My condolences. I'm sorry for your loss."

"I'm hoping nothing terrible happened to her?"

"It wasn't an accident. I'll tell you that," Cooz said flatly.

"Ah, this is awful," she said glumly.

"Where were you that evening?"

"We were on vacation in Italy."

"Excuse me for the question, but what was your daughter's sexual orientation? Was she attracted to women?" Cooz asked in an easy manner.

"How is this relevant?"

"I'm trying to establish motive why your daughter was murdered."

"Why would someone do this to her?" she asked, somewhat baffled at the question of her daughter's sexual orientation. "She had boyfriends over the years. She wasn't seeing anyone lately."

"She was never involved with another woman?" Cooz pressed the questioning.

"There was…" the woman said and paused. "There was an incident with her high school volleyball coach, where the coach got fired over some sexual involvement with her players," the woman solicited.

"Your daughter was one of the players?"

"Yes, she was. Are you saying a woman killed her?" she asked, thinking of the absurdity of her daughter being killed by another woman. "She did have a very close friend. Her name was Misty. She could have been involved with her. But I don't know," the woman said, unsure of herself.

"Did she ever mention Marty Remy? That she had any feelings towards her?"

"Her boss?" the woman questioned with raised eyebrows. "She admired her, but I never got the impression that Tina was attracted to her," the woman said as her mood shifted to a perplexed sadness.

Cooz picked on the signal. "My apologies. I'm not trying to insinuate anything about your daughter. Are you aware that Marty Remy was Marty Kittering? She was the prime suspect in the chef murders several years ago in Los Feliz."

"No, I had not known this. My God, are you saying that she killed Tina?" the woman asked, distraught.

"I was the lead detective in the case. And when we had her for the murders, some new evidence suddenly appeared that cleared her. But to this day I am still convinced it was her."

"Why aren't you arresting her?" the woman asked in a sudden rage.

"We need evidence. We haven't found any yet," Cooz said. "But we will. Be assured of that."

"This has been so troubling for my husband and me," the woman said as she began to tear.

"I'll be in touch with you as soon as we establish something. You take care of yourself," Cooz said and then exited the shack more determined to catch Marty Remy for something.

Chapter Ten

Marty tracked down Officer Robbins at a public basketball court where he was involved in a four-on-four pick-up game. She felt guilty about standing him up, but not as guilty as she was horny, especially given how athletic and sweaty he was and with the Amoros kicking in. Marty would have spread-eagled in broad daylight. She didn't care—she wanted it. And needed it. And with no panties on, she could feel the moistness in her vagina. As soon as Officer Robbins recognized Marty standing behind the fence she was peering through when the game ended, he headed straight toward her. And just like a pickup scene at a bar where boy meets girl, they were off to a nearby beach motel after a few words of greeting.

Officer Robbins and Marty both jumped into the shower together at the motel room where Marty lathered his rock-hard penis with soap. She then pressed herself against the wall of the shower and arched her rear end in the air. Robbins inserted himself in Marty, cupped her breasts and rhythmically maneuvered his groin against her supple body. Marty moaned at each thrust. Robbins nibbled on her shoulder and neck as they came together. Marty smiled while she shuddered and realized she had a new fuck buddy she not only felt desire for but who would be an ally, presumably, in law enforcement.

Marty secured the deal with her patent testicle sucking and tonguing while stroking the officer's penis. She had become quite adept at this since taking the Amoros. It was a skill that was serving her well, and one she enjoyed. Which reminded her, she needed to get some more of the sex drug from the good doctor.

"Yoohoo, Marty. Are you in there?" Didier called out as he pressed his face against the glass shower door. Sookie followed suit and peered through the glass.

"You are making me so excited," Sookie said in a lustful voice. And before long, Sookie and Didier were rolling together on the bathroom floor. Marty thought they were fighting, but they began to have sex together. Marty was pleased because they were at least not at each other's throats.

Officer Robbins entered the Santa Barbara Police Station for his late afternoon shift when a detective on the Simms case, who was talking to Cooz, stopped him. "Robbins, you ever have any run-ins with a Marty Remy by chance?"

"Marty Remy. The wine store owner?" Robbins asked.

"That's her," the detective responded.

"No. Can't say that I have," Robbins replied. "Why's that?" he asked.

"A murder case I'm working on involving Tina St. Clair. She worked for Marty Remy," Cooz said.

"Is she a suspect?"

"I'm trying to establish that. You know she was our prime in the Los Feliz chef murders."

"It obviously wasn't her, though," Robbins said, appearing to become somewhat territorial, not just in regard his new sex partner, but for Marty who was a local business owner and resident.

Cooz, who didn't want to come across as overzealous, picked up on the tone and said, "Thanks." Robbins nodded and then stepped away. "Just to verify. Gallagher Simms made no claims that it was anything other than an accident when he fell down the cliff. Is that right?" Cooz asked the detective.

"That's correct," the detective said. "But his ex-wife was adamant. She was upset with Marty Remy."

"Any threats made by her or Remy?" Cooz asked.

"None that I know of," the detective responded.

"Have you checked the phone records? For possible messages between them?" Cooz asked.

"There were no threats that we can ascertain. Misty Simms' death was deemed to be a shark attack. No reason to investigate either situation further than what it was," the detective said. "As far as the phone records, there's no probable cause for a search warrant. I still don't see how you're trying to connect a shark attack with a possible murder."

"It's outlandish, but I know Marty Remy. She's involved somehow," Cooz said as he thought about the two surfboards. *Something was wrong with that.* "Don't you think it's odd that her surfboards were found on her car?" Cooz asked.

"Maybe she went for a swim? We have had shark attacks in the past."

"Swim at your own peril. You think I can get the make and model of Marty Remy's vehicle?"

"Certainly," the detective said.

Cooz received a text from Detective Janson stating that the autopsy report on Tina St. Clair came up negative on any DNA other than that of the deceased. She was choked. Contusions on her head and body matched the DNA found on the grated stairs at the fermentation shack. She was obviously moved from the stairs and placed in the wine tank. *Any progress?* asked Janson.

Cooz answered with regret, *not much.*

Cooz made a stop by Remy Wine and Spirits' parking lot. When no one was around, he inspected Marty's car tires for any gravel lodged between the threads. Nothing. But he did notice a scratch on her car near the passenger side taillight, which also looked new compared to the other taillight. He then drove away and headed towards the Santa Barbara General Hospital.

Cooz stepped inside Gallagher's room. He was awake and sipping orange juice through a straw. Cooz introduced himself and said, "I'm sorry for the loss of your ex-wife. I'm here investigating the death of Tina St. Clair. I gather you and your ex-wife were friends of hers?"

"I can't believe both of them are gone," Gallagher said.

"Not easy on you, I'm sure. Can you tell me what happened the night of your accident?"

"I thought this had to do with Tina?"

"It does. I just need to establish a connection between you, your ex-wife, Tina St. Clair, and Marty Remy."

Gallagher was cognizant but still slightly sedated on painkillers. Even though he was curious about the Marty connection and his accident, he responded without pause. "We had driven over to the cliffs. One thing led to another, and we got naked. She was on her knees, and I was about to take her. We both were excited. I mean, after all, she's a hot woman. I lost my bearings and tripped backward. And that's when I fell down the cliffs."

"She didn't push you over?"

"Oh, no. It was me. I just got too excited," Gallagher said.

"Did Tina ever mention Marty? That she had liked her as more than just a boss or friend?"

"She had. She thought Marty was a sexy woman. But she was reluctant to approach Marty. She didn't think Marty would have been interested. Sexually and all that."

"Had Tina and your ex-wife ever been involved, romantically?"

75

Gallagher paused and then responded, "They had. It's one of the reasons why we divorced."

"And you all remained friends?" Cooz asked inquisitively.

"I'm just one of those guys. I loved Misty very much. But she had drifted, and Tina was there for her needs, whatever they were," Gallagher said. "Did Marty do something wrong?"

"It's possible that she was threatened or felt threatened, which may have caused the death of Tina. And maybe even Misty. Was your ex-wife upset with Marty?"

"I don't know. I was pretty out of it. But, knowing Misty, I'm sure she had words with Marty," Gallagher said. "But what do you mean about Misty?" Gallagher asked with a concerned note to his voice.

"We detectives speculate about a lot of things. And through deduction and evidence we examine possible scenarios," Cooz responded. "Emotions, jealousy to be precise, sex are all motives for murder. Maybe Misty found out about Marty and Tina being involved, coupled that with your accident and threatened Marty. Or Tina got upset about you and Marty, became enraged with Marty, and it got physical. Tina was choked at some point before she died."

"Oh, man. I can't believe that," Gallagher exasperatedly said. And with squinted eyes of disbelief asked, "You're saying Misty was also murdered?"

"If I can prove there were actual threats made, then it's possible Marty could have murdered Misty and put her into the water where sharks or whatever tore at her body. Two of her surfboards were found on her car," Cooz said.

"That's because she used to swim to keep in shape. But, man, that's some heavy shit. You're saying Marty did all this to protect herself? And you're a detective?" Gallagher said sarcastically.

"I'm a private investigator. I was a detective with the Los Feliz Police Department. I just need some tangible evidence. You've been very helpful with my own theories, though. Best of luck getting better," Cooz said and then abruptly left the room.

Cooz had a possible motive in the Tina St. Clair case since she was attracted to Marty and a probable motive with the Misty Simms case since there was clear animosity toward Marty from Simms. But unless Simms threatened Marty with bodily harm, the evidence against Marty was *nada. No threat—no motive.* He had nothing to go on unless a witness stepped forward claiming to have seen Marty with Simms the day of her disappearance or street cameras could show Marty in her car at or near Simms' residence or at Surf Beach.

The Santa Barbara detective assisting Cooz had called him and told Cooz he had pulled Misty Simms' phone records. The two comments made by Simms, 'You need help with your thing' and 'You bitch!!!' proved interesting but not actual threats. No return calls or text messages were made by Marty. *She knew better—less evidence to pin her with.* Cooz was a veteran of the detective game. Although he was frustrated, he questioned whether Marty was asked by Janson to account for her whereabouts on the night Tina St. Clair was killed. He looked in the St. Clair file. It mentioned she was at home most of the day studying, made a delivery around 7:00 to a restaurant, stayed an extra hour to have something to eat and then went home after that.

If Marty had murdered St. Clair, the time to drive there and back, including the incident, could have feasibly taken three hours, maybe less. The time of St. Clair's death was ascertained as between 4 and 8 p.m. the night of her murder. Which left a one-and-a-half to two-hour window for Marty to have committed the crime and driven back to Santa Barbara. Considering it takes one hour from the scene of the murder to Santa Barbara, that left thirty minutes to an hour for Marty to have killed St.

Clair and disposed of the body in the wine tank. *That was plenty of time*, Cooz surmised. One hour.

Cooz had Janson question the other associates at the wine store to ascertain when they last saw Tina St. Clair at work. Her shift ended at 4:00 p.m. Why Janson did not ask that question before made Cooz wonder. No other mention of where she was going, least of all if she had met up with Marty for some reason. But one of the associates stated that she had run errands for Ms. Remy earlier in the day. Did Marty and St. Clair have an altercation? Did they meet for a sexual liaison? Lots of speculation. Cooz suggested to Janson that they bring in Marty for questioning. There was now sufficient evidence that Marty Remy could have committed the crime, at least regarding opportunity.

Marty arrived at the Santa Barbara County Sheriff's east county of-fices. She was lawyer-less and dressed in a black skirt suit. Janson escorted her into an interrogation room and had her sit at a table. He said he would return shortly and left. It was more than twenty minutes before he returned with Cooz.

Marty looked up at Cooz with a straight face and said, "You've re-turned. Are you on loan?"

"You could say that," Cooz said casually. "No lawyer?"

"I'm fine fighting my own battles," she said with a smile.

"Ms. Remy, you're not under arrest, but according to California law, I have to read you your Miranda rights before we begin. Are you okay with that?" Janson asked. "I will also be recording this interrogation."

"Yes, I'm fine," Marty said, and then Janson turned on the recorder and proceeded to state his name and Paul Cooz's name and Marty's and the reason for the taping. Then he read Marty the Miranda Rights.

"Now, you stated that the night of Tina St. Clair's death, you were at home and then you had made a delivery to La Boca Tapas Restaurant in

Santa Barbara and stayed for something to eat. Had you seen Tina at any time during that day?" Janson asked.

"Yes, she dropped off some work papers around ten that morning," Marty replied.

"And that was the last time you saw her?" Janson asked.

"Yes."

"Other than Tina, who knew you were at home? Did you have any guests over to verify your whereabouts between the hours of 4 and 7 p.m.?"

"I was there alone. Just little ol' me," Marty said coquettishly. "I've been studying for the California Grand Master Sommelier Competition. It's very intense and requires a lot of time," Marty offered.

"Were you and Tina..." Janson said and then he coughed. "Were you and Tina sexually involved?" he continued.

Marty paused a moment and said in a drawn-out fashion, "No." And then continued, "I'm heterosexual."

"Is that right?" Cooz interjected. "What about the dominatrix in San Francisco? And the French woman over in Nice you had trouble with? And what about Evie Ann? She said you hit on her," Cooz stated with a certain animosity.

"What's the matter, you still bitter about Evie Ann? She was cute. But can't say that I had a thing for her. Or, in fact, for any other woman, let alone a dominatrix," Marty said.

"Okay, what about the lesbian jamboree you had going on in New Orleans?" Cooz said, adding more fuel to the fire.

"You mean that all women jazz band when I was drugged and held captive against my will?"

"That's not what I heard. It seems like you really enjoyed yourself," Cooz returned the volley of touchés.

"I think you're obsessed with fantasies about me," Marty said. "Just because you have a badge…" Marty said as she was interrupted by Cooz.

"…Used to. I'm a private investigator now," Cooz said.

"Just because you have a penis, it doesn't give you the authority to stalk someone. Like you did in Hawaii," Marty said with a show of anger.

"Oh, you lie with a velvet tongue. Don't you?" Cooz insisted.

"I have you on tape," Marty said emphatically.

"Ms. Remy, would you be willing to submit to a DNA test?" Janson asked while looking over at Cooz and pondering the B&E Marty was referring to.

"I suppose," Marty said, knowing if they had found her DNA at the crime scene, they would have arrested her by now. It was a ruse to get her anxious. But she was as calm as could be because she was thorough the night Tina died.

"You choked her, didn't you? You two had something going on. You had gotten into an argument and threw her down the stairs, and she broke her neck. Isn't that what happened?" Cooz pushed.

"That's terrible. But no, I did not kill her," Marty replied. "I'll submit to your DNA test, but I know you won't find anything. Whoever killed her probably knew her. I knew her, but not on any intimate terms. Why would I have killed her? She was a valued and trusted employee."

"She was attracted to you. You never sensed that?" Janson asked.

"She was a warm and friendly person to everyone. Ask her yoga students."

"Did you know Misty Simms?" Janson asked.

"Yes, we met once at Tina's yoga class and had wine afterward."

"She contacted you after the incident with her ex-husband?"

"She was obviously upset about what happened to him. Purely an accident."

"Maybe she was upset about Tina's affection toward you. She was jealous and came after you?" Cooz asked.

"Paul, your conclusions are wrong. As if everything revolves around sex and murder. This is all tragic. First, the accident with Gallagher. And then Tina and then Misty. I'm very upset about all this. It's overwhelming," Marty said to elicit sympathy.

"Really? How about you tell us what actually went on with the surfer? His ex thought you wanted to kill him. While you were doing the nasty. Like some black widow who kills its mate after having sex," Cooz said as he motioned his hips back and forth.

Marty looked at Cooz with disdain and said, "Detective Janson, on second thought, I'll take a pass on the DNA test. But if you insist, you can contact my attorney." She then stood from her seat and said as she exited, "Have a good day, gentlemen."

"I think it's time we start looking at some other suspects. Maybe the groundskeeper did it. Somebody in the local area. A vagrant even?" Janson suggested.

"You honestly fell for that routine of hers. She's as smooth as cheesecake with whipped cream and strawberry coulis," Cooz said.

Janson got a little lost in the analogy. "Maybe we should wind this thing down? I'll have administration cut you a check. I can handle this. I'll give you a call," Janson said, trying to dismiss Cooz.

"She's as guilty as silk pie. But, whatever you say, Janson," Cooz said, feeling the letdown.

"Maybe you are infatuated with her? She is an incredible-looking woman."

"I'm going to get her. Guaranteed. You watch," Cooz said while chewing on the humility he was feeling.

Outside, Marty entered her car, started it up and drove away. When she looked in her rearview mirror, she saw Stan Kravitz and Angela Jordan in a make-out session in the back seat. "You have to do that in my car?" Marty asked sarcastically.

"Join us, Marty?" Stan suggested.

"Not now, I'm driving," Marty replied.

"Then how about we take a trip to the Russian River Valley? I'm in the mood for a nice pussy and wine tasting," Stan said. "My treat."

"Sounds tempting, but I have to deal with some potential legal problems," Marty said.

"I'll call my cousin Marvin Steele. He's one of the best lawyers in the business. He can even get you a settlement for the harassment," Stan said.

"Stan the man," Angela crooned.

Chapter Eleven

Cooz recovered from having his tail between his legs by sending Dorothy Lanore of Wine Chat a bottle of Friberg J. Frye 2008 Vintage Sparkling Wine from North Coast, California. Cost: $120 a bottle. According to Wine Merchant, Inc, the sparkling wine was an 87/13 blend of Chardonnay and Pinot Noir grapes that opened up with baked pears, Meyer lemon, and candied pineapples followed by nuances of honeysuckle, toffee, and cinnamon-toasted almonds. The wine also had notes of pears with layers of ripe persimmon, rich, long textures, and a citrus finish. He also sent an anonymous e-mail to her regarding the death of Tina St. Clair. His attitude was fight fire with fire, threaten the threatener, and outface the brow of bragging horror, as he remembered the Shakespeare quote. Even though he was off the case of her murder, he was even more determined to get Marty. With whatever means he had at his disposal.

Marty was busy at the store interviewing a replacement for Tina. After reviewing several applicants, from students who had recently graduated from local colleges to restaurant servers who wanted a change of pace to more mature individuals looking to keep themselves busy with employment, Marty settled on a twenty-five-year-old woman named Michelle Sloane who reminded her of a beach bunny with her bushy blond hair, tender round face and smiling green eyes. Marty liked her vibrant attitude and wine knowledge. Although her sales experience was limited to working at cellular stores, she had a soft yet encouraging vibe that Marty felt would result in wine sales.

After Marty called Michelle Sloane and requested to have her come in for a follow-up interview, she turned on the Public Broadcasting

Radio app on her computer. Although she was still miffed at Dorothy Lanore, she did like the show. It was very informative. And she needed to stay focused on wine since the competition was only a few weeks away.

Blue Oyster Cult's, "Don't Fear the Reaper" opened the show. And then Dorothy Lanore came on and said, quoting the song, "Come on baby, don't fear the reaper. It's Halloween time, and this is Dorothy Lanore of Wine Chat. One quick and inauspicious note. We lost a promising young winemaker last week by the name of Tina St. Clair from Santa Barbara County. It happens that she also worked for Remy Wine and Spirits, the owner of which just happens to be connected to the infamous Los Feliz chef murders. Spooky, isn't it? It sounds more like Remy Witches, Ghosts, and Goblins to me."

An enraged Marty picked up a wine bottle off her desk and threw it against the wall where it made a "thunk" and stuck suspended in the drywall. "That fucking bitch!" Marty screamed out. She quickly popped an Amoros and texted Officer Robbins. "Need a quickie," it said. Then she texted Dr. Bollinger. Her supply was running low. In the next two weeks leading up to the competition, she needed all the focus she could get. Dr. Bollinger responded first with "I'll meet you at your place in an hour." Marty was in no mood for compromising, knowing that she would most likely have to give something in return. She reluctantly texted back, "Okay."

An hour later, Marty had pulled up to her condo and parked her car on the street when she noticed Cooz sitting in his car, waving at her. She decided to give him the middle finger. Cooz replied with a condescending smile. As Marty approached her doorstep, the good doctor was waiting there. He tried to kiss her, but she brushed him off as she opened the door. Meanwhile, she received a text message from John inquiring about her upcoming visit to see Jackie in two weeks. Marty read the text and feeling frustrated said, "Oh, God," realizing that the competition, which was going to be a week-long event, conflicted her trip to Maui.

While Marty returned John's text stating that her trip would have to be in three weeks, Dr. Bollinger began to grope her. Marty elbowed him in the belly, which angered the doctor. "New rules, Marty. For every three pills I give you, you're going to have to show your gratitude," the doctor said.

"Every ten," she said. "And it will just be a hand job."

"So, you must have been a naughty girl going through all those pills so fast?" he questioned Marty's sexual activity.

"I need them to be mentally focused. Not for the sex," she said as she read John's new text. In three weeks, they would be in New York.

"Oh really? It's not what you said when you brought up the subject of your shriveling pussy," Doctor Bollinger said. "Every five pills and intercourse."

Marty really had no time for the doctor's antics, let alone the scheduling concerns she was facing. She texted John, "Let me know when it's convenient for me to see Jackie, then." She replied to the doctor, "Every eight pills and a blow job. With a rubber on." And then she realized how horny she was getting and between John, Cooz, and the doctor's bullshit, she said angrily, "All right, fucker, you can have me this one time and it's every eight pills and a hand job." And then she pulled down her skirt and panties and bent over. "Here, have at it."

While the doctor was taking care of business, Marty read a new text from Officer Robbins. "I'm just pulling up to your condo. Get ready, cream pie." Marty immediately pulled herself away from the doctor. "Time's up, I have company. Where're the pills?" she asked as she pulled up her clothing and then held her hand out.

The doctor pulled his pants up and handed Marty the pills. "You drive a hard bargain. But I don't think I can get much more of the Amoros," he said with a smirk.

"That's your problem. Isn't it?"

The doctor blew her a kiss and exited the condo. He passed Officer Robbins on the walkway. Robbins looked back at him, then saw Marty and asked, "Who's that?"

"My personal physician," she replied, grabbed Robbins by the collar, pulled him inside the condo, and planted a wet kiss on his lips while she closed the door behind them.

Cooz was watching every move. He was amazed yet knew of Marty's sexual appetite. He watched the doctor get into his car and wrote down his license plate number, delighted with himself. He was slowly making progress with catching Marty. At what, he didn't know.

Inside the condo, Marty tore off Robbins' clothes. He did the same with her and they ferociously engaged in a sex marathon that lasted for almost two hours. Marty and Robbins were sweating profusely. He took a shower while Marty planned her initial trip up the coast to visit her nemesis, Dorothy Lanore. When Robbins left the condo, Cooz watched him get in his car and drive away. He took down the license plate number. He then texted a friend and former co-worker at the Los Feliz Police Department. He already had Dr. Bollinger's information. He would have Officer Robbins' shortly. "Gee, I'm hungry," he said to himself gleefully and decided to have some lunch. He drove away while having a fantasy of Marty and Evie Ann kissing.

As Cooz had his lunch on the terrace of Petit Pacifica, a local French bistro, eating a grilled ribeye steak with a rosé-infused béarnaise sauce, pomme frites and a mixed green salad with a lemon-thyme dressing, he pondered his next move. He wondered if he had played the situation with Evie Ann a little differently, could they still be together? Accusing of her conspiring with Marty to commit murder wasn't one of his finest moves as a detective. It cost him the relationship with Evie Ann. She was in Maui now, running her own restaurant. He realized that ship had sailed. *One false move lead to everlasting consequences,* he reflected.

Yet one false move was all he needed to pin Marty. *So, what was she doing with a psychologist and a cop, at her home no less*? he questioned himself. If he tried questioning Dr. Bollinger about Marty, he wouldn't be too helpful, let alone forthcoming with any information concerning Marty due to patient/doctor confidentiality, that's if he was actually her doctor. If he sought any pertinent information about Marty, specifically about her current emotional makeup, it would require a B&E. He didn't want to risk getting caught, lest he lose his private investigator's license.

She was obviously fucking this cop. But what was she getting out of it other than sex? He was a cop and had to know somewhat of her past, especially with the Gallagher Simms thing. So he was just in it for the sex. Cooz wondered where Robbins' beat was. Maybe he met her on a pullover. He remembered the scratch on Marty's passenger side near the taillight and what looked like a new taillight. In lieu of a ticket for some infraction, had she offered sex? Not the first time that happened. *If there was a pullover, could a traffic camera have captured it?* And would he be lucky enough to get a copy of the recording if it were the night Tina St. Clair was killed, considering it was for a broken taillight?

Cooz decided to take a drive up to the St. Clair residence. After paying the bill, he left with a renewed mission. When he arrived, he was greeted by Mrs. St. Clair at the door. She let him in, and they had a seat in the living room. "I don't know if you know this, but I am technically off your daughter's case. The Santa Barbara Sheriffs don't think it was Marty Remy who killed your daughter," Cooz stated.

"Do they have any suspects?" Mrs. St. Clair asked.

"No. Not one. If you and your husband agree to have me investigate the case, I would have the legal authority to pursue it. Would you agree to that? Of course, you would need to confer with your husband," Cooz remarked.

"No, I don't need to. We want closure. So, yes, we would grant you authority to pursue the case," she said with sad but reassuring eyes.

"Good, I'll e-mail you a contract with all the pertinent information. Two thousand a week plus expenses. Do you agree to that?"

"That's fine. Let's make sure we get her. My daughter had so much to live for," she said as her eyes welled up.

"I'd like to look around the premises if you don't mind?"

"Please, feel free," she said. Cooz stood up, shook Mrs. St. Clair's hand, reassuring her of his efforts, and then stepped towards the door.

Cooz went straight towards the fermentation shack and stopped in front of the wooden fence, bent down and sifted through the grass. He then shifted his focus near the bush, sifted through the dirt and suddenly found what he thought he'd find—the broken piece of taillight. That's all he needed. He got in his car and drove away.

On the way back to Santa Barbara, Cooz called Fajida, his old partner from the days on the Los Feliz police force. "I thought you'd be in Costa Rica enjoying retirement," Fajida said when she saw Cooz's number on her phone.

"Not a chance. I'm doing some private investigation for some clients. A murder case. And guess who's the prime?" Cooz prompted Fajida.

"No. Don't tell me," Fajida said rhetorically, knowing the answer.

"That's right. Marty Kittering. She's Marty Remy now," Cooz proffered.

"Holy shit. What the hell did she do?"

"She killed one of her employees and stuck her in a wine fermentation tank."

"Fucking A. So she's up to her old tricks again," Fajida said, amused. "What was her motive?"

"You know her. It's all about sex. Listen, I remember you said you had a cousin on the Santa Barbara Police force. I need to get some traffic camera footage from last Thursday. Can you help?"

"What time frame?"

"Good question. Ah, between 6 and 8 p.m. I'm looking for her car being pulled over for a broken taillight. I think she sweet-talked herself out of a ticket," Cooz said. "I found a piece of broken plastic from the crime scene. I'm pretty sure it's from her car."

"I can't believe you're chasing after her again, Cooz."

"Yeah, it's like marrying your ex-wife looking to fall in love," Cooz remarked.

"Not with this one," Fajida said. "She's deadly. You just be careful."

"I'm a big boy. Let me know when you get something? See you later, Fajida."

Chapter Twelve

The store was closed when Marty grabbed a bottle of Roaring Eagle Cabernet Sauvignon 2012 from a locked case in the storage room and stuffed it inside a carry bag. Retail list price of the wine: $899. She exited the store, set the alarm, hopped in a van and drove away. She decided to take a leisurely drive up along the coast towards San Francisco. It was a beautiful sunny autumn day and she opted to lay off the Amoros and instead squeezed some Valerian tincture underneath her tongue. It was time to relax and enjoy the scenery. She figured she'd get to her destination, the Cliff House, by noon and then back to Santa Barbara by dinner time. She had plans with Officer Robbins.

When she hit the 101, she kept looking at the time and soon realized that she had to make better time and hopped on the I-5. She got a little anxious, fished through her pocketbook, pulled out the vial of Amoros, popped one in her mouth and then another. She downed the sex pills with some bottled water, kicked up the radio, some jazz station, and hit the gas. "Why are we in such a rush?" Didier asked from the back of the van.

"I have to drop some wine off to a friend

"I know who it is," Sookie crooned like a little girl.

"Who?" Marty toyed with her.

"That lady from the radio station," Sookie replied.

"You're right."

"That old gasbag?" Didier smartly asked.

"Yes, Dorothy Lanore," Marty said.

"Why didn't you mail it to her?" Sookie asked.

"It's a surprise," Marty said with a smile.

"Oh, you are a bad girl," Sookie said.

"And so am I," Didier said as he began to fondle Sookie, who in return socked Didier in the eye.

"Hey, I thought you liked that the other night?" Didier asked curiously, befuddled.

"I was excited. You got me when I was vulnerable watching Marty have sex in the shower," Sookie said.

"Just say no, Sookie. He'll get the message," Marty said.

"He's a real *cachon*," Sookie complained.

"I know," Marty said.

"You want it. Lorraine's not here to give it to you anyway," Didier said, teasing Sookie.

Sookie "tutted" and cringed her face at him. "Of all the men in the world, I had to be stuck with him."

Marty laughed and said, "Better him than to be stuck in jail like Lorraine."

"My poor *cherie*," Sookie moaned. "Don't you miss her? I do."

"No. She belongs where she is for exploiting people. If it weren't for her, you and Baron would still be alive," Marty said.

"Baron was a bad apple. He would have been put away in some sanitarium," Sookie said.

"I really showed compassion for him. You know I made love to him?" Marty stated.

"Oh, my God, you did?" Sookie asked in disbelief. "He was my poppa."

"It wasn't him. It was Emile," Marty said. "So, in theory, it wasn't your father."

"You're so horny, Marty," Didier said.

"I know. Like how I'm getting now," Marty said as she squeezed her crotch together. "This is going to be a long ride."

"I'm always here for you, Marty," Didier said, offering himself.

"Not in this lifetime," Marty responded.

Marty made good time. She arrived at the parking lot of the Cliff House, overlooking the Pacific Ocean on the western shoreline off San Francisco, in less than six hours. She stepped in the back of the van, dressed in a pair of brown khaki pants and a matching buttoned-down top and then applied a thin-trimmed beard and put on a brown cap as she stuffed her hair underneath. She then pulled out a vial of a liquid sedative called alprazolam (generic Xanax) and a syringe from a small tote bag and filled the syringe with the drug. She grabbed the bottle of Roaring Eagle, extended the syringe needle into the top of the bottle through the cork and emptied the contents into the bottle. She placed the bottle in a Brown Shipping padded box, sealed it and then put a pre-printed label on it addressed to Dorothy Lanore at Wine Chat.

Marty grabbed one of the hand-held inventory devices from the store, took the box and exited the van. "You two stay here, I'll be right back," she said as she closed the sliding van door.

She stepped into the lobby of the Cliff House where Wine Chat recorded its show every Friday afternoon. "Delivery for Dorothy Lanore," Marty said to the hostess as she placed the box on a table nearby.

"More wine?" the hostess asked.

Marty shrugged her shoulders and began to exit the restaurant.

"I'll make sure she gets it," the hostess said. Marty raised her arm, acknowledging her statement, and then left the Cliff House and drove away.

Marty's plan was in play. Once Dorothy saw the bottle, Marty sensed, she wouldn't be able to resist having at least one glass on air. That was her M.O. Marty knew this because she always seemed a bit more boisterous towards the end of her show, which meant she had had a few glasses of wine. After all, it was a show about wine. And Marty was aware she drove south along the coast to go back home because she, Dorothy, always spoke of how *splendid* of a drive it was on the way to Monterey Bay on Highway 1.

Marty pulled off the side of the road, took off her masquerade, and continued to drive south back to Santa Barbara. She tuned into Wine Chat on the radio. "Where are we going now, Marty?" Sookie suddenly asked.

Marty put up her index finger to her lips and whispered a 'shush' as Bruce Springsteen's "Badland" played. Dorothy Lanore came on the radio as the clatter of china and the hum of the restaurant chimed in the background. "I want to go out tonight. I want to find out what I got," Dorothy said, quoting the song. "Well, baby, I just got a fabulous bottle of Roaring Eagle, vintage 2012, from an adoring fan. Not so bad. Thank you, my lovely," Dorothy said with more excitement than usual. "I also want to thank our wonderful host at the Cliff House where we are coming live to you as we do every Friday afternoon. And this is Wine Chat with your one and only, Dorothy Lanore."

Marty giggled condescendingly and said out loud to the radio, "I hope you enjoy it, you bitch."

"And before I forget, I will be at the Regency Hotel in the Embarcadero in San Francisco from November twelfth through the fifteenth signing my new book, *My View of the World as Seen Through a Wine Glass*. I will also be broadcasting live from the California Grand Sommelier Challenge on Friday the sixteenth. I welcome all you wine enthusiasts in the San Francisco area to come and join us for a fun-filled week of Wine Chat, the sommelier challenge and all things wine because wine is an adventure," Dorothy said.

Dorothy wasted no time. She let the Roaring Eagle breathe just a bit and began to partake of the aromatics of one of the finer Cabernet Sauvignons on the market, which the vintners boasted had plenty of black cherry, licorice, tanned leather, violets, and an espresso nose. Subtle, yet complex and elegant. At $900 a bottle it had better be, Dorothy noted in a conversation with the general manager of the Cliff House, with whom she did not share any of the wine. Dorothy only savored a half a glass, corked the rest of the bottle and stored it away for later indulgence at home—if it made it that far. And it didn't.

After the show, Dorothy got into her later model Volvo and drove away, heading southbound as the sun gave way to the usual fog that seemed to creep its way along the coast every time she drove home. Before she hit Highway 1, Dorothy pulled to the side of the road, lit a cigarette, pulled the bottle of Roaring Eagle Marty delivered to her from her carry bag and let out a smile of delight. Then she placed the bottle back in the bag and began to drive away. She stopped suddenly, grabbed a red go-cup from her backseat and poured herself some of the Roaring Eagle. She took in a waft, sighed in delight, and sipped the wine as she drove with the cigarette in her steering wheel hand.

With every sip, Dorothy kept 'umming' and 'ahhing' with such gusto that she didn't realize the effect the wine was having on her. Normally, she was a stout drinker and could handle even a full bottle of wine. But she was feeling no pain, as the saying goes, and began to sing along with Johnny Mathis performing "Misty" on the radio as she swerved more than normal, considering the winding drive along Highway 1. "And I feel like I'm clinging to a cloud," she sang with a slur as the fog became denser. Oncoming headlights from the other direction seemed blurry. Cars blew their horns as she crossed the meridian line. She continued to drink more of the wine and lit another cigarette.

When she took a drag on her cigarette, all she could hear was a horn blaring. She cut the steering wheel to the left, immediately scraping her car along the steep rocky wall and then cut the wheel to the right. She headed back into the southbound lane, but on an angle, and hopped over the guard rail and was lodged there, teetering, only feet away from the edge of the cliff. She had lost her cigarette in her carry bag, which caused a fire. Dorothy was slightly unconscious as she leaned toward the passenger seat where her carry bag was, and her hair caught fire. Her orange hair was ablaze.

Dorothy somehow had the presence of mind to pick up the bottle of Roaring Eagle and doused her hair with the remains of the wine, which was maybe a glass. Then she rubbed her head against her carry bag, which extinguished the blaze. She then heard yelling from a passerby who had stopped to help her. "Don't move. Help is on its way!" Dorothy looked at herself in the mirror. Her hair was charred as well as her eyebrows, and blood trickled down her face. "Are you okay?" the passerby asked as he stood outside her car while traffic in both directions came to a halt. Dorothy looked over at him, realized her predicament and then passed out. She had no idea she was drugged. A tow truck eventually secured her car with a tow chain. She was able to exit her car, stumbling, but without harm.

Dorothy was brought into an ambulance where she was quickly administered a breathalyzer test by a sheriff, who found her legally over the alcohol limit by a mere ten one-hundredths of a percent, and then was taken to the nearest hospital where she was treated for some charring of her scalp. A blood test revealed she had alprazolam in her system. The doctor in charge of her treatment, who knew of Dorothy Lanore, having seen a promotional placard of her when he frequented the Cliff House with his wife for occasional dinners, suggested she ease up on the Xanax. "Oh, I didn't know I had taken any today," she responded coyly. The results of the blood test were conveniently misplaced prior to Dorothy being escorted back to the local sheriff's station where she was then administered a breathalyzer test for alcohol. The doctor had told the sheriff he would fax the results of the blood test when they finished it. Two hours had passed since the first breathalyzer and the test showed she was under the legal limit. She was then released and let go, after being ticketed for reckless driving.

Marty had arrived back to town feeling energetic, although she had endured the twelve-hour drive to San Francisco and back with a charged-up libido, her pussy twitching every mile of the way. She had texted Officer Robbins confirming their date an hour before arriving in Santa Barbara and had not heard back from him. She nonetheless popped two more Amoros. She took a quick shower, primped herself, put on a black satin short dress and black pumps, a spritz of her favorite tangerine-infused perfume and headed to the Ravenous Feline Restaurant.

Marty waited almost an hour at a table for Officer Robbins. He was a no-show, so she decided to leave, although she had not texted him at all. She figured something must have come up. If he had given her the brush-off, she didn't want to appear too eager. She had her pride. She finished her wine, paid the bill, and began to exit when she noticed Michelle Sloane at the bar, sitting alone. She decided to say hello. Michelle was sipping on a Rosé spritzer that was made with the wine, muddled strawberries, lemon, and mint. Normally, it was more of a summer drink, but the Ravenous Feline made the finest in town and besides, it was her favorite drink, and she was in the mood.

As they say, there are no coincidences. When Marty arrived at the restaurant, the hostess, who just happened to be a good friend of Michelle's and her one-time lover, sent Michelle a text saying, *Marty Remy is here. May be your lucky night.* What Michelle's friend inferred was not that Michelle was hoping she would land the job at Remy Wine and Spirits and that bumping into Marty might give her a chance to further impress her. No, Michelle had the hots for Marty, and her friend knew it because that's all Michelle had been talking about.

Michelle had been waiting to make her move, but Marty beat her to the punch. "Oh, hi, Michelle," Marty said to Michelle whose back was to Marty.

Michelle turned around with eager excitement and said, "Oh, hi, Marty. I hope you don't mind me calling you Marty?"

"No, not at all. What are you doing here?" Marty asked as she looked at Michelle, who was wearing shiny lip gloss and a green silk dress that matched her own sparkling eyes. "You look nice," Marty said.

"Oh, thanks. You too. I come here for the drinks. They make a great Rosé spritzer. Here, try it?" Michelle handed Marty her drink.

Marty sipped at it as she watched Michelle stare at her. "Tasty. But I'm more of a purist."

"Of course, you are. You own a wine store," Michelle said with a giggle of affirmation while Marty admired Michelle's ornate dangling jade earrings.

"I love your earrings," Marty said, caressing them, which excited Michelle. They stood face to face.

"My father brought them back from India. They're my favorite."

"They complement your eyes. So stunning," Marty said in an amorous way. "Are you with anyone? Let's make it a night on the town?" Marty offered.

Michelle knew you had to make chance happen and said, "I would love to."

After a night of drinking and dancing with men, with other women and with each other, Michelle suggested they go back to her apartment for a jacuzzi. Marty agreed. She followed Michelle back to her place. When they got there, Marty asked, "Do you have a bathing suit for me?"

Michelle laughed and said, "Naked only jacuzzi."

Marty smirked and said, "Only in California."

"All the way. I'm born and raised here," Michelle said with a smile.

"Are you related to Justin Sloane? The big investor?"

"He's my father."

"And you want to work at a wine store?"

"I make my own way. Besides, we had a falling out a couple of years ago," Michelle said somberly. "But I'm okay. You're here."

Marty politely smiled and asked, "So, do you have any wine?"

"Too bad we're not at my parent's house. He has one of the biggest and best wine cellars in Southern California, if not in the whole state," she said almost apologetically. "I have some Gruet Rosé."

"That'll be fine," Marty said with a 'who cares' attitude. Michelle poured them both a glass and then proceeded to undress herself in the kitchen where they were standing.

"Are you going in with your clothes on?" Michelle asked Marty, who then took off her clothes. Michelle pulled out some beach blankets from a small closet and handed one to Marty. They wrapped themselves. Michelle opened a pair of French doors that led to an open terrace. They walked twenty feet towards the pool area. It was a bit cool out, so no one was there. Michelle let her towel down and quickly entered the Jacuzzi. Marty stuck her toe in, shrugged her shoulders, unwrapped the towel and eased herself into the very warm spritzy water, while Michelle scanned Marty's naked body.

Michelle took notice of Marty's raven tattoo on her shoulder and said, "Let me see your tattoo? What is it?"

Marty turned her back towards Michelle, who touched the tattoo with soft caresses. Marty gave the impression she liked her touch. "It's a raven. I got it in Marseille."

"I dig it. It's so Edgar Allen Poe the way it looks, so surreal," Michelle said as she rubbed Marty's back.

"That feels good," Marty said, which prompted Michelle to nibble and kiss Marty's shoulder. Marty turned her head towards Michelle, and they began to kiss tenderly. After some serious petting and kissing, Marty and Michelle continued their encounter inside Michelle's bedroom. Marty was not only on the Amoros, but was so adept at making love, especially to a woman, which seemed natural after Dominika and Lorraine, both of whom taught Marty how to make love to women, that Michelle came numerous times.

Michelle had no idea what she was in for when her friend texted her. It was Nirvanic. She had never climaxed like this before as Marty suckled her clitoris while massaging her bunghole with moist fingers and tongue. Marty sucked on Michelle's vagina, tasting all her flowing juices. Michelle, in turn, provided Marty with the same pleasure. She was immediately hooked on Marty's nectar. It was sweeter than any she'd ever had. They tribbled each other, staring into each other's eyes, expressing utter delight. Michelle cooed and was lost in the moment. The hours passed. They eventually fell asleep in a sixty-nine position. When Michelle awoke in the morning, Marty was gone.

Chapter Thirteen

Three days later, Marty had one of the store associates contact Michelle informing her of a job offer, to start immediately if she were available. Michelle eagerly accepted the position. When she showed up for work at Remy Wine and Spirits, Marty made no mention of the lustful night that started off at the Ravenous Feline. Marty was professional, to the point of being curt with Michelle. There was a little more than a week until the California Grand Sommelier Challenge, and Marty was in focus mode. This bewildered Michelle. She pouted inside yet knew better not to bring 'it' up with Marty, lest she risk her job. She was aware that Marty was a convoluted, complex woman who had a lot on her plate. Her desire would have to be put on hold. *Until when?* Michelle wondered.

Michelle decided to get in Marty's good graces by working hard and performing well and to eventually introduce her to her father, who could prove quite lucrative for Marty, in the hopes of brokering wine deals between her father and high-end oenophiles and wine merchants. But first, she would have to make right with her father. That would be well worth it to prove her value to Marty, with all the benefits that offered, including rewarding the love she was beginning to feel for Marty. *Oh God, Marty, please say something to me that expresses your mutual feeling,* Michelle whispered to herself as Marty spoke with one of the managers, offering some last directives before she left the store.

The following day Michelle felt extraordinarily agitated. It's that feeling you get when you're on the losing end of unrequited love—an affair that had begun in her head after one night of outrageous sex. And one night is all it took to convince Michelle she was madly in love with Marty. Her usual prescription meds didn't help her anxiety any, yet she didn't want to take more than what was prescribed. So she decided to visit her therapist, Dr. Bollinger.

In Dr. Bollinger's office, Michelle waited for him fully clothed. She was fidgeting when the doctor entered the office. He noticed right away and asked, "What's going on?"

"I'm feeling anxious. I need something stronger than what I'm on," she said in an agitated voice.

"Anything new in your life to explain why you're feeling this way?" the doctor asked.

"A new job. A new girlfriend," she said, realizing she just called Marty her girlfriend.

"Seems like a lot at once for you," he said. "What type of work?"

"I'm a wine associate. At Remy Wine and Spirits. I'm seeing the owner."

Dr. Bollinger was beside himself. Not only was he hoodwinked by Marty, he was having to endure salt rubbed in the wound. And at his own expense. Marty was a patient having sex with another of his patients. And he was getting none. Well, at least from Marty. He tried with Michelle, but she wasn't buying for obvious reasons. So, he decided to fight fire with fire and gave a handful of Amoros to Michelle. At least he would have fun with this serendipitous occasion. *To be a fly on the wall*, he smirked to himself. "Take one a day of these and if you need to, double your dose of the Xanax," he said.

Michele downed an Amoros inside her car and drove away. An hour later she stopped at the store. She asked one of the associates if Marty was around. She was told she had left for the day and was probably at home. Reluctant to ask where Marty lived, Michelle Googled her address and headed for the unknown. When she arrived at Marty's condo, she knocked on the door. Marty opened the door wearing a cream-colored cashmere sweat suit. *Even dressed down, Marty looks ravishing*, Michelle said to herself as she felt fire in her loins.

"Michelle, what are you doing here?" a surprised Marty asked.

Michelle's heart was racing. She paused and then finally said, "Marty, we made passionate love the other night. And now I'm working for you. Do you have any feelings about what happened?"

"Michelle, that was, ah…" Marty said when she was interrupted by Michelle.

"What, a one-nighter?" Michelle said bitterly.

"Yes. I'm studying for the sommelier challenge. Can we talk about this some other time?" Marty pleaded.

"No. I have desire for you. You have desire for me. I know what that is. You can't fight chemistry," Michelle said.

"I had desire. Just that night. I'm a busy woman. I really can't do this," Marty said firmly but softly. "You're a sweet girl. I like you. I think you have a lot to offer, but not right now," Marty said a little more gingerly and convincingly.

"Maybe when you finish with the sommelier challenge, we can see each other?" Michelle asked submissively.

"We'll talk when I get back from San Francisco. In a couple of weeks."

Michelle kissed Marty on the lips and said, "Good night, precious." She gazed into Marty's eyes and then ran to her car, feeling enraptured by her renewed prospects. Meanwhile, Cooz sat across the street in his car. He had taken photos of Marty and Michelle. Marty had not noticed when she shut the door behind her.

"And Marty continues to spin her web," Cooz said out loud.

As Michelle drove around the block, she began to pant with sexual desire and then began to rub her crotch. It wasn't enough—she had to have Marty. Michelle pulled up to the curb, parked her car, got out of her car and meandered her way through the condo complex towards Marty's back terrace. It was walled, so she eased herself up and supported her body with her arms stretched out on top of the wall. She was able to see inside Marty's kitchen where Marty sat at the table. She was smelling what must have been scents from individual vials and then describing them to someone, but Michelle couldn't see anyone else.

Michelle watched Marty go through the routine of smelling and describing for more than an hour. Marty then got up from the table and shut the kitchen light off. A few moments later the bedroom light went on, Marty appeared, slipped into bed, and the light went off. *Was the other person in the room with her? Had they also slipped into bed with Marty?* The idea enraged her. *She has a lover. She's cheating on me.* Michelle ran towards Marty's front door and knocked on it heavily. A light went on inside Marty's condo. There were footsteps and then a pause as Marty looked through the peephole. Marty finally opened the door.

"What is it, Michelle?" Marty asked in an annoyed tone.

"You have a lover in bed with you?" Michelle asked, shivering with rage.

Marty began to sense that Michelle had some psychological issues of her own. "What's going on with you?" she asked.

"Ever since we made love, I've been having anxiety. So I went to see my therapist. He gave me these pills and my desire for you has gotten worse. I can't control it."

"What kind of pills and who's your therapist?" Marty asked reluctantly because she knew the answer.

Michelle pulled out the Amoros pills from her pocket and showed Marty. When Marty saw them, she realized her fear for Michelle. "Don't tell me you're seeing Bollinger?"

"Yes, he's my therapist. Why?" Michelle asked.

"Because he's also my therapist and those are sex pills. Like Viagra for women. Come inside?"

They stepped into the living room. "You shouldn't be taking those pills. They're only going to get you all horny and you'll be knocking on my door. Just give them to me, and I'll deal with it," Marty said.

Michelle obligingly handed the pills to Marty. "Why would he give me sex pills?"

"Did you tell him about us?"

Michelle nodded.

"He's fucked up. He thought he was playing a joke," Marty said.

"We should report him," Michelle said emphatically.

"That's not a good idea."

"How do you know they're sex pills? Are you taking them?"

"They help me have clarity. But the side effects…well, you saw what happened the other night," Marty professed.

"So, what, you don't really care for girls?" Michelle asked.

"I generally have sex with men," Marty said.

"But you were so into it."

"That's what happens when you take two at time," Marty said.

"Oh, my God, I can barely handle one."

"You have to know how to control yourself. I've had lots of practice."

"So, who were you talking to?"

"I'm just preparing for the sommelier challenge," Marty said. "But you shouldn't be stalking me, Michelle. Don't you have any other friends?"

"I'm sorry, Marty," Michelle said as her eyes began to well up. Marty hugged Michelle. Michelle, in turn, caressed Marty affectionately.

Marty stepped away from her and said, "I'm your boss now. It's not a good thing to have going on, let alone at work."

"I want you so badly," Michelle begged.

"Go home and take a cold shower," Marty said and then she stepped towards the front door.

"What am I going to do?" Michelle asked rhetorically.

"Not think of me so much," Marty said as she opened the door. "Have a good night."

Michelle tried to kiss Marty on the way out, but Marty skirted her approach. "Good night," she said and exited, as frustrated about Marty as she had been before.

Marty resigned herself to accept that the situation between her and Michelle was partly of her own doing. *Maybe it wasn't a good idea to have hired her? But it is what it is.* Yet something needed to be done about Dr. Bollinger. What he was doing to other female patients, especially Michelle, forfeiting his professional responsibilities for a few jollies, angered Marty. She also realized that she didn't have to see him as a patient. There were certainly other therapists in town. Scoring the Amoros was another issue. *But would he tattle on me to John's attorney out of spite for abandoning him as a patient? He could, considering his sophomoric behavior.* Marty slipped back in bed and fell fast asleep.

Marty was awoken by a gentle but incessant knocking at her door. She looked over at her clock radio for the time. It was almost 2:00—in the a.m. "What now?" she said as she dragged herself out of bed. She looked through the peephole of her door, rolled her eyes and shook her head when she saw Michelle for the third time that night. "What is it, Michelle?" Marty asked from behind the closed door.

"Marty, I need your help. Please!" Michelle pleaded.

"With what at this hour? I'm not giving you sex," Marty said.

"I have Dr. Bollinger in my trunk," Michelle said in a whisper.

Marty quickly opened her door. "Don't tell me you…?" Marty questioned her, wide awake now.

"No, he's alive. He's just passed out," Michelle said.

"Why?!" Marty asked excitedly.

"Oh, come on, Marty, I know you were involved with those chef murders."

"That was all mistaken identity," Marty said, lying through her teeth.

"We need to do something with him," Michelle said.

"How did you get him in your trunk? Did he see you?" Marty asked.

"I snuck up behind him when he was entering his house and knocked him out."

"What has gotten into you? If he had seen you, you could go to jail for abduction. Don't you know that? And you don't want to kill him because that's pre-meditated murder," Marty said as she slid her thumb along her throat.

"What are we going to do?"

"We? Just drive him back near his house and dump him on the curb. And hope he doesn't recollect a thing. That's what you're going to do," Marty said didactically. And then the doctor's muffled yelling voice could be heard from the trunk. "You didn't tape his mouth?" Marty asked, baffled.

"I've never done this before," a confused Michelle said.

"You need to cover up your face and then knock him out again," Marty said.

"Help me, Marty?" Michelle cried out.

"Oh, Christ!" Marty said and ran back in her bedroom, pulled off her pillowcase and then grabbed a rolling pin from a kitchen drawer. She then ran out the door toward Michelle's car. "Give me the key," Marty said. She then put the case on her head, popped the trunk open and swatted several times at Dr. Bollinger's head with the rolling pin. She quickly shut the trunk and said to Michelle, "Get going." Michelle kissed her through the pillowcase and then drove away. Marty took off the case, stepped back inside her condo, went back to bed and said to herself, *she's a lot like me.* And then slept like a baby—a piece of cake.

Two days later, Marty went to her monthly check-in with the good doctor. When Marty saw him with a bruised forehead, she asked in a surprised yet sardonic voice, "What happened, one of your patients decline your unwanted advances?"

"Funny," Dr. Bollinger said with much consternation. "You're going to have to find yourself a new supplier. I'm moving my practice back East."

"Oh, how unfortunate," Marty said disappointedly.

"My partner can handle your case. And don't try to hustle her, you're not her type."

"As if I hustled you?" Marty said ironically.

"You have it upside down, darling. Who invited whom to inspect their vagina? I'm a clinical therapist, for God sakes," the doctor said with a quiver in his voice.

"It's that shit I'm forced to take that made me into an old school-marm."

"Without the proper medicine, you would have kept on having schizophrenic episodes. I'm surprised you're not having any now. Are you?"

"I guess I substituted the devil for Satan."

"Are you saying you are having psychotic episodes?" the doctor asked with professional concern.

"You go wherever you are going, and I'll be just fine," she responded.

"Maybe it's for the best. Although you were a great lay," he said in a conciliatory voice.

"It was fun while it lasted. But maybe there's a lesson to all this," Marty said.

"What's that?"

"It's that you should use greater discretion when fucking your patients," Marty said as she stood up from the chair. "Looks like someone hit you with a rolling pin," she said.

"That or a baseball bat," he said, knowing that Marty had something to do with his bruised head considering her jaded past. *Best that you leave town,* a colleague who knew about his propensity for having sexual relations with his patients had recommended.

Marty was faced with a conundrum. She no longer wanted to be on anti-psychotic drugs for her own mental stability as well as for her sexuality. If she stopped taking the clozopine, she risked losing her rights to visit her son, Jackie. Yet the relationship with him was strained and would probably continue to face obstacles as time progressed. Particularly, that she could only see him once a month. Unless she moved back to Hawaii and really cleaned up her act, she was stuck with the arrangement. She didn't see John wavering on his demands.

Would she have to give up Jackie to become naturally whole again, without any drugs, even the Amoros, which had been incredible and reminded of her sexual exploits when she was younger? If she chose that path, she would need something more holistic to keep her mind, body, and spirit in homeostasis. Yet could she live with the results of giving up her son for a healthier life? This is what she faced because if she continued on this path, her life and possibly that of others could come into harm's way.

Her life in Hawaii had been the healthiest and the most productive and loving right before she left for her business trip to France. Her experiences when she arrived there triggered a deep recession in her mental state. Albeit Lorraine had pushed her over the edge into the abyss that awoke the demons within her psyche, she needed to exorcize the past and that's why she subconsciously chose to go to France where she wound up being abducted. It was the accident with Dominika that held her prisoner, yet she had to become a prisoner herself to achieve catharsis, which ultimately led to her being at the Alala Holistic.

She had resolution with Dominika, yet she needed to make amends—to apologize to Dominika, in her own way. *Perhaps that will come in time.* But why was she experiencing the ghosts from the past—Sookie and Didier and Bubba Arnet, Angela Jordan and Stan Kravitz, even? *Am I really psychotic—having episodes? Or were they real in some way?* Was it an accident that she was given the Amoros that awakened these spirits or was it just happenstance? She needed to find out. And she needed to become healthy again. And she needed to stop doing away with people out of convenience. It was time to get healthy.

Marty pulled out the vial of Amoros from her pocketbook. There were only a few left, and she tossed them out her car window. She had virtually weaned herself off the clozapine, and then and there decided she was done with it. Which meant that she also had to give up her rights to see Jackie. *It's for the better for everyone involved. In time, he will understand.* Marty suddenly felt reassured. She smiled knowing, everything would be okay and then she took notice of an Angela Jordan film marathon at the Hitchcock Cinema. She pulled off over and parked her car, purchased a ticket and went inside.

Marty took a seat towards the back. *Love Be Damned,* produced by Stan Kravitz, had already begun. Marty recollected the film as one of Angela Jordan's better ones. Her character was the wife of a WWII captain who was a prisoner in a Japanese War camp. She has an affair with his best friend, thinking that her husband had been killed, to only have him return after the war. But she already had fallen in love with his best friend. Marty couldn't help but think of what happened to John and

Jacqueline when she was under treatment at the Alala Holistic. *John needed comfort and who was there for him?* A pretty French nanny. How could she blame him?

During a sex scene between Angela Jordan and the husband's best friend, Angela appeared in the seat next to Marty. "The director didn't know we were actually making love," Angela said.

"Better than make believe. No wonder why you won so many awards," Marty replied.

"I think it's because they liked my tits and ass," Angela said cynically.

"You were one of the hottest actresses in Hollywood," Marty said.

"You're sweet, Marty," Angela said.

"It's terrible what happened to you and Stan," Marty said and then a man in a couple of rows in front of her "shushed" her.

"Let's get out of here?" Angela said and then Marty and she exited the theater.

Chapter Fourteen

It was cold and damp when Marty arrived at the Regency Hotel in downtown San Francisco. The hotel was bustling with the upcoming California Grand Sommelier Challenge activity. She checked in and had her luggage dropped off in her room. She was feeling energetic and stopped by the banquet rooms where there were several speakers on various topics on wine already in progress. The one that intrigued her most was on the burgeoning Santa Barbara County Wine industry. Some of the top names in the wine and hospitality business had sponsored the event, including Friberg J. Frye Winery, Reinhart Vineyards and Cutiella-Sampson Furnishings. The challenge would begin in two days, but Marty wanted to study and stay focused. She decided that she should have a bite to eat and then go back to her room.

As she walked by one of the banquet rooms, she saw an advertisement of Dorothy Lanore's book signing. Marty decided to take a quick look and then she would be off. When she stepped into the banquet room, Dorothy was signing her books and gabbing about her recent accident. "I was dangling on the side of the cliff, and I was inches away from going over as my car teetered back and forth. It was terrifying, but here I am," Dorothy Lanore said with a smile, penciled eyebrows and the fake orange wig she wore in lieu of her singed hair. Marty laughed to herself at how hideous she looked.

Marty picked up a copy of *My View of the World as Seen Through a Wine Glass* and browsed through it. "Would you like me to sign it for you?" Dorothy Lanore asked.

"Sure," Marty said and then handed it to Dorothy.

"What's your name?" Dorothy asked.

"Marty. Marty Remy."

"Oh? You came all the way up here to San Francisco just for my book signing?" Dorothy asked coyly, knowing that it was far from the truth.

"Not quite. I'm in the challenge."

"You think you really know your wine?" Dorothy shot at Marty.

"I do. Especially Roaring Eagle wines," Marty said with a straight face. She picked up her book and read the inscription: *To Marty, The truth always meanders between fantasy and reality. But always trust your olfactory bulb—it never lies. Dorothy Lanore.* "I'll remember that," Marty said as she tilted the book towards Dorothy. Marty paid the cashier and left. Dorothy Lanore never knew the truth about the Roaring Eagle wine Marty gave her, only that it must have been she who sent it. She sensed Marty wanted acknowledgment for her presumed acumen as a well-informed wine merchant. *Why else would she be at the challenge?* Dorothy questioned rhetorically.

Although Dorothy was provided a hotel room by her publisher, she opted to drive home instead. On her way along the coast, just a mile past Devil's Slide, while listening to Harry Nilsson's "Jump into the Fire," Dorothy ran into trouble. Under normal circumstances, she would have had no problem navigating the winding coastal highway, even after several glasses of wine. But as a result of her most recent accident, her confidence in her own driving had been diminished. That, combined with the fast pace of the song and the alcohol level in her blood, meant her judgment was impaired enough that she miscalculated a swerve in the road and hit a car in the other lane head-on. She was killed instanta- neously. A faulty seatbelt was an additional culprit in her death— something that was a result of her last accident and had been overlooked. The other driver survived with just a concussion and some minor bruis- es.

112

On the way out of the hotel, Marty asked the concierge for a good Italian restaurant nearby. He suggested Giacomelli Ristorante in North Beach. Marty hopped into a cab and took a quick ride to the restaurant. The restaurant was a local favorite for four generations of ownership and had been recently renovated in a modern style—the brick-and-mortar walls had been painted white and there were plenty of stainless steel accents. The floors were refinished in beechwood. Several blown-up celebrity photographs, remnants from the restaurant's early years, hung on the walls. One of Joe DiMaggio and Marilyn Monroe as they were about to kiss captured Marty's attention. She was mesmerized as many patrons had been when they first saw the life-sized image of one of the most admired couples of the day.

It was early lunchtime and there was a modest crowd. Marty was seated and was immediately taken by a strikingly handsome man who was tall, dark, and handsome and who was as solid as an NFL tight end with long wavy black hair. He wore a brown Armond suit, and he wasted no time, stepping towards Marty's table. "Hello, I'm your host Fabrizio. My friends call me Fab," he said as he handed Marty a menu.

"I'm sure they do," Marty said smartly as she admired his looks.

"You can call me Fab if you like," he said.

"And we haven't even had a drink yet," she replied, playing a little cat and mouse.

"There's plenty of time for that. Are you a local or just passing through?"

"I'm here for the challenge."

"To see if you can pick me up in one wink?" he asked.

"Hah," Marty as she laughed off his pass. "No, the sommelier challenge being held at the Regency."

"As an observer or participant?"

"Strictly a participant," she replied. "So, what does a girl have to do to get a drink around here?"

"I'm your man," Fab said. "You really think you're going to win the challenge?" Fab said with an air of cockiness.

"I grew up with wine. I'm a trained chef and I own a wine store," Marty remarked casually.

"So. I also grew up with wine. I'm a trained sommelier and I own a restaurant."

"Oh, a participant?" Marty asked.

Fab nodded and then asked, "I tell you what. How about you and I do a little challenge of our own? To see who is the better."

She paused and then said, "Okay. But for every question answered correctly we keep one article of clothing on. And for every question answered incorrectly, one article of clothing shall be removed." Marty then winked at him.

"The stakes aren't high enough. I get to do whatever I want to you," he said as he looked over at several patrons being seated. "I get off at 11:00," Fab said. "What are you drinking?"

"Surprise me," she said as she thought about the foregone conclusion that they'd wind up naked anyway. He'd get to do whatever he wanted at that point.

Marty looked at the menu, which dazzled her culinary senses with entrees that included pan-seared chops in a roasted garlic cream infused with sun-dried tomatoes; braised lamb shanks *fagioli*; cured pork cheeks and white truffles served with a porcini ravioli; and the *bistecca al Fiorentina*—a grilled ribeye steak prepared with extra-virgin olive oil, green peppercorns, fresh lemon, and *erbaco* (fine herbs).

Fab brought Marty a glass of red wine. *He was smooth*, Marty thought. *And he had this finesse like a Donatello sculpture.* Marty felt suddenly smitten. "Oh, bring your bathing suit," he said as he left the table.

Marty sipped the wine. *Pinot. Good boy*, she said to herself. *He can read his customers well. Bathing suit? Not much to take off.*

Marty opted to eat light. She had to study. So she chose to have a salad of warm radicchio, chèvre, pear, and walnuts with a balsamic honey dressing. And the house-cured salami with fennel, garlic, and red wine. She couldn't have been more pleased. Later, Fab brought over a complimentary dessert. "It's our house specialty. *Ama la mela.* Love apple," he said.

"Is this how you lure all your women?" Marty asked.

Fab flipped back his hair and asked, "You think I have to lure them? Before you leave, take a look at our wine cellar. I think you'll be impressed."

Marty bit into the cake and said as Fab left the table, "It's lovely. Thank you."

Marty did saunter downstairs with Fab to the wine cellar before she left. It was cool and dank. The brick walls provided the right climate although it was temperature controlled and secured with a locked, grated-steel door and a bolted alarm-sensored glass door. Fab walked her through the cellar towards the back where the higher priced wines were and planted a kiss on Marty's lips while he cupped her breasts. "Do you like my love apples?" Marty whispered into his ear.

"I do. But are they as supple as I think they are?" Fab said and kissed Marty's neck as he ground his groin into hers.

Marty eased him off and said, "You're not going to find out because I'm going to win that challenge of ours."

"Okay. New bet. I win, you come with me to Catalina for a weekend," he said as Marty perused the cellar.

"Fine. But if I win, which I will, I get to have this." Marty pulled a bottle off one of the racks and showed it to Fab.

He read the label and yelled, "That's a 2007 Richebourg."

"All the more incentive to get me naked. Losing your confidence?" she asked, goading him.

Fab gave Marty's body a long glance and thought of how he desired to indulge himself on her pussy. He pondered the upside of the bet and then stuck a curled pinky towards her.

Marty hooked his pinky with hers. And then she grabbed his crotch with her other hand. She got right up into his face and said, "I guess that apple cake worked?"

"Every time," Fab responded. "But you better get going; I need to go back upstairs."

"You don't want any more love apples?".

"I'll be having them later," he said confidently and then walked toward the front of the cellar.

Marty followed him, admiring his ass along the way and said seductively to herself, *Fabulous.*

When Fab and Marty came onto the floor of the restaurant off the cellar stairs, one of the female servers noticed them and smiled at Fab as she passed. She knew what Fab was up to since he had ripped through most of the female servers like a hot knife through butter. His sexual appetite was commensurate with his huge penis. She had been one of his many exploits—obligingly so.

When Marty arrived at the Regency, she was informed of Dorothy Lanore's tragic death by the concierge when she asked where she could purchase a bathing suit. *The grim reaper finally caught up to her,* Marty thought and then replied to the concierge, "I'd like to send some flowers." He recommended she have them sent to the PBR radio station

116

Lanore worked for. He personally assisted Marty with the flower arrangement order. Marty tipped him generously for his efforts and then went into one of the hotel's gift shops and tried on several bathing suits. She settled on a black two-piece designer suit.

Back in her room, Marty picked up one of her study manuals. The breadth of knowledge that a Master Sommelier must accrue to pass the written exam that would be held on the first day of the challenge was overwhelming. This part of the challenge would eliminate over half of the one hundred challengers. Remembering the general laws pertaining to each and every wine locale across the globe was inconceivable yet would be a part of the exam she had to pass. But as long as she had the fundamentals down, she stood a chance at continuing with the challenge, even though she might miss a few questions here and there.

She had all the regions and their varietals, including general price points, reasonably memorized. Obscure questions about acreage prices of growing regions would certainly find their way into the exam. What little knowledge Marty had on the subject, outside of California's Napa Valley, Sonoma Valley, Russian River Valley, Santa Barbara County, etc., would have to do. But since it was the California Grand Sommelier Challenge, questions would likely be more specific to the California wine industry. *Yet it was best to be prepared,* Marty thought.

The second day of the challenge was when it became a little more rigorous. There was a full day of sniffing, gargling, tasting, and spitting. This was where each individual's olfactory skill was put to the test. Blind tasting of specific wines tested the challengers to properly identify specific varietals, regions, makers, vintages and the wine's profile—the smell, taste, and feel of the wine, ergo the nose, nuances, flavors, alcohol content, acidity, tannins and the like. Part of this challenge was to appropriately pair each specific wine with food items.

On the third day of the challenge, the real fun would take place—taking orders from a table of four judges who were mock patrons ordering wine and/or mixed drinks. If wine was chosen, the challenger would have to select the wine, bring it to the table, present the wine, cut the foil, uncork the wine and present the cork to the person who ordered the wine. Then the wine was poured into the correct wine glass. Each step of the challenger's moves was carefully observed and later judged on a point system. If mixed drinks were ordered, the challenger had to properly mix the drinks, garnish them and serve them. In many cases, the challengers who had serving experience in restaurants passed this phase of the challenge. Marty was adept at wine and mixed drinks service and could handle this. This part of the challenge would ultimately whittle down the challengers to five.

On the fourth and final day, the five remaining challengers would sit on a stage and be asked random questions about the wine industry. Three wrong answers and they would be excluded. They would be seated one through five by order of their overall score. The challenger with the lowest overall score would be seated in the first chair, the second in the second chair, the third in the third chair and so forth. The first challenger would be asked the first question. When only two challengers remained, the last remaining person to answer a question correctly became the overall winner of the challenge. If the last challenger answered incorrectly, then that person and the previous challenger got one question. The person who answered it first and correctly won the overall challenge unless they both answered it incorrectly. In that case, the two would repeat the process until one of them answered a question correctly.

Marty walked with Fab towards his three-story executive home on Pfeiffer Street. He took her inside his home that had been renovated by the same architect and contractor that did the renovations at his restaurant. Marty was immediately impressed with the angles, the spaciousness, and the large windows. The home was impeccable and very modern with its pale white walls, white trim, and varnished white pine flooring. *It was reflective of Fab's persona*, Marty gathered— meticulous, vibrant, and strong. The first floor contained the dining room, the kitchen, a bathroom, and a utility room. Fab brought her to the second floor where there was the master bedroom, a walk-in closet, and a relaxation room with a large window that contained only a leather chaise lounge. Marty imagined all the sex that Fab must have had on the chaise. On the opposite side of the bedroom was a sauna room.

The third floor was one big entertainment room with a full-sized pool table and a video layout complete with a high-end 75" flat screen and surround sound and an L-shaped plush leather couch. Fab pulled on the drawstring that opened up collapsible stairs that led to the roof. "After you, my lady," he said to Marty. Marty ascended the stairs and then poked her head through the opening. She was hit by the cool air of the bay, and then she saw the dazzling view of Alcatraz Island.

"Wow," she said amusedly as she continued toward the roof.

"Pretty impressive, hah?" Fab said as they stood on the roof looking out at the one-time infamous prison.

"That's very cool," Marty replied.

"You ever been there?" Fab asked.

"No. Never have," Marty said. "You?"

"High school field trip. I had sex in Al Capone's cell," Fab said with a smirk.

"Now that's a story. How am I not surprised?" Marty said.

"I was very shy in high school. It was my girlfriend who initiated it," he said, attempting to defend his honor.

Marty laughed. "I'm sure you didn't resist."

"I've been debauched ever since," Fab said devilishly. "So what would you like to do, a sauna, music, and wine?"

"Music and wine. Not so compromising," Marty said.

"Music and wine it is then," Fab said and led Marty down to the playroom, left her and continued to the first floor. Marty made herself comfortable on the couch and took her shoes off. Fab returned shortly with a bottle of wine and two glasses. He poured the wine and slipped the bottle down on the side of the couch. He handed Marty the glass.

"What's the secret? What are we drinking?"

"You tell me," Fab prompted.

Marty swirled her glass, raised it towards the light to look at the wine's viscosity and then took a sniff. She raised her eyebrows, took a sip and savored it. Mesmerized, she cocked her head, not completely sure what she was tasting and curiously asked, "Is this a Richebourg?"

Fab grinned and asked, "How did you know?"

"Because it's incredibly ripe and spicy and supple and it's tighter than a virgin's pussy. That's why. And there are a few wines in the world that drink like this," Marty said enthusiastically and took another sip.

"What year, dear?"

"I'll go out on a limb and say 2007," Marty said.

"I think I'm starting to worry," Fab said as he poured Marty some more wine.

Marty took the bottle from him and examined the bottle. "I guess you have to take your shirt off," she said.

By the time they finished the Richebourg and were onto another bottle while listening to the jazz of *Offramp* by the Pat Metheny Group, Marty and Fab were challenging each other on all aspects of wine. Marty was down to her bathing suit, and Fab had only his briefs on. "One more wrong question and I win," Marty said.

"Not quite. I'm known for the walk-off home runs," Fab said. "It's my turn, right? So, what region in the U.S. produced the most wine, pre-Prohibition?" he asked.

Marty thought. It had to be somewhere in California. Something to do with the Catholic Eucharist and drinking of the wine that's representative of the blood of Christ—sacramental wine. "That's easy, Napa Valley."

"Wrong," Fab said. "It was New Mexico."

"I question that one. Just might have to Google it," Marty said. "But I'll give it to you," she said and then she unhooked her top and dropped it on the floor. Fab gazed at her breasts. They were as supple, firm and luscious as the Richebourg.

Marty then asked, "How much is an acre selling for in Napa?"

"Half a million," Fab said quickly without a thought about the question.

"Shit," Marty said under her breath. It wasn't as much about being naked as it was losing. Marty was extremely competitive, whether it was on the high school debate team where she helped win the Oregon State Championship, or in college when she graduated summa cum laude with a 3.9 GPA, she always strove to be the best.

"Total wine sales in California for 2016?" Fab asked without hesitation. "Within a few million."

"Thirty-two billion," Marty said, remembering an article she read on the subject on WineMerchant.com.

"Thirty-four point one billion."

"Who's the authority?" Marty asked poignantly.

"The Wine Academy," he replied.

Marty said with joking consternation, "Come on. That's like asking a priest, 'who has the biggest breasts in porn.' "

"You're a funny one, Marty," Fab said with a laugh.

"Stick around, I have more," Marty said and then she stood up, took her bathing suit bottom off and kissed Fab on the lips. Fab eased Marty onto the couch and kissed her breast tenderly, then down her belly. Marty sighed, enjoying the warmth of his lips against her flesh. He continued to kiss her thigh and slowly put his lips on her moist vulva and inserted his tongue into her vagina. The pleasure was immeasurable. She didn't know if it was the deftness of his cunnilingus ability or the wine or how she felt in Fabrizio's presence; all she knew she was about to orgasm like she hadn't done in a very long time. Perhaps it was the most natural she had felt in a while. Taking the Amoros was more conducive to frenzied sex, not what she was currently experiencing. It was intimate and driven by desire, not artificially induced.

Fab took off his shorts, which exposed his rock-hard penis that had plenty of girth and length. Marty swooned as she took a quick glance at his genitalia before he eased inside her. She paused for just a nanosecond, realizing they were about to have unprotected sex, but it was a flash of a thought before she allowed herself the immense pleasure she was about to receive. She was lost in the sudden moment—in the tenderness. She couldn't believe how she felt, not just physically, emotionally, with the scent of a man permeating her senses. *Could this really be happening? That I'm falling in love? In one day?* She had thought falling in love with John was fast, in less than a week. But one day? In less than twenty-four hours she already started to feel that elation, that sensation of love. She then let out a 'woo.' Fab knew the effect that he had on women. He was a skilled lover, yet Marty was different than any other he had experienced.

Their lovemaking continued in the sauna where there was a profusion of perspiration and body nectar. Marty and Fab's bodies became one on the towel that lay on the floor of the sauna. There was a moment where they gazed into each other's eyes, and both knew something special was happening. Afterward, they showered together and slipped into bed, and what began as pillow talk turned into the hubris of rivals. As much as Marty hated to leave, she not only didn't want to spoil the spectacular evening they'd had; she thought it best she go back to her hotel since the most critical part of the challenge was looming, and she needed to be in good form. Marty caught an Uber back to the Regency. All she could think of was each tender moment of that evening until she finally fell asleep in her room.

Chapter Fifteen

A motorboat docked at the pier of Alcatraz Island. Marty, dressed in broad-striped horizontal black and white prison garb and with her wrists and ankles shackled with irons, was escorted by two armed guards off the boat onto the walkway that led up to the prison. At the end of the walkway in the courtyard, Marty and the guards were met by Jack Holden, the warden of Alcatraz prison, and his assistant. Marty felt that she had met the warden before. Something familiar about his cherry red hair and deep blue eyes. One of the guards unlocked her shackles as the warden introduced himself.

"Welcome to the Alcatraz Federal Penitentiary. Every prisoner here on the Rock is expected to work. You'll be given a choice of what tasks you would like to perform, like the laundry, cooking, library assistant, mechanic. You have a preference?"

"I'm a trained chef. So, a cook," Marty replied.

"This is not the Ritz-Carlton, but I think we can find you a place in the kitchen," the warden said. "You'll be given thirty cents a day for your efforts. You're also given 2400 days of good time. But, since you were sentenced to life and a day, good time won't apply."

"Why am I here?"

"That's something you'll have to figure out on your own. A few rules while you're here. No fraternization with the guards or the other inmates. No fighting. No inciting trouble of any kind. And no hunger strikes. Please. Otherwise, we'll be forced to feed you. And that's not pleasant. Breaking the rules can get you thirty days in the dungeon. You like the cold and damp?" the warden asked.

"No," Marty said obediently.

"Good, because the Rock can get very unpleasant, especially in the dungeon where the rats like to feast on your tender flesh," the warden said. "And another thing. Whatever you do while you enjoy your stay here, do not try to escape. No one has ever made a successful attempt. That will get you sixty days in the dungeon, guaranteed. But, if you do try to escape, you better not get caught." The warden walked Marty over to a small gravesite. "Half of all those decayed carcasses failed at an escape."

"Yes, sir," Marty said as she turned her head towards the San Francisco skyline and knew that's what she had to do to survive the miserable existence that lay ahead of her.

"Good, because what we don't want is a failure to understand each other. That's why my door will always be open if you have any concerns. Enjoy your stay," the warden said. Marty was escorted by the two guards to the main gate station and then to her designated cell on B block where prying eyes were on her along the way. When she arrived at her cell, her cellmate was stretched out on the bottom bunk. The cell door was opened, and Marty entered. The door closed behind her with a clank of permanence. Her gut wrenched at the reality of her new prison life, for what she did not know. All she knew was that she was in an enclosed, locked 5' x 9' space.

"Finally, my new roomie has arrived," Lorraine Lacroix said in her French accent to the guards who just stood there outside the cell.

"That's right, L, and she's a looker," one of the guards said. They both walked off.

"Not you?" Marty said with consternation.

Lorraine stood up from her bunk and hugged Marty. "It's yours truly. Oh, it's so good to see you, *mon cherie*," she said in a loving tone.

"Why did it have to be you?" Marty said disgustedly.

"My little *corbeau*, you'll soon find out that you are lucky to have me because when you meet the other inmates, you'll be washing my panties and brassiere," Lorraine said.

"Do me a favor and keep to yourself. I know how amorous you get."

"I love it when you get ornery. I get so excited."

"I can't win for losing with you."

"So you got to meet the warden?" Lorraine said to ease the tension coming from Marty.

"He reminds me of someone that I know. But I don't know who. He seems like a nice guy."

"Don't be fooled by his demeanor. They call him 'Blackjack' Holden because he personally knocks out the inmates with a rubber-coated lead pipe," Lorraine said.

"I'll just stay out of trouble, then."

Lorraine snickered. "Being the new girlie on the block, I doubt that will happen," Lorraine said. "But I'm here to protect you."

"I feel safe already," Marty said sarcastically. "How come you're not working?"

"My day off," Lorraine said.

"Lucky you. What do you do?"

"I help in the warden's office. Clerical work, and I polish his knobs. The sacrifices one must make to make it a little more comfortable."

"It's polish his *knob*," Marty said.

"No, he likes me to rub his hairy balls," Lorraine said. "While I suck him off."

"That's what you get for killing off Baron."

"It was an accident. Who knew the creep Henri would show up?" Lorraine said in a perturbed voice. "But at least I didn't sink a ship full of Portuguese sailors."

"Rapists," Marty said curtly.

"It was only two of them," Lorraine retorted.

"Not one of those twelve men on the *Duzia de Diablo* gave a shit what happened to me. They deserved to die," Marty said angrily.

"You're your own judge, jury, and executioner," Lorraine said, poking at Marty's bravado.

"I live by my own rules," Marty said.

"In here, you live by Blackjack Holden's rule," Lorraine said.

Not wanting to acknowledge the reality of Lorraine's words, Marty changed the subject. "I've seen Sookie lately."

"Oh, my little Asian lover. I miss her so much," Lorraine said reminiscently.

"That's what she said about you."

"How could you see her? She's dead."

"I don't know. She just appears."

"That's spooky. I don't understand," Lorraine said. "Maybe she'll come here and visit with me?"

"I don't know," Marty said and watched tears flow from Lorraine's eyes. Marty consoled Lorraine by hugging her.

Lorraine took advantage of the situation and began to rub Marty's rear end. "When we take a shower, let's make love," Lorraine suggested.

Marty pushed herself away from Lorraine, "You never change. Always hustling for a piece of ass," Marty said with disdain.

"Can you argue with me? Look at you, you're gorgeous," Lorraine said, gazing upon Marty in her prisoner garb.

"No, that's not going to happen."

"Marty, you'll find yourself lonely and wanting to caress something warm. And who will be there? Me. Either now or later, we'll be lovers again. So, why wait?" Lorraine proposed. "Besides, you have a lifetime in here."

"How did you know?"

"I read the papers. Your lover Fabrizio was found strangled in his sauna."

"No, no, that didn't happen."

"You're like the others. Always denying that they did something wrong, especially murder," Lorraine responded as she shook her head back and forth.

"Poor Fab. I loved him. That wasn't me."

"Believe what you want to believe. You live in a fantasy anyway," Lorraine said, and then the cell door opened. "It's time for dinner."

"I bet the food is awful," Marty said as they walked down the cell block.

"Actually, I taught the cooks how to make French food," Lorraine said.

"Only you could have pulled that off," Marty replied.

Marty and Lorraine grabbed their grub and sat down on one of the picnic benches inside the mess hall. All eyes were on Marty—their new prison mate. An older woman with gray hair and glasses sat opposite Lorraine. "This is Birdie, Marty. If you ever have the urge to get high, she's the woman. Right, Birdie?" Lorraine said.

"If you say so," Birdie said with a half-smirk as she nodded at Marty. "The chicken is good today."

"Coq au vin," Lorraine said.

"You have wine on Alcatraz?" Marty asked.

"It's called the Rock. The alcohol is made from orange juice and moldy bread and added to grape juice. How would you say? It is very crude, but it's the best we're going to get. Unless you brought some with you, Marty?" She was enjoying her meal of mock coq au vin and ratatouille.

"I was going to say the next time I'm sent here. But there won't be a next time because I'm getting the fuck out of here. And they're not going to catch me."

Birdie and Lorraine had heard it before, especially from the new prisoners. "The last inmate that escaped was found washed up on the shore. Dead as a drowned rat. So, get it out of that pretty little head of yours," Lorraine said to Marty, looking straight into her eyes.

"You forget, I escaped Baron's island."

"There's a lot of bars and a lot of angry men in lousy relationships who wouldn't hesitate to shoot you in the back just to get some satisfaction," Birdie said as a word of caution.

"Don't worry about me, I'll be fine," Marty quipped.

"How would you do it?" Lorraine asked, looking like a curious cat.

"When I was being held in the jail before coming here, I met a former Alcatraz prisoner who tried to escape from the dungeon but didn't have enough time to dig through the walls, which are soft from the sea water. The dungeon runs along a drainage pipe that leads out into the bay. I dig my way through, and I'll never be seen again," Marty said.

"You don't want to go to the dungeon," Lorraine said.

"Have you been in there?"

"No, but I've seen people return from solitary. They looked like corpses. How would you get off the Rock?"

"Does the warden leave every day to go home on the mainland?" Marty asked.

"No, but there are boats that make trips to the Van Ness Pier," Birdie said.

"When's the last one leave?" Marty asked.

"Around 5:30," Birdie replied.

"Then twenty-eight days after I've been in the dungeon, at 5:00 pm, you girls are going to start a riot in the mess hall. A small one, but enough to distract things. Maybe enough to delay the boat some. That way it will be darker out when I hitch a ride on the side of that last boat. Before they dock, I'll swim to shore with the tide," Marty said.

"You are crazy, Marty," Lorraine said emphatically.

"I've always been a little crazy," Marty said. Lorraine and Birdie then stood up with their trays in hand. Marty followed.

On their way back from the mess hall to their cells, Marty asked, "Where did you get that feather, Birdie?"

"Birdie is the bird lady of Alcatraz," Lorraine said. "That's how she gets her pills. Her ravens fly to her contact on the mainland and return with a small stash."

"During the riot, the dungeon will be the least of their worries, but just in case, I'm going to fill my bunk with dirt to make it look like my body and use the feathers to make it look like my hair," Marty said as she eased the feather out of Birdie's hair.

"I have plenty of feathers. They make sleeping a little more comfortable," Birdie said. "But how are you going to get in the hole?" Birdie asked.

"A fight," Marty said.

Two days later, Marty and Lorraine were in the cell block B showers. Marty dropped a bar of soap on the shower floor. A large, imposing woman picked up the bar and as she was about to hand the soap to Marty, she said, "I know you. You're the one that killed Dominika. Because of you, I'm stuck in this place." She then hauled off and punched Marty in the belly. Marty buckled slightly and then charged the woman, pushing her up against the wall of the shower. Marty grabbed a bar of soap from a dish along the wall and shoved it in the woman's face. The woman then kneed Marty in the crotch. A crowd of naked inmates formed around Marty and her opponent who was now on top of Marty on the floor of the shower.

"Punch her in the face, Marty," Lorraine yelled out. Most of the women cheered on the other woman. Marty and her opponent looked like Greco-Roman wrestlers putting each other into various holds like twisted pretzels. It was not long before a handful of guards came rushing in and broke up the fight.

Marty and the other woman were brought to the warden's office just as they were caught in the shower. They stood there at attention, naked and still wet. "All right, which one of you started the fight?" the warden asked.

The other woman was about to speak up, but Marty said, "It was me, Warden. I instigated the fight." The other woman kept silent while she glanced over at Marty.

"Thirty days, sweetheart," the warden said. "That didn't take long. Enjoy the comforts." The two women were escorted out of the office and brought to their cells.

On the way out of the warden's office, Marty apologized to the woman by saying, "I'm sorry. I never meant to kill Dominika."

Marty got dressed in her prison garb and discreetly slipped the raven feathers down her panties and then was taken off to the dungeon. Lorraine blew Marty a kiss as she walked down the cell block with a guard by her side.

That evening as Marty lay asleep, having felt damp and cold ever since she was put into the dungeon, she felt a tickle at her nose. She swiped at her nose and brushed up against a furry animal the size of a large cat. Marty was startled and quickly awoke. She realized it was a rat and knew it was going to be a long four weeks before she could escape. Sleeping would be almost an impossibility unless she was willing to risk being bitten by some vermin. But how did the rat get into the cell? She thought about it. The rat must have come through the tunnel. She felt for holes in the walls since the lighting was poor. She covered the expanse of the cell, except for underneath the makeshift cot that she slept on. She lifted the cot, found the rat hole and put her ear against the hole. She heard the trickling of water. *Which meant?* That it had to be the tunnel.

When Marty was served her breakfast of gruel and a tin of water, she used the spoon to dig around the sandstone rock that was a part of the original construction of the prison, which was formerly a military fortress. She returned the spoon to her meal tray so when the guards came to retrieve it after leaving her next meal, there would be no suspicion. After several weeks of digging and hiding the stones, some mortar and dirt underneath her cot, Marty was able to make a hole big enough to fit through. She then shimmied through the hole and inched her way towards the tunnel. It was completely dark, but she could see daylight at the end of the tunnel, which was about fifty yards away.

Marty gingerly made her way down the tunnel, bracing herself against the wall as she stepped closer to the entrance. She had to wade through the water as she got closer to the opening. When she got there, she peeked out to her left toward the dock of the prison, which was about two hundred yards away. She would have to swim the distance to the boat two weeks hence. Hopefully, it would be dark enough out that she would not be seen by any of the guards who were in the lookout tower. Marty stepped back toward her cell, slipped back through the hole, covered it up with the loose stones and dirt and waited another two weeks.

On the twenty-eighth day at 4:30 p.m., Marty received a bowl of beef stew, a piece of stale bread and a tin of water. She quickly ate her food, drank the water and then stuck a raven feather inside the cup. She made her bed, arranging the stones and dirt to conform to the shape of her body and several of the stones to look like her head, and covered it all with the remaining raven's feathers. She then slipped through the hole and made her way down the tunnel.

At 5:00 pm, the prison sirens blew. Marty eased herself in the water and waited. It was frigidly cold, but a fog covered the island, so she felt a little secure. She then began to wade toward the dock where her escape boat awaited. Marty stopped about halfway and braced herself on some rocks along the edge of the shoreline. By then the sirens had stopped blowing. She had to time it so that she didn't get to the boat too early or risk getting caught. Too late and she'd miss her ride. The boat engines began to chug, and she continued to wade closer.

Marty was able to hide next to the boat. All she had to do was get hold of it for little more than a mile in the frigid water, and she would be free. The boatman released the dock ropes, and the boat hoisted off as Marty held onto to the side. She was able to grab hold of one of the dock ropes, securing her ride. The fog got thicker as they got closer to the mainland. She got the sense they were close. Or at least she was hoping they were as she began to shiver uncontrollably. She somehow lost her grip on the rope and began to drift off into the water as the boat motored away. She tried to wade toward shore but slowly began to sink into the water. Suddenly, she felt paralyzed as if she had been knocked in the head by a blackjack.

There was a constant sound of knocking. Marty then heard a familiar voice call out for her. She opened her eyes and looked around. She was in her room at the Regency. She got up out of bed and answered the door. Fab was standing there. He said, "Jesus Marty, you're going to be late."

Marty took hold of Fab, hugged him and whispered in his ear, "God, I'm so glad to see you."

Chapter Sixteen

After the exam, Marty and Fab drank some of the wines from several of the vineyards that sponsored the challenge while they waited for the results of the exam. The top fifty challengers were sent text messages stating their overall score and told to report at designated times for the second phase of the challenge the following day. The other fifty were sent texts offering an apology that they had not received a high enough score and were thanked for their participation. Both Marty and Fab were very happy. Fab left to go to his restaurant and planned on meeting Marty later at his home. Marty felt as if she was walking on clouds, having received a high score on the exam. She also was feeling smitten that Fab had gone out of his way to wake her that morning. She felt wanted, desired.

She had received several text messages from one of her managers at the store wishing her well and saying everything was fine. She also received a text from Michelle wondering how things were going. Marty called Michelle. She had to talk to someone from back home. "Hi, Marty, how are you? How did you do?" Michelle said in a spirited voice.

"Hey, Michelle. Everything is great. I'm still in it. But I met a guy. He's so wonderful. His name is Fabrizio and he owns a restaurant," Marty said in a whimsical voice

"Oh? That was quick. Did you two…?"

"I don't know if I should be telling you this, but my God, he's such a great lover," Marty exulted.

"You sound like you've fallen for this guy?"

"I have. I haven't felt like this since my ex-husband," Marty said. And then there was silence for a moment.

"So where did you meet him?" Michelle asked.

"At his place, Giacomelli Ristorante. It's so nice," Marty responded. "And he has a beautiful home in North Beach with a sauna in his bedroom. And there's a view of Alcatraz from his rooftop. It's incredible. He's incredible," Marty swooned with exuberance.

"I'm happy for you, Marty. You deserve it," Michelle said in a veiled condescending voice. "Well, I'll let you go. You must be busy," she said curtly.

"I'm sorry, Michelle, I just had to tell somebody. I consider you a friend. Right?"

"I suppose," Michelle said in a distant voice.

"Well, I'll let you know how it goes tomorrow. You take care of yourself," Marty said. She got the sense that Michelle was jealous. *Maybe I shouldn't have told her about Fab.* "Bye," Marty said.

"Okay," Michelle said and ended the call.

I hope she's going to be okay? Marty pondered. She was going to go back to her room, but that dream she had of Alcatraz was so vivid in her mind that she decided to take a quick trip out to the prison just to satisfy the urge. She walked over to Alcatraz Landing and took the ride over to the island. When she arrived, she was taken on a tour of the prison with several other tourists. When the tour arrived at cell # B-206, the tour guide said, "This is the infamous Al Capone's cell. He arrived here in August of 1934. He spent four and half years at Alcatraz Federal Penitentiary. Worked in various job capacities. He was involved in an altercation with another inmate that cost him eight days in isolation."

As the tour continued down Cell Block B, Marty heard a man's husky voice say, "Hello, doll face. Aren't you the looka?"

Marty turned to the man who was robust with slick dark hair. He was wearing bluish-gray prison garb and sitting in cell # B-206. "Are you a part of the tour?" Marty asked amusedly.

"No, I'm Big Al. Al Capone," the man said as if Marty should have known that.

"Yeah, and I'm Marlene Dietrich," Marty said smartly.

"You look more like Vivien Leigh."

"Well, it was nice meeting you. I have to get back to the group," Marty said and took off at a quickened pace.

"I'll be seeing you real soon," the man said through the cell bars.

Marty caught up to the tour and asked the guide, "Does Alcatraz have a dungeon?"

The guide responded, "Yes, it does. It's called the Spanish Dungeon, and it's below Cell Block D. And Cell Block D is where some of the penitentiary's more hardened criminals were locked up. The dungeon was used for a period for solitary confinement until James A. Johnston, the warden from 1934 to 1948, ceased to use what were actually chambers from a Civil War-era citadel."

"Will you be showing us the dungeon?" Marty asked.

"You'll have to get the special tour to see the chambers below Cell Block D," the guide responded.

"I guess some other time, then. Thanks."

On the boat ride back to the Embarcadero, Marty couldn't help but think about how real her dream was about Alcatraz and how accurate it was, considering she had never seen the prison before. She couldn't recall ever seeing a history show or looking at a book about the prison. She couldn't explain it. *And then seeing Al Capone? He had to be a part of the tour, but why didn't anyone else see him? He just appeared.* Seeing Sookie and Didier and Bubba Arnet and Angela Jordan, Marty speculated that she was just having episodes, which she controlled in her mind. But Al Capone? He was the first dead person to appear to her whom she had no personal connection to.

She Googled him—there it was, "Al Capone," "Big Al," "Scarface." Prohibition-era bootlegger and one of the most notorious gangsters that ever lived. There were photos of him looking very much like the man she saw. There were also movies, like *Al Capone* with Rod Steiger, *The St. Valentine's Day Massacre* and *The Untouchables* about this larger-than-life character. Movies that Marty had never seen, albeit the first two were produced well before her time. She didn't know much about him, other than hearing the name Al Capone over the years in her three decades of life. Yet it was "Big Al" that got Marty to really think about actually speaking to a ghost, a spirit. She was starting to believe that she could, and she wanted to somehow prove it. When she arrived back at her room at the Regency, she showered, hitched herself on her bed and Googled San Francisco psychics. There was one by the Fisherman's Wharf. She called the number and set up an appointment for later that evening.

Marty hopped a cab ride over to the Wharf and was let out by a storefront. In the window, a pink neon sign read: 'Readings - Psychic Medium.' The banner above read 'Donna Anglin World-Renowned Psychic.' Marty entered the store as a bell jingled to announce a prospective customer arrived or maybe it was a wake-up call for the spirits. Marty got a feel of energy emanating from the waiting room that was done in a 70s style with a green velvet sofa and chairs and few chrome glass side tables. Perhaps it was the mood of the room. A woman in her fifties with fluffy blonde hair and striking hazel eyes stepped into the room, held out her hand and said, "Hi, you must be the woman I spoke to earlier? I'm Donna Anglin."

"Yes, hi. I'm…" Marty was saying when she was interrupted by the psychic.

"No, don't tell me your name. I don't want to taint the reading with superfluous information.

"I'm sorry."

"No, don't be. It's Martha, right?" the psychic asked.

"Yes," Marty said in surprise.

"How about we go inside?" the psychic said and then she brought Marty into the back room that was dimly lit and had a faint scent of beeswax. "What would make you more comfortable, the table or the sofa?" she asked in a soft, unassuming voice.

"The sofa," Marty said and proceeded to take a seat upholstered in red velvet. Marty eased into the chair and thought as she rubbed her hand on the velvet, *Nice.*

Donna Anglin took a seat opposite Marty in a matching chair. "Marty, what I would like you to do is a take some deep breaths and let them out. And then try to clear your mind," she proposed to Marty.

Marty followed her commands, breathing in through her nostrils then exhaling through her mouth.

"Now sit back in the chair and try to relax," Donna Anglin said. The psychic closed her eyes, put her hands together in a prayer position and then leaned against her chin as she began to deeply absorb Marty's aura and sense of being. This took Donna Anglin a brief moment and then she opened her eyes and put her hands on the armrest of the chair. "On the surface, you are conflating visceral with emotional love. This with someone you just met. You think you are in love, but it's just infatuation. Maybe it's the sexual relations you are having?" the psychic asked.

"It is very good between us," Marty responded.

"This may not last long. There's someone else who has strong emotions for you. This person is very demonstrative. You may want to use caution when dealing with her."

"Okay," Marty replied with concerned eyes.

"Have you been to the Devil's Island, Alcatraz, lately?" the psychic asked. Marty nodded. "You saw Al Capone's ghost, didn't you?"

"That was actually him?" Marty asked.

"Yes. I've only met a few people who have seen his ghost," Donna Anglin said.

"I spoke with him. He called me doll face."

"And you've spoken with other spirits, not just seen their ghosts?" the psychic asked.

"How is it that I'm able to talk with them?"

"Some people are gifted with it. It also can be a curse," Donna Anglin said.

"Why do these spirits appear?"

"Through verbally or cognitively asking for their presence. Sometimes it can happen subconsciously without you being aware," the psychic said. "It's possible you have clairvoyant ability. You have a business with 'Spirits' in the title?" the psychic asked.

"Clairvoyant ability?" Marty questioned. "But, yes, I do. My business is called Remy Wine and Spirits," Marty replied.

"That's not a fluke. Can you do me a favor and close your eyes and relax while I probe deeper into your psyche? There's a reason why 'Spirits' is in the name of your business," Donna Anglin said. Marty sat back in her chair and closed her eyes while the psychic meditated on Marty's mind and soul. The psychic twitched, and her closed eyes moved rapidly. She picked up on Marty's deep psychological trough. And then she got a sense of the spirits connected to Marty. She paused for a moment, opened her eyes and stared at her. "I'm sorry, but I think we should end the reading," Donna Anglin said in a disturbed voice.

"Why?" Marty asked, knowing that the psychic must have some greater power than Marty presumed.

"I think you know."

Marty pulled out a one-hundred-dollar bill from her pocketbook and placed it on the arm of the chair as she stood up and exited the store.

Donna Anglin quickly locked the store's front door and turned off the neon sign.

So, I have clairvoyant ability? Marty mockingly laughed to herself. But she felt let down after leaving the psychic—she had hoped that her love for Fab was real and would be long-lasting. *And who was the person that was being demonstrative?* Marty pondered but knew right away that it had to be Michelle. *It was a mistake telling her about Fab,* Marty opined. That was her personal business. She wouldn't mention Fab to her again, regardless of what happened with the relationship. *If it is a relationship?* Marty questioned herself. *But it feels like one, and it's real because I have strong feelings for him. It wasn't just the sex.*

Marty went back to the Regency and decided to dress down in a sweatshirt and sweatpants. *Let's see if he'll still be attracted to me in these,* she said to herself as she looked in the mirror. Maybe she wouldn't brush her teeth either, but that would be pushing it.

"Going to the gym? What, no big date tonight?" Didier said as he appeared next to Marty in the mirror.

"How come you're so nosey? Where's your sidekick?" Marty asked.

"Because you fascinate me. She's over there," Didier said as he pointed towards Sookie on the bed.

"Hey, Marty, how's your new boyfriend?" Sookie asked.

"Hi, Sookie. He's fabulous," Marty said with a smirk.

"Oh?" Didier questioned with French hubris in his voice.

"He's probably the best lover I've ever had," Marty said.

"You've never had me," Didier said.

"Agh," Sookie spouted through her throat.

"You think too highly of yourself," Marty said.

"Your cousin Janine said I was a great lover," Didier said.

"Oh, really. She was with her old boyfriend Ben the day after you had your accident."

"That fucking slut," Didier said angrily as Sookie began to laugh. "*Pitre,*" he shot at Sookie.

"*Enfoire,*" Sookie shot back.

"I'll show you an asshole," Didier said, pulled down his pants and spread his rear end cheeks at Sookie. She gave him the middle finger.

"Clit licker," Didier spat at her.

"That's what I like about you two, there's no love lost between you," Marty said with a chuckle.

"You must be getting it good. You're in such a great mood," Didier said as he motioned his fist back and forth, emulating sex.

"That I am. And it's better than good. It's great," Marty said.

Marty decided to jog over to Fab's house so she would be nice and sweaty. But she had that look of love. When he answered the door, he kissed her, glanced at her attire, pulled her inside, closed the door and proceeded to pull off her sweats while he kissed her body. They didn't even make it to the bedroom and made passionate love at the base of the stairs.

Marty and Fab did make it to his bed later and continued their love-making through a good part of the evening. Afterward, they spoke about the challenge and how they each felt that they had a chance at winning it all. Then Fab asked, "Marty, I'd like to see you after this whole thing is over. Maybe, you can come up some time, or I can come down by you?"

"I would like that very much," Marty replied. "Whatever is easiest for both of us." 'Us' meant that 'they' were a couple and that they both desired to spend time together in the future meant they were officially in a relationship. They shared stories about their lives, where they grew up and the schools they attended. Marty talked about Jackie and how it was a challenge.

"If you don't mind me asking, why does your ex-husband have full custody of your son?"

Marty paused and then said, "I had a breakdown after I was abducted for ransom in France."

Fab pulled back as if it were unfathomable. "You were abducted?" he asked disbelievingly.

"By two women and a man who had a split personality. I escaped and wound up on a ship as a cook where I was raped," Marty said confidently, seeking sympathy.

"That's...?" Fab said as he tried to find the words to describe the heinous nature of what happened to Marty.

"Horrific," Marty said.

"My God, Marty," Fab said, trying to understand the emotional impact on her. He consoled her by hugging her. "I can see how you had a breakdown. I'm sorry," he said but withdrew himself emotionally, not knowing how to proceed if Marty had deep psychological issues that could rear up at some point. He now had second thoughts about the relationship.

"And, I don't know if you know, I was working at the food channel in Los Feliz when those chefs were murdered. I was accused of the killings."

"That was you?" Fab asked, not fully comprehending it all.

"Yeah, I hid in a monastery and then got into a car accident," Marty continued with full disclosure. Fab was utterly befuddled.

"Jesus Christ, Marty! What in God's name possessed you to go to such extremes?" Fab asked exasperatedly.

"I got scared. But it was an enlightening experience with the monks. I had dressed up like one. They didn't know I was a woman. Except my son's father, whom I had sex with."

"A monk?!" Fab asked in a thoroughly stunned voice.

"I was cleaning the bathroom floor and he came in to urinate. One thing led to another and before you know it, we were getting it on," Marty said amusedly.

Fab got up out of bed and said, "I need a drink."

Chapter Seventeen

Marty, Fab and twenty-three other challengers who made it past the tasting phase of the competition filled one of the smaller banquet rooms at the Regency Hotel. They were all participating in the third leg of the competition—the service. Although the four judges who sat at the table had some of their own criteria that they used to evaluate each participant, they also had the ones set forth by the California Grand Sommelier Challenge committee. In particular, all the judges wanted to see how quick each participant was on their feet, especially when it came to suggestions of food pairings. Pairing a wine to complement two or more courses was high on the list of each judge and was not a simple task. Salesmanship played a part when it came to wine pairing. Striking a balance of appropriate wine pairings without overselling was what the judges were keeping an eye on. It was a matter of customer courtesy, which the challenge committee advocated as one of their mantras—*a California Grand Sommelier must treat a customer as a valued guest and not a commodity.*

It was Marty's turn. She introduced herself as Marty, their beverage server. She kept it simple. Received orders for a Bloody Mary, an Appletini, a Fabiola and a white wine. Marty had to make her first sale. "Would you like a glass or a bottle, sir?" she asked the judge.

"A glass," the judge responded and took a mental note—a knock against Marty he later annotated on Marty's score sheet.

"Would a Sauvignon Blanc work for you?" she asked.

"That would be fine," the judge retorted.

"Thank you. I'll be right back with your drinks," Marty said and quickly went behind a makeshift bar and began mixing the Bloody Mary and the Appletini. No problem. Poured the wine and then pondered the

Fabiola. She had to go off memory and only vaguely knew what it was. She had no *Cocktail Codex* or mixology book to reference.

Luckily, Chef Bubba appeared by her side. "Don't worry. I'm here to help ya', chitlin'. Equal parts of Grand Marnier, dry vermouth and brandy," he twanged.

"Thanks, Chef," she muttered under her breath and quickly mixed the cocktail.

She garnished the drinks and served them to the judges. One of the judges had timed her with a stopwatch. She had a half a minute of allotted time to spare. The judges tasted the drinks, scored her on her performance and then had Marty take their appetizer and main entrée food orders and suggest wine pairings accordingly. Marty didn't want to outguess the judges by assuming what they would want her to suggest, so she used her intuition and experience with each item. Luckily, two of the judges ordered seafood appetizers, crab cakes and steamed mussels. For their entrees, the two judges ordered seared lamb chops and roasted black sea bass, respectively. Marty suggested a nice California citrus-driven Pinot Blanc would work well with both their appetizers and entrées. The two judges were satisfied with that.

The other judge ordered fried quail with a raspberry chipotle sauce and the fourth judge, beef tenderloin street tacos with salsa verde. Marty suggested a Russian River Valley Pinot Noir since the wine had plenty of rich fruit, smokiness, and spices and would pair well with the quail as well as the grilled Petit Filet with red peppercorn béarnaise and smoked wild boar they ordered for their main entrées. Marty asked the judge who ordered the taco if he would prefer a beer, Mexican, perhaps *Tres Noches*? He agreed.

Marty left the table and came back with a bottle of the Pinot Blanc and two narrow aperture glasses. She set the glasses in front of the judges, displayed the wine on the napkin on her arm and then corked it.

Set the cork on a small plate. Poured a sample for one of the judges, who proceeded to sniff and gargle it. She said, "It's fine." Marty poured the glasses, set the bottle on the table and went to get the Pinot Noir.

Marty left the table again and brought back the Pinot Noir and two slightly triangular shaped glasses. She then went through the service. And when she went to pour the second glass of Pinot Noir, she spilled some on the table. Marty looked up at the judges who were all writing down the incident on their score sheets. She went for the beer and poured it into a frosty mug, which gave it a decent head. The judges were making some evaluations, particularly to note that she made too many trips back and forth to the bar.

When it came to the last course—the dessert—Marty was asked by one of the judges, "What is *Botrytis cinereal?*"

"It's a fungus. It's known as noble rot. It's what sweet or dessert wines are made from when the grape shrivels up like a raisin on the vine," Marty answered succinctly.

"How about suggesting a wine to go with my tangerine souffle?" the judge asked.

"I wouldn't go with a dessert wine, per se. I think a Chenin Blanc would pair exquisitely with the tangerine. But how about we see what the other judges are getting? Would that be fine with you? Marty asked politely and professionally, to which the judge concurred with a smile.

"Your dessert?" Marty asked the female judge.

"The lemon candied ginger crème brûlée," she said.

"And yours, sir?" she asked the next judge.

"The chocolate sampler."

"And you, sir?"

"I would just like something to sip. I'm thinking of a Port," he responded.

"Portuguese or Californian?" Marty proffered.

"Californian, of course," he shot back.

"We have the twenty-year-old Ficklin Tawny Port. Does that work for you?" Marty asked. The judge nodded.

"I would also suggest then the Tawny Port to go with the chocolate sampler. And with the brûlée, I would go with Toad Hill Sparkling. It's a perfect fit," Marty suggested. The female judge agreed, and Marty left the table.

Overall, Marty scored okay on the service. Good suggestions and reasonably good pairing, but the spilled wine and timeliness cost her points. Collectively, the judges felt she could have been a little more cordial. *She seemed a little stiff,* the female judge wrote in her notes about Marty during the service. Yet she had taken a good lead over most of the other challengers between the initial exam and the tasting. Consequently, she and Fab would be two of the five who would continue to the next and last leg of the challenge—the Q & A.

On the way out of the service challenge, as Marty and Fab were about to catch a cab to go to dinner in Chinatown at Fab's favorite noodle house, Marty was pulled aside by John. "What are you doing here, John?" Marty questioned. John let go of her arm with a look of disdain on his face. "What is it?" she asked in a frustrated tone as Fab looked on with concern. "It's okay, Fab. My ex-husband. It will only be a minute." Marty and John stepped to the side while Fab waited within hearing distance.

"Not only did I find out you stopped taking your meds, I get a call from that detective from Los Feliz. Paul Cooz. He tells me that you're connected to two murders, and one of them was your employee. And you also threw the husband of the other woman over a cliff," John said angrily, wanting answers.

"Keep it down, John," Marty said as she looked over at Fab who had his back turned to them.

"What, your next victim?" John asked.

"I resent that. Fuck that Paul Cooz. He's nothing but trouble. He's been stalking me," Marty said, showing her angst.

"See. This is exactly what I knew would happen if you went off your meds. You invite trouble somehow. I don't want to know what happened with these women, so don't tell me because somehow I would be complicit."

"I didn't kill them," Marty said and then she looked over at Fab hoping he didn't hear what she just said. But he had.

He mouthed, "I have to go. I'll call you later."

"See what you just did. He's the best thing that has happened to me in a long time. And you scared him off," Marty said.

"Yeah, when he finds out about your past and this latest shit, you're in because Cooz found a piece of your taillight where your employee was found dead, he'll be long gone. Can you explain yourself, Marty?" John asked. "Why is it that everything you do, there's murder around it? The only time I can remember you were never in trouble was before you left to go on the trip to France."

"What can I say? I'm unlucky," Marty said. "You know you're not Jackie's real father?"

"You think I didn't know that with his red hair and blue eyes? But he is my son, regardless," John said solemnly. "I recommend you get a good lawyer."

"It's all assumptions, John. People making up stories, but they don't know the truth, or they just can't find the truth," Marty said flippantly.

"Explain the broken piece of taillight?"

"From some other car. And Gallagher slipped down the cliff. He lost his balance. And his wife was mauled by some sharks while she was surfing. She already had been bitten by a shark. A big chunk was missing from her calf," Marty said as she described the injury with her hand next to her own calf.

"Sounds like she was the unlucky one. You always have some exotic explanation. Why is that?" John asked, not looking for a real answer. He always found himself getting sucked into Marty's web of duplicity.

"Exotic is why you married me. You fell in love with me for it. It's just what I am. How is Jackie, by the way?"

"He's fine. Jacqueline takes good care of him."

"She's a sweet person. Jackie is better off with the both of you."

"You knew this would happen?"

"I just can't be on those drugs anymore. I need to be me first before I can give myself to anyone else. Besides, all of you are better off not having me in the picture," Marty said, feeling like she had been punched in the belly, even though she had tried to rationalize the truth about letting go of Jackie before.

"So, this is what you want?"

"It's what has to be. As much as it hurts me to let go of Jackie…I'm sorry, John," Marty said as tears began to fall from her eyes. "I have to go," she said and ran off down the banquet area hallway and then to her room at the hotel.

Marty sunk her face in a pillow and cried, feeling deeply hollow inside. She loved Jackie, and she had missed him very much. The happiest days of her life were during the first two years of Jackie's life in Maui with John. *Where were those days?* Marty asked herself. Just then she received a text from Fab. It read: M…I have to work tonight. I'll catch you some other time…F

If being punched in the belly earlier, figuratively speaking, wasn't hard enough, getting the vague, yet distinctive brush off by Fab was the blow that knocked her out emotionally. Marty opened the hotel room refrigerator, grabbed two mini bottles of Jack Daniels and drank them both. She then grabbed her pocketbook and left the room.

A sudden winter storm hit the city with a torrential downpour of rain. Marty caught a cab by Van Ness and Geary where she had once gone to see a dominatrix who forever changed her life. Marty instructed the cabbie to stop at what she remembered was Dominika's place of business and residence. It was now a nightclub called *The Hunky Dory Club*. Marty paid the cabbie and ran to the front door of the club as the rain pelted her. Her mascara ran from underneath her eyes, but she fit right in with the avant-garde décor of the club, which had a six-foot-high copy of David Bowie's *Hunky Dory* album cover hanging on the wall just as she entered. Some obscure techno-pop played through the club speakers.

Marty passed an androgynous, tall, thin couple. They both wore heavy mascara and were clinging to each other. Mirrors were everywhere in the club—on the walls, the ceiling, behind the bar. Marty got herself a red wine at the bar. The bartender's face, nose, and ears were covered with piercings. "First time here?" he asked Marty.

"Yes. Interesting place. You know, a dominatrix used to work out of here," Marty remarked.

"Is that right? Well, Marlene Dietrich inspired Bowie's album cover," the bartender said.

"Seems to fit," Marty responded.

"Yeah, Marlene was into that kinky stuff," the bartender said.

"So was I."

"I'll play along," the bartender said.

"Was. No longer. Is the bottom floor still open?"

"It's used for storage. Were you the dominatrix?" the bartender asked.

"No. It was a woman named Dominika. But it's funny, now that I'm talking about her, she sort of resembled Marlene Dietrich. She was

Eastern European and striking," Marty said reflecting on the night she met Dominika.

"So, why did you come here tonight? Were you friends with this dominatrix?"

"We were lovers. Just for that one night."

"What happened to her?" the bartender asked with keen interest.

"She just disappeared. Until she came back into my life a couple of years ago," Marty said somberly.

"And then she disappeared again?"

"How did you know?"

"Sounds like she's a ghost," the bartender said. "But that's why you're here."

"I'm haunted by her memory."

"You think she's going to walk in that door?" the bartender said as he pointed towards the club's entrance.

"She just might," Marty said with a smirk.

"I think you and I have a better chance at making love than you seeing this woman by chance."

"You may not be able to see her, but I will be able to," Marty said.

"So, she is a ghost after all?" the bartender speculated.

"She died the night I met her."

The bartender raised his eyebrows in surprise and asked, "Oh?"

"She was electrocuted by her lover. Right upstairs," Marty said as she pointed toward the ceiling as if she were making some veiled confessional.

"Here, in this building?" the bartender asked as if he were spooked.

"I guess you didn't know that."

"Are you able to see her now?" the bartender asked, questioning her sanity.

"No. I'll need to summon her," Marty said. "Maybe you can let me go downstairs?"

"I don't know if I can do that. To tell you the truth, this seems a little far-fetched."

"What's it worth? A couple hundred dollars?" Marty asked, trying to bait him.

He contemplated. "That's possible. And how about you and me?" the bartender asked taking his chances.

The club had emptied out as David Bowie's, *Life on Mars?* played through the club's speakers. The bartender proceeded to lock the front doors and turn off the outside lights. He stepped back toward the bar where Marty was seated. "I can give you twenty minutes," he said to Marty.

"Thanks. So, what's your name?"

"Roberts," he said and then he stepped towards a stairwell. Marty followed him as Bowie sang the lyrics, "But her friend is nowhere to be seen/Now she walks through her sunken dream."

The bartender turned on the light to the basement and walked down the stairs till he got to a chain-linked door. He unlocked it, turned to Marty and said, "I trust that you are going to do your thing. Nothing funny. Okay?"

"Yes, no funny stuff, I promise you," Marty said and then slipped past him and entered the storage room. Boxes of beer and alcohol lined one wall. She stepped further into the room, which previously had been a preschool for children, but no traces of that remained. Marty put her mind on Dominika. She envisioned Dominika in a black leather cupless corset and stilettos. She called out to her, but nothing happened. No sign of Dominika. She called out again. She pleaded for Dominika to appear. Marty closed her eyes and saw Dominika in her mind. She could only see Dominika's dead body floating in the bathtub—her soapy breasts bobbing in the water through her bathrobe. She called out again for Dominika, but to no avail.

As Marty began to ascend the stairwell, she heard Dominika's voice. She said, "Marty, be a good person, find love and go on with your life." Marty turned back towards the storage room. There was no sign of Dominika. She continued up the stairwell where the bartender waited for her by the bar.

"Well, did you get what you wanted?" he asked.

"Do we always?" Marty asked rhetorically.

"You didn't see her. Did you?"

"She spoke to me."

"That's good. So, where are you headed now?" the bartender asked.

"Not sure."

"I guess you wouldn't want to go upstairs to my place?" he asked. "Have a drink or two?"

"You own this club? How convenient. But going upstairs might be too painful."

"I'll be gentle as a lamb," Roberts said with a warm smile.

"One drink," Marty said.

Roberts poured two red wines and handed one to Marty. He stepped towards a door that led to his upstairs apartment and shut the clubs lights off.

Marty and Roberts sat on his couch and talked briefly about the club. Marty was distracted, though. She couldn't help but think about when she was young and innocent, and how she lost that innocence in one fatal act, taking the life of Dominika. Roberts then kissed Marty on the lips. She was reciprocating half-heartedly when she heard Dominika speak from the bathroom. "Marty, go to Fab, he needs you," she said. Marty looked over at the bathroom and saw Dominika standing there in her wet bathrobe. "Marty, you need to go," Dominika said in an urgent voice.

Marty got up from the couch and said, "Sorry, Roberts, I have to run. Thanks." But she was really thanking Dominika. She slipped down the stairwell, leaving Roberts frustrated and with thoughts of how a strange an evening it was. He didn't even get her name. He chased after her. By the time he got downstairs, Marty had caught a cab. The earlier rain had given way to a hazy fog. He quickly jumped in his car and sped after the cab. *Why am I chasing after her?* He questioned himself in a bemused way. But Marty had that effect on a lot of people she met.

The cab pulled up in front of Fab's house and Marty got out. Roberts pulled over and watched Marty, who was reluctant at first as she stood on the sidewalk. She looked up toward the second floor where the lights were on. She was eager to see him—to hold him. She rang Fab's doorbell. No response. She texted him that she was out front. She rang the doorbell again. She even called his cell phone, which went straight to his voicemail. "I'm downstairs. I need to see you. I love you," she wrote on her message.

She walked around back of Fab's house. She ascended the fire escape to the roof and then looked out to the bay—Alcatraz was lit up. She stepped toward the roof door. It was ajar, much to her surprise. She slipped her head inside the door and called out, "Fab, are you home? It's Marty." She then descended the stairs to the playroom and continued down to the second floor. "Hello, Fab," Marty called out again. She then stepped into his bedroom where suddenly she heard the roof door close while she sensed the shower running. "Fab, it's me, Marty," she said not to startle him. She was shocked at what she saw.

Marty stood outside the shower, stunned. It was Fab—he was on the floor of the shower in a huddled position. He was cut up and bleeding. He had been slashed. Obviously, by the chef knife that lay next to him.

The shower water and his blood were a murky wash. Marty called out to him. He was unresponsive. She opened the shower door. It was gut-wrenching for her. "Oh, my God," she moaned. She shut the shower nozzle off and then checked his pulse. There was none. She called out, "Fab. Please, Fab." But she knew it was too late. *Who could have done this?* she pleaded to herself yet was afraid of the answer.

Outside, Roberts observed a woman wearing a black hoodie over her head slowly appear from Fab's back alley. And then she disappeared into the darkness of the street.

Marty wiped down the shower nozzle and the shower door handle. She then made a call to 911 on Fab's house phone and told them a murder had been committed. She ascended the stairs towards the roof and left down the fire escape, wiping the rail along the way. She stepped out from the alley, looked down towards the street and then headed in the opposite direction from the front of the house. As she did, she ran directly into a couple who were out walking their dog. They got a good look at Marty underneath a streetlamp. She had been startled. The dog barked.

Marty was in over her head, so she lost herself in the foggy streets of San Francisco, distraught and bewildered.

Chapter Eighteen

Word of Fab's murder quickly spread on all the local social media outlets. The couple with the dog came forth that evening with a description of the suspicious woman they ran into by Fab's back alley. They assisted the police with a composite drawing of Marty and gave an account of her sighting, which was at approximately 12:45 a.m. By 6:00 a.m., Detective Harris of the San Francisco Police Department-Homicide Division had several DNA samples from the crime scene that were being processed. The chef knife was bagged and tagged—later to be identified as the murder weapon by the City Coroner. No fingerprints would be found on the knife.

By 9:00, Detective Harris' suspicions began to run to an old murder case that was never truly solved. It was the composite drawing and the eyes that looked back at him. But due to bureaucratic manipulation, in his professional belief, the case was incorrectly solved. The wrong person was accused, tried and convicted. They had a suspect with opportunity, means, and motive to have caused the death of a woman—a dominatrix who lived and operated her business in the Van Ness Neighborhood. But how could he ever forget their suspect, Martha Kittering—the young beauty whose file was sealed by Spuds Florez, the city's District Attorney at the time.

Harris kept his own file on Martha Kittering. He took it personally when Florez sealed her file. So he copied most of the documents pertaining to their prime suspect, including her fingerprints, and stored them away for safekeeping in a box he kept in his garage above the rafters. It had been thirteen years since he stored the box away that was marked MK. He placed the box on the garage's workbench, wiped off the dust from the box and used his car key to slash open the masking tape that sealed the box. He rifled through the docs—a photo of her at seventeen caught his attention. She was sexy and had trouble in her striking blue eyes. The same eyes as in the composite drawing.

What interested him most was the fingerprints that were taken off the cell phone that was found in the stairwell of the victim's residence. He knew that what he was doing did not follow evidentiary procedure, but he had to satisfy his hunch about Martha Kittering. *The question was, if she had killed Fabrizio Giacomelli, did she know him? Had she been seen with him? If so, where? The first place to begin was at his restaurant.*

Harris grabbed a coffee and a cherry cheese Danish down in North Beach and went back to his car to read the background check on Martha Kittering on his laptop. It stated that she had lived in Maui for several years. Owned several businesses—a restaurant and a perfumery. Was married to a John Abruzzo. Had a son by the same last name. Currently lived in Santa Barbara. Name change to Marty Remy. Owned a business called Remy Wine and Spirits. No outstanding warrants or convictions. But of course, there were the chef murders in Los Feliz she was connected to several years back that he recalled. *This woman is at it again*, he felt it in his gut.

Harris walked by the Giacomelli Ristorante. A sign on the window said, *Closed Temporarily*. There were several people inside cleaning for a shutdown. *For how long?* They didn't know. He stepped inside. His badge was on his belt indicating his authority. He stepped towards the bar where a woman was cleaning out the refrigerators. "Hello, I'm Detective Harris. San Francisco P.D. I'm here investigating Fabrizio Giacomelli's death," he stated to the woman.

"Yes. What can I do for you?" she asked in a somber voice.

"My condolences. I'm sorry for your loss," he said sincerely. "Your boss. Had he been with a woman with dark hair? In her early thirties. Very attractive."

"Sounds like several. But there was one woman he had been seeing lately. They were involved with the sommelier challenge over at the Regency. I guess that's where they met," she said.

"Was he with her last night?" Harris asked.

"He was here for a time and then left by himself," she said. "But no, I didn't see her."

"What time was that?" he asked.

"Around 11:30," she responded. "You think she did it?"

"Couldn't say. But would you happen to know her name?" Harris asked.

"Marty. She was all Fab was talking about. I think he liked her a lot."

"This sommelier challenge. Is it some type of competition?" Harris asked.

"It's to do with being a wine expert. I think Fab was one of the top finalists. They were supposed to compete today," she said.

"Both him and her?"

"I believe so."

"Was he seeing anyone else?"

"He sees a lot of women. But she was the only one he was focused on," she said.

"Got it. Thank you for your help," Harris said and then left the restaurant.

Harris walked over to the crime scene where he met his partner, Detective Shandra Jones, a tall woman of color. He stepped inside Fab's home, slipping past some crime scene tape. He stopped to look at an alarm system and continued to walk through the hallway toward the kitchen. He opened the drawers. Looked at some chef knives of various sizes and closed the drawer. He then proceeded to climb the stairs to the second floor. He heard his partner on the roof and made his way there. She was inspecting the door. "Harris," she said to him.

"Good morning, Shandra. So, what do we have?" he asked.

"Looks like it was shimmied open."

"What about the bolt lock?"

"No signs of it being tampered with."

"The alarm?"

"The security company said he rarely set the alarm unless he was going out of town for a while," she said.

"Picked a wrong time to be careless," he said. "But I think we may have a potential perp."

"So soon?" she said, surprised. "I did find a piece of cloth on the sill. I guess forensics missed it. Might amount to nothing," Jones said as she showed Harris the bagged evidence of a quarter-inch patch of heavy black cotton.

Harris and Jones drove over to the Regency where the California Grand Sommelier Final Challenge was taking place. The challenge committee decided to replace Fab with the next runner up. The banquet room where the top finalists, who were down to three, were seated on a stage was jam-packed with wine enthusiasts. Marty was seated in the third chair. "That's her in the middle," Harris said to Jones.

"You want to get her now?" Jones asked.

"We'll wait till it's over," Harris said.

"Ms. Remy. How much does an acre of land cost in Napa Valley?" the challenge moderator asked as she read off an index card.

"Five hundred thousand," Marty replied.

"Correct. Mr. Johansen. What percentage of California wines are produced in Napa?" the moderator asked.

"Eight percent," Mr. Johansen said.

"Sorry, that's incorrect. It's four percent. Thank you for your participation," the moderator said. Mr. Johansen exited the stage. "And then there were two. Ms. Woods. How many acres of Chardonnay grape vines were planted in California last year?"

"One hundred thousand," Ms. Woods answered.

"You were so very close. But I'm sorry. There were ninety-five thousand acres planted in California last year," the moderator said. Ms. Woods was not happy, not so much that she missed the question but because of how close she was to being correct. "Ms. Woods, please remain seated. Ms. Remy. This is your opportunity to win the challenge. If you answer incorrectly, you and Ms. Woods will be asked another round of questions. Ms. Remy. What are the four top wine grapes grown in the Santa Barbara Wine Region?"

"Chardonnay, Pinot Noir, Syrah and Sauvignon Blanc," Marty answered.

The moderator smiled and said exuberantly, "Ms. Remy, you are this year's California Grand Sommelier Challenge Champion. Congratulations." Applause erupted in the audience. Marty pursed her lips as tears came to her eyes. They were more to do with Fab's death than winning the challenge. Ms. Woods shook Marty's hand and gave her a comforting shoulder. The moderator and the other challenge committee members came on stage to congratulate Marty. She was given a check for ten thousand dollars, several cases of premium California wines and a crystal chalice decorated with bunches of grapes.

Harris and Jones approached the stage. Marty got a sense that they were there for her as she looked at them making their way to the stage amongst the commotion and congratulations. "Ms. Remy, can you come with us? We're with the San Francisco P.D.," Harris said.

"Now?" she asked almost defiantly.

"Yes, now," Jones said with widened eyes.

Marty handed the moderator her gifts and told her she would be right back. She then slipped off the stage and proceeded to walk with Harris and Jones toward the exit. "What's this about?" she asked Harris.

"I don't know if you remember me. I was assigned to the dominatrix murder case thirteen years ago," he said.

"I thought that was settled?" Marty said.

"New case. This has to do with the death of Fabrizio Giacomelli."

"I see," Marty said quietly.

"You were expecting us?" Harris asked. Marty didn't answer.

Harris had his hand on the door of the interrogation room where Marty sat awaiting the inevitable when Jones said, "She's pretty cool under pressure, this one."

"Yeah, I know. I couldn't tell you the difference between a Pinot Grigio and Pinot Noir, except for their color," Harris said as he entered the room with a file in his hand and then shut the door behind him as Jones stood outside. Harris took a seat opposite Marty. "You have the right to remain silent. Anything you say can and will be used against you in a court of law. You have a right to an attorney. If you cannot afford an attorney, one will be provided for you. Do you understand the rights I just read you? With these rights in mind, do you wish to speak to me?" Harris asked Marty.

"Am I under arrest?" Marty asked.

"Not yet. It's protocol. So, do you understand those rights?" Harris asked.

"Yes," Marty responded politely.

"Good, Ms. Remy. It's funny you had changed your name. Trying to hide from your past?"

"It's my mother's family name. I like it. It fits with my business."

"And what may that be, murder?" he asked smartly. "You knew Fabrizo Giacomelli. You were at his place last night. So, what happened? Were you getting rid of the competition?" he asked sarcastically.

"I was falling in love with him, if you really want to know."

"Lovers do kill each other from time to time. I mean, you killed that dominatrix over jealousy of another woman," Harris said, hitting Marty with a verbal jab.

"I was young and curious. But you have it turned around. It was the other woman who killed her," she said.

"So you say," Harris replied.

"That's what the court said. Don't you remember?" Marty said coyly.

"You just had luck on your side. And guess what? It's about to run out," Harris said. He then showed Marty a copy of the composite drawing of her. "This is you, isn't it? Harris asked. Marty shrugged her shoulders. "Well, we'll soon find out when we do the lineup." A knock came at the door. Harris opened it and Jones had him leave the room so she could talk to him.

"Just got off the phone with the cab company. A woman meeting her description was picked up by Van Ness and Geary and dropped off at the vic's around 12:20 last night," Jones said. Harris went back in the room.

"Ms. Remy, we know you were there. The cab company confirmed you were dropped off at his place the time of the murder. You can avoid the lineup if you just admit to killing your lover. He was your lover, right?" he asked.

"Yes, he was."

"So, you went over to his place. Did he let you in?" Harris asked.

"No. I rang the doorbell. There was no answer. I called him on my cell phone. It went to voicemail, and I left a message. I rang the doorbell again and then I went around the back and climbed the fire escape to the roof. The door was open, so I went inside."

"And then what?"

"I went down the stairs to the second floor and that's when I found him in the shower. I checked his pulse and called 911. You'll find my fingerprints at his place. And my DNA in his bed, and on his couch and in his sauna. But I didn't kill him."

"Then why did you run off and not wait for the police to arrive?" Harris asked.

"He was already dead. I know how you guys operate. You would have locked me up, right then and there. But I did hear someone up on the roof when I was in the bathroom."

"Right," Harris said with a look of disbelief. "So, what were you doing around Van Ness and Geary? Were you reminiscing about the dominatrix? Did you have that old feeling of killing again? Hell, you've been on some wild spree. The dominatrix, the chef murders, the escapade over in France. Oh, and I forgot, the culinary instructor at Chapman. Who else, Ms. Remy? Who else have you killed?" Harris asked fervently.

"You must fish for a hobby?" Marty said indignantly. "All coincidence," she said ironically, thinking about the ship full of tainted Portuguese sailors he had missed, and Mr. Persimmon, her neighbor who killed his dog.

"I give it to you, you are a sharp cookie. In the fallout of killing your lover, you pull off that wine challenge by winning the whole thing," Harris said. "What's the saying? You're as cool as a cucumber. But you're not as smart as you think because you admitted to being at the scene of the crime last night." Jones knocked on the door and then entered the room. "She's under arrest for murdering Fabrizio Giacomelli." Jones gestured for Marty to rise from her seat. She handcuffed Marty behind her back and then escorted her out of the room.

Chapter Nineteen

The arrest of Marty hit social media with a torrent of postings that made Marty out to be some modern Lizzie Borden, the infamous axe murderer who hacked to death her father and stepmother in 1892. A posting of a photo of Lizzie Borden and Marty side by side was shared by tens of thousands. An older video of her in a brawl at the Vatel Toque Awards in Nice, France, where she was on the floor pantie-less and intertwined with the now dead Chef Didier Gaston, had resurfaced. Suggestions were made that she had murdered Chef Gaston by causing a gas leak at his restaurant where he went ablaze when he went to light the pilot of a stove.

The news media made a field day of Marty, much more interested in her than the death of Fab. She was castigated as they used innuendo just short of false accusations that she had barbecued Chef Bubba Arnet of Bubba's Place and poisoned Chef Matt Comatos with "Death Cap" mushrooms. Even a connection between Marty and the death of Chef Johnson, formerly of Chapman Culinary Academy where Marty was a student, had been conjectured by one San Francisco media outlet—a possible tip by Detective Harris. Marty had already been tried and convicted in the court of public opinion before her arraignment.

Traumatized patrons of Giacomelli Ristorante expressed their condolences and horror over the death of Fab in front of his restaurant where dozens of flower arrangements decorated the sidewalk. A handful of Fab's ex-lovers were interviewed. "He was such a wonderful...lover. I will miss him tremendously," one woman reminisced while the other women sobbed uncontrollably.

Marty was housed at the San Francisco City Police Jail when she stepped into an interrogation room escorted by a female police officer.

Her attorney, Spuds Florez, awaited her. "Hello, Marty. Are you doing okay?" Spuds asked.

"I could use a drink, Spuds," Marty said.

"Can't help you. You doing okay with your meds?"

"Stopped taking them."

"Is that prudent?"

"I feel better without them."

"As long as you're okay," he said. "Your father sends his regards, by the way."

"I'm sure he took the news in good stride."

"He'll be coming into the city tomorrow," he said. Marty nodded. "What the police have is several witnesses stating they saw you or someone that looks like you at the scene of the incident. You've admitted to being there. Not so good, Marty. But what they don't have is any fingerprints on the knife used to kill the victim. At the arraignment today you'll be asked whether you are innocent or guilty of the murder. To which you will respond, not guilty."

"Is that going to help?"

"I'm not going to lie; you're getting hammered out there," Spuds said. "Let's go over the events of last night. Set it up for me?"

"I went to the Hunky Dory Club around ten o'clock. After the place closed, I hung around with the owner till around midnight. I then took a cab over to Fab's place. Rang his doorbell. No answer. Texted him. No response. Rang the doorbell again and then decided to go to his roof thinking he might be in his entertainment room on the third floor," Marty said when Spuds interjected.

"Was he expecting you?"

"No," she replied.

"You were involved with him romantically?"

"Yes."

"So, you decided to drop in on him unannounced?"

"Yes."

"Had you known him for a while?"

"I first met him several days ago when I came to San Francisco for the sommelier challenge."

"So, you went to the roof via the fire escape, I'm assuming?" Spuds asked.

"Correct," Marty replied.

"Had you been to his place before?"

"Yes," she said.

"So, what happened next?"

"The roof door was open. I went inside, down the stairs to the second floor. Went into his bedroom. The shower was running in the bathroom, and I called out to him. Peered into the shower and saw Fab bleeding. Cried out to him. Checked his pulse. He had none. Shut the water off and then called 911. And then I left," she said.

"Why didn't you stay and wait for the EMT and the police? Or should I ask?" Spuds queried Marty.

"Actually, I was spooked because I heard a noise from upstairs."

"So you heard someone leave the house from the roof?" Spuds asked.

"Yes, I did," Marty replied emphatically.

"You didn't happen to see them?"

"No, I did not," Marty said.

"Then what?"

"I went back down the fire escape and rushed down the alley to the street. That's when a couple with a dog saw me."

"They're the ones who described you?"

"I would imagine so."

"Hmm," Spuds contemplated. "Is it possible they saw this other person come out of the alley before you? How much time elapsed from the time you heard this person leave the house and the time you ran into this couple?" Spuds asked.

"Three or four minutes," Marty replied. "So they probably didn't see this other person?"

"You never know. Certainly, I'll interview them," Spuds said, trying to lend encouragement to a situation that looked bleak for Marty.

"You think I will be able to get bailed out of here today?"

"All we can do is petition the court. But let's see what happens," Spuds said.

"I need to get back to Santa Barbara. It's been almost a week since I've been away. I have my business down there," Marty said.

"We have the probable cause meeting and then pre-trial to go through, to see if they have enough evidence against you. The fact that you were there weighs heavily. Then we have the trial. And I don't see how we are going to avoid that, at this point."

"It wasn't me, Spuds. Just so that you know," Marty said in a serious tone.

"I understand," he replied.

At her arraignment, Marty pleaded not guilty to the murder charge against her and was denied bail. She was then sent to the San Francisco Hall of Justice Complex for lockup until her hearings. Marty was given a pair of orange coveralls to wear while she was held in the jail. Many of the female inmates' eyes were upon Marty as she entered the general population. "Hello, sweetheart. You want to date?" one of the older inmates toyed with Marty.

Marty kept to herself as several other inmates smiled at her, seeking her attention and possibly her affection. Marty condescendingly smiled back at them, not wanting to interact with ladies of ill-repute as she tried to assimilate the reality of her new situation. "What's the matter? You too good for us?" a Latin inmate with tattoos on her arms and face asked.

"Hi," Marty responded, but kept to herself.

"Hi," the Latin inmate said as she stepped closer to Marty, who took a seat in a chair. "What're you in for?" she whispered in Marty's ear.

"Murdering my lover with a knife," Marty said as she gave her a stern stare.

"Well, aren't you a tough chick," the inmate responded and then made a noise with her cheek and tongue as she stepped back towards her sisters-in-arms. "She tango-downed her lover," she said sarcastically to the other inmates as she waved her head back and forth.

"I'd like to tango down on her," another inmate said, and the others snickered.

Marty just stared off into the distance. There was a pit in her stomach. Not since she was held captive on Baron's island off the coast of Nice had she been this scared. But she didn't show it. She had to remain cool, just in case one of those girls started trouble. "That's right, Marty. Don't take any shit from them," Bubba said as he appeared next to Marty.

"What are you doing here?" Marty said under her breath so as not to be heard by anyone else except Bubba.

"I'm here for moral support. Shit luck you're in here. If it weren't for that little hussy who works for you," Bubba said.

"What do you mean?" Marty asked.

"Exactly what I mean. Michelle. She was the one that killed your boy," Bubba said.

Marty raised her eyebrows in disbelief.

"That's right. She not only fucked you once by killing him. She fucked you right into jail," Bubba said with eyebrows raised as he nodded his head.

"Fucking bitch," Marty said. But this time louder.

The Latin inmate then charged Marty and threw her to the ground. She got on top of Marty and proceeded to punch Marty in the face as she ground her groin against Marty's. Several of the other inmates quietly huddled around them. Bubba cheered on Marty as she punched the Latin inmate in her right eye, which knocked her out. By then, several prison guards proceeded to break up the fight that had already ended. Marty was escorted to her prison cell as the Latin inmate was attended to by the other guard.

The following day Marty was visited by her father who sat on the other side of a heavy paneled glass partition. Marty sat down opposite him with a bruised eye. "What happened to you?" he asked.

"Hello, Dad," Marty responded.

"You okay? Does it hurt?"

"No," Marty said sternly.

"You've been in some situations. But this one is pretty unbelievable. Don't tell me that was you?"

"They have the wrong woman," she replied.

"Let's hope so. I spoke with Spuds. He's going to do everything he can. But you were seen leaving the scene."

"Number Three, no speaking of her case," the visitor moderator said didactically.

"Sorry," Marty's father said to the moderator.

"How's Mother these days?" Marty asked.

"You know. In and out of the clinics," he said. "Between you two, I don't know who's concerned me the most."

"Same DNA," Marty said.

"I know. So, can I do anything for you?" he asked.

"Yes, I need someone to check in on my business. I don't know how long I'll be in this place. I don't even know if I'll ever get out of…" she said as her father intentionally interrupted her.

"Spuds is good. Let's hope he can pull this off for you," her father said. "I'll go down to Santa Barbara tomorrow."

"Thank you, Dad."

"Time's up, Number Three," the moderator said.

Marty's father stood up from his chair and waved at Marty who waved back as she was escorted by a guard back to the lockup.

Later, Marty was allowed to make a phone call, which she placed to the wine shop. "Remy's Wine and Spirits. This is Michelle. How can I help you?"

"Just the person I wanted," Marty said.

"Oh, my God, Marty. It's all over the internet. I can't believe what's happened," Michelle said in a whiny concerned voice.

"All a mishap. Right, Michelle?" Marty queried her.

"I hope so," Michelle responded. "Are you okay, Marty?"

"Been in worse situations. At least I'm alive," Marty said. "My father will be down at the store tomorrow. He's going to check in on things. Let the other guys know. Okay?"

"Anything. Anything at all," Michelle said.

"I'll be in touch."

"I'm sending you a hug and a kiss," Michelle said.

"Whatever. But thanks. I have to go." Marty hung up the phone. She then received a sudden tap on her shoulder. Marty turned around to a diminutive woman. She looked down at her and said, "Yes?"

"Shanise wants to see you," the diminutive woman said.

"Who's Shanise?"

"Let's put it this way. She's someone you're going to want to know," the diminutive woman said.

"As long as she's friendly."

"Follow me, then," the diminutive woman said, and she escorted Marty down a block to a cell where an attractive, dark-skinned woman wearing reading eyeglasses was perched on a cot reading *The Art of War* by Sun Tzu.

"Sun Tzu once wrote, when you wage war against another, one must be whole. And to be whole, the source of your strength comes from unity," Shanise said in a Jamaican accent.

"*The Art of War,*" Marty said. "You're speaking of an alliance?"

"You're an educated woman. But you picked a fight against someone you know nothing about. They call her Conejita. The little rabbit. But she isn't so cuddly. She'll be coming after you," Shanise said.

"What are you proposing?" Marty asked with some apprehension.

"Don't worry, I have a man on the outside," Shanise said.

"What do you want in return?"

"Spuds Florez is your lawyer. He's the best there is. I need him to get me out of this place."

"I'll give you his number," Marty said.

"I'm afraid his fees are beyond my means."

"So you want me to pick up your tab for some protection?" Marty asked.

"It's the price for remaining whole. Meet me in the laundry room just before we go to the showers."

"A roll in the sheets? I thought you had a man?" Marty questioned her.

"Just be there."

Several hours later, Marty made her way to the laundry room. It was quiet; no one was there. Marty peered around and then Shanise appeared out of nowhere. Marty was startled because she thought maybe it was a setup and Shanise was allied with Conejita.

"Good, you're here," Shanise said and then handed Marty a bar of soap with a shank encased inside of it. "Here, put this away."

"What's this for?" Marty asked in surprise and tried to hand it back to Shanise.

"Put it in your coveralls. Now!" Shanise said urgently. "There's a shank inside. You're going to slash Conejita's achilles in the shower."

"I thought you were going to protect me?"

"I am. Right after you slash her, you hand off the shank to me, and I'll get rid of it. Because if they catch you with it, it's trouble," Shanise said.

"Why do I have to slash her?"

"Because when you're not looking, she'll do it to you. It's either her or you. And I'm sure you don't want to be hopping around the rest of your life like some bunny rabbit," Shanise said with certainty. "And make sure you get her good. Down on an angle," Shanise said as she mimicked the slashing on Marty's own achilleas. "That tendon will snap like a rubber band, and she'll drop to the floor like a water buffalo being shot."

"What if she bleeds to death?" Marty asked.

"Unlikely. But why are you so worried? You killed your man with a knife."

"It wasn't me. Just bad timing."

"Right," Shanise said as if she heard that one before.

The shower was quiet time for the female inmates. It was almost zen-like as many of them shared washing each other's backs. As Conejita washed one of her fellow inmate's back, Marty pulled the shank from the soap, approached her foe, stepped near her and slashed Conejita's tendon with precision of a surgeon. Conejita fell to the floor on her side. She winced in pain but made no sound as she held her achilles, knowing precisely what had happened to her.

Marty then palmed the knife and slipped it off to Shanise, who stepped by two women who shrouded a floor drain that had its cover slung to the side of the hole on one of its screws. Shanise slipped the shank down the drain. One of the women replaced the cover over the hole with her foot and stepped on it to give it a good seal.

Two of Conejita's posse helped her to her feet as she held her right foot off the ground as if she had sprained her ankle. Blood dripped onto the floor of the shower and commingled with the water. A guard approached Conejita and her posse and asked, "What happened?" Conejita just gave a grimace as if she had been beaten at her own game as she held her slashed achilles.

Chapter Twenty

The court deemed that Marty's murder case would be bound over for trial at the probable cause hearing based on the two witnesses who identified her leaving the crime scene, the cab driver who identified her as the person he dropped off at Fab's residence prior to his murder, and the 911 recording of Marty stating that Fab had been stabbed to death. At the pre-trial hearing, the discovery stage of the trial process, Spuds Florez appealed for a dismissal of the case since Marty's fingerprints were not found on the murder weapon, nor was her DNA found on the victim. Dina Wineberg, the judge presiding over the case, found that there was enough circumstantial evidence and denied Spuds' request for a dismissal.

Jeffrey Koontz, the San Francisco City District Attorney, a stout, black-bearded man in his mid-forties, headed the prosecution against Marty and successfully won a motion for one count of first-degree felony murder with a deadly weapon that was deliberate and with premeditation and one count of breaking and entering for good measure. Witnesses for the prosecution included Detective Harris, the couple with the dog, the cab driver, several Giacomelli Ristarante employees, a California Grand Sommelier Challenge member, Dr. Bollinger (with limitations), and Paul Cooz. The DA was denied in his motion to unseal Marty's juvenile record pertaining to the murder of Dominika.

At the jury trial, Marty was dressed in a royal blue suit dress and sat next to her attorney, Spuds Florez, and his co-counsel, a tall blonde woman named Linda Brice. Marty was surprisingly relaxed at the one of the biggest murder trials in San Francisco since the George Moscone and Harvey Milk assassinations back in 1978. As one court reporter stated, *It makes for tentpole theater*. The courtroom was jam-packed, alive with a hum of excitement.

Judge Dina Wineberg was a women's advocate who liked high-profile cases, which Spuds felt could help with Marty's defense if it came down to a guilty verdict. *Possibly she would be lenient*, he surmised. Yet his argument was going to hinge on a piece of evidence, the black cotton swatch that was found on the door jamb by Harris and Jones. It was very weak because there was no way he could disprove Marty was at the crime scene at the time of the murder. In the interview he had with the couple with the dog, they said they only saw Marty that night and no other person.

Spuds had to create some reasonable doubt with the jury that Marty was the killer, surmising that there was another person, the actual killer, who was in Fab's home that evening. Which meant that he had to put Marty on the stand as much as he hated to do so because it would open her up to attacks by the prosecution. And Marty's credibility was going to be hotly contested by Koontz, who Spuds knew was fearsome and had no remorse when it came to demolishing a defendant by whatever means at his disposal. Spuds knew his opponent very well. He had groomed Koontz as a young assistant when Spuds was the city DA.

Judge Wineberg entered the courtroom. "Superior Court of California—County of San Francisco, is now in session. Judge Dina Wineberg presiding," the court clerk called out to all those who sat in the electrified courtroom. Several eager law students were present, as well as local and national media court reporters who were there for the hot story of the day. A few of Fabrizio's family members and former lovers also were present. An illustrator smartly sketched Marty in a dark and ominous way, making her resemble a raven with piercing eyes and jet-black hair. Paul Cooz was certainly present. Yet Marty's father was not there. He was back in Santa Barbara taking care of her wine store.

"Good morning, everyone. Marty Remy, who is here today in court, has been charged with one count of murder in the first degree with the use of a deadly weapon. She is also charged with one count of breaking and entering. The charges were pled not guilty, ergo, the trial by jury. On January 13, 2018, the accused willfully, deliberately and with premeditated forethought murdered Fabrizio Giacomelli in violation of Penal Code 187. As to the jury, every person guilty of murder in the first degree shall be punished by imprisonment in the state prison system for life without possibility of parole. Do not let bias or prejudice by friends, family members or the internet influence your decision," Judge Wineberg said, making finger quotes when she said the word "internet." "Let's proceed with opening statements."

Koontz stood up, smiled and introduced himself. "Ladies and gentlemen, the state has irrefutable proof that the defendant, Ms. Remy, is the perpetrator of this monstrous act, the premeditated murder of Fabrizio Giacomelli. She broke into his home, went into the kitchen, grabbed a knife and then went into his bathroom where he was taking a shower and stabbed him repeatedly with the knife. He fell to the shower floor and bled to death.

"Out of guilt or shame, she called 911 to report the incident and fled the scene. She was seen by a couple walking their dog who later identified Ms. Remy as the person they saw coming out of the alley behind the victim's home. Now, this is not the first time the state has encountered Ms. Remy. Thirteen years ago, when I was a young assistant attorney with the city of San Francisco, Ms. Remy was picked up for questioning in the murder of a dominatrix…"

"Your Honor, my client was a juvenile at the time. Her file was subsequently sealed," Spuds said, interrupting Koontz.

"That is true. Strike the last two remarks. Mr. Koontz, stick to the case at hand," Judge Wineberg said. But the cat was out of the bag.

Koontz had already cast suspicion on Marty, and in Spuds' opinion, as expressed by the displeased look on his face, the judge was far too lenient with Koontz.

"Ladies and gentlemen, you see, my opponent, Mr. Florez, and his client have a long history together. He was the city's district attorney thirteen years ago and was the state's attorney general when Ms. Remy was a suspect in the infamous chef show murders several years ago," Koontz said when he was interrupted by Spuds again.

"Your Honor? Am I on trial here?" Spuds demanded.

"Were you not the state's attorney general?" the judge asked of Spuds who then kept quiet, knowing if he objected too much, it might cast doubt on his whole defense of Marty.

"And now he is representing her again. What's the old saying? Three strikes and you're out. Ms. Remy committed this murder, and we will show to you through testimony that she is mentally flawed, which is why she killed Fabrizio Giacomelli. It's up to each one of you to make sure she is put away for a long time, so she doesn't commit another murder. Thank you, ladies and gentlemen," Koontz said to the jury and then took his seat at the prosecution table.

"Mr. Florez. Your opening statement," the judge said.

Spuds stood up and gave a quick glance at Koontz. "Thank you, ladies and gentlemen of the jury. I apologize for my opponent's miscued representation of the facts. I have only represented my client once, and that is today. She stands before you in the murder of Fabrizio Giacomelli. But this is not so. She did not kill him. Although they recently just met, they fell in love with each other. My client, Ms. Remy, excited with anticipation, went to go see her new companion at his home on the night in question. She rang the doorbell and, not knowing he was already dead, entered through a door on the roof, which was open. When she found his body on the floor of the shower, she checked to see if he was still alive and then she called 911. In the meantime, she heard someone on the roof, apparently the killer. She was scared and left the residence in a hurry." He then paused a second to let the jury absorb the facts he'd just told them.

"We will prove to you that the person my client heard leaving Fabrizio Giacomelli's home was real and not some phantom she made up as an alibi. There was a piece of clothing found on the doorjamb that contained a hair fiber that is inconsistent with my client's own hair fiber. Obviously, the person left in a hurry, catching their clothing on the doorjamb as they fled. I want you to consider that throughout this whole trial is reasonable doubt as to her guilt. The prosecution will try to paint my client as a murderous vixen through conjecture and hearsay. They will try to say she is a bad person. That she even killed the victim because he was a threat in the sommelier competition they were both involved in. As if getting rid of him improved her chances of winning the competition. All absurdities," Spuds said and then took his seat next to Marty.

"Thank you, Spuds," Marty whispered into his ear as she leaned towards him. He reciprocated by putting a hand on her arm.

"Your first witness," Judge Wineberg said to Koontz as she hand-gestured to him.

"We call Detective Frank Harris to the stand," Koontz said.

Harris took the stand, was sworn in by the judge and then took his seat. "Detective Harris, tell us, where do you work and what you do?" Koontz asked.

"I'm a homicide detective with the San Francisco Police Department," he said.

"How long have you been with the department?" Koontz asked.

"Seventeen years," he replied.

"On the night of January twelfth of this year, did you respond to a possible homicide?" Koontz asked.

"Yes, my partner and I proceeded to 268 Pfeiffer Street in North Beach after we got the call from patrolmen who had been on the scene," Harris said.

"The home of Fabrizio Giacomelli, the deceased?" Koontz asked.

"Yes," Harris stated.

"Describe the scene?" Koontz asked.

"Mr. Giacomelli was lying on the floor of his shower on the second floor. He was naked with multiple stab wounds to the body and hands," Harris said. "A kitchen knife was found next to him."

Koontz flipped through photographs of Fabrizio Giacomelli's wounds on a portable flat screen so the jury could see. "We'd like to introduce these as exhibits 'a' through 'f,' " Koontz said. "Now, Detective Harris, was Mr. Giacomelli dead at that time?"

"He was unresponsive when the patrolmen arrived. Later, the medical examiner pronounced him dead shortly before my partner and I arrived," Harris said.

Koontz picked up a bagged ten-inch chef knife off his table and held it up. "Was this the knife that was found lying next to Mr. Giacomelli?"

"Yes," Harris said.

"We'd like to introduce the knife as exhibit 'g,' " Koontz said as he held it up for everyone to see. "Was that knife a part of a set obtained from Mr. Giacomelli's house?"

"A kitchen drawer housing other knives was open. Based on similar knives in that drawer, it appears that it was part of a set," Harris replied.

"Detective Harris, did a break-in occur during the process of this crime?" Koontz asked.

"To the best that I can ascertain, the roof door, which had been locked, was shimmied open," Harris said. "The door was found open when the patrolmen arrived."

"So, the killer entered that door and also exited that door?" Koontz asked.

"The front door and a side door off the kitchen were locked, so that's my presumption," Harris said.

"Is there a fire escape leading to the street down below from the roof?" Koontz asked.

"Yes," Harris said.

"So, the killer entered the house from the roof, stepped down two flights of stairs to the kitchen, grabbed the knife—exhibit 'g'—went back up a flight of stairs to the second floor, entered the bathroom and proceeded to stab Fabrizio Giacomelli to death while he was taking a shower?" Koontz asked in a slow methodical tone as he showed a flow chart on the flat screen describing the sequence.

"That is how I see it based on the evidence," Harris said.

"And then the killer exited the roof and fled down the fire escape?" Koontz asked as he displayed a photograph on the flat screen of the fire escape.

"Yes," Harris said as he peered over at Marty.

"Did anyone see the killer fleeing Mr. Fabrizio's house?" Koontz asked.

"Objection. Speculative," Spuds said.

"Sustained," the judge replied.

"Were there any witnesses who saw a person leaving Mr. Giacomelli's home via the fire escape?" Koontz asked.

"No, but they saw a person matching the description of the defendant coming out from the alley behind Mr. Giacomelli's residence at the time of the murder," Harris said. "They assisted with a composite drawing of her."

"The defendant being Marty Remy who sits before us today in court?" Koontz asked.

"Yes," Detective Harris said.

"How were you able to match the drawing with Ms. Remy?" Koontz asked.

"A staff member at Mr. Giacomelli's restaurant stated that he had been with a woman who matched the composite drawing, which led us to the sommelier competition at the Regency," Harris said.

"You're referring to the California Grand Sommelier Challenge that was just held at the Regency Hotel?" Koontz asked.

"Yes," Harris stated. "Marty Remy was a part of the competition. That's how they met. Mr. Giacomelli and her. I assume. Of course, I had seen Marty Remy before, thirteen years prior. So, when I saw the composite drawing, it hit me like a ton of bricks. My instincts said it was her."

"Because she was a suspect that got away?" Koontz asked coyly.

"Objection, Your Honor. My client was never tried in that case," Spuds said adamantly. "Her records were sealed in the matter since she was a juvenile at the time."

"Strike the last question by the prosecution. Lead counsels approach the bench, please?" Judge Wineberg said with a two-finger gesture. The judge leaned forward as the two men stepped forward toward her. She spoke in a soft tone. "I know you two have history together, but this is not going to be some Ali-Frazier match. Mr. Koontz, you need to keep it relevant to this case. On the other hand, Mr. Florez, I've had the opportunity to go over your client's sealed records, and although specifics of that case may be prejudicial, cursory references can be applied." And then with a two-finger gesture, she excused the two.

Al Capone, dressed in a black pin-stripe suit, leaned over the railing behind Marty and said, "Hello, doll face. You're in a little jam, heh?"

"Hi, Al. Yeah, you could say that," Marty whispered through the side of her mouth toward Al Capone.

Spuds took notice. "Everything alright, Marty?"

"Fine. And you?" Marty asked. Spuds just nodded.

"Detective Harris, where did you pick up the defendant?" Koontz asked.

"She was at the Regency Hotel," Harris said.

"What was she doing?" Koontz asked.

"She was on stage at the sommelier competition," Harris said.

"Where she had won the challenge? Where, if Fabrizio Giacomelli were still alive, he could have easily won that competition?" Koontz asked.

"Speculative," Spuds objected.

"Sustained," Judge Wineberg responded.

"Was the defendant identified in a lineup?" Koontz asked.

"Yes, by the couple with the dog who saw her come from the alley behind the victim's residence and by the cab driver who dropped off Ms. Remy in front of the victim's residence the night of the murder," Harris said.

"Did Marty Remy admit to killing Fabrizio Giacomelli while she was in your custody? Koontz asked.

"Objection. Prejudicial," Spuds said.

"Overruled," the judge responded. "Please continue, Detective Harris."

"Marty Remy did not admit to killing the deceased. But she did claim to be at his residence the night of the murder and admitted to making the call to 911," Harris said.

"I'd like to play a recording of that 911 call and admit it as evidence 'h,' " Koontz said.

The jury and everyone in the courtroom got to hear Marty's voice. The recording was a little grainy, but it was distinctly her voice that as some have stated was as smooth and husky as a shot of Grand Marnier or well-aged whiskey. There was no stress in her voice, only grief as she said, "Fabrizio Giacomelli has been murdered in his home. He's on the floor of his shower." She hung up before the 911 could ask her to stay on the line.

"Was that the voice of Marty Remy on that 911 call we just heard?" Koontz asked.

"Yes," Harris said.

"Would you consider that call an admission of guilt by the defendant?" Koontz asked.

"Objection. That would be a presumption," Spuds said.

"Sustained," the judge said.

"Okay, let's back it up. Where had the defendant been prior to arriving at Fabrizio Giacomelli's home the night of the murder?" Koontz asked.

"She was at the Hunky Dory Club on Van Ness visiting with the owner of the club after hours," Harris said.

"Did she engage in amorous activity?" Koontz asked.

"Objection. Hearsay," Spuds said.

"I'll allow it," the judge said.

"Do you mean was she having sex?" Harris asked.

"The club owner kissed me. And that's when I left," Marty whispered into Spud's ear.

"You tell us," Koontz asked.

"According to the club owner, they had gone up to his apartment above the club and had sex together," Harris said.

"Objection. Irrelevant," Spuds said firmly.

"Overruled," the judge replied.

"Can you tell us if this was the same location where a murder took place thirteen years earlier?" Koontz asked.

"Yes. It happened on Halloween night in 2005. A dominatrix named Dominika Slovovice was murdered. She was found electrocuted in her bathtub," Harris said.

"Objection. Relevance? My client was never indicted for that murder," Spuds called out.

"Counsel, is there a conclusion with your line of questioning?" the judge asked Koontz.

"Marty Remy was at the same location the night of Dominika Slovovice's death thirteen years prior. Don't you find it a little ironic?" Koontz asked.

"I said cursory. Counsel, you need to check yourself. Strike the last question by the prosecution and the answer by the witness. Jury, please disregard that last question and answer," the judge said with a disgruntled face.

"Your Honor, I'm done with the witness," Koontz said.

"That's good because you were almost in contempt of court," the judge warned Koontz.

"Your witness, Mr. Florez," the judge said.

Koontz took his seat as Spuds stood up.

"Sweetheart, you and I need to break some bread over some Chianti. You're my kind of gal," Al Capone said to Marty.

"As long as it's not on Valentine's Day," Marty whispered like a ventriloquist.

"You're a funny dame. I like dat'," Al Capone said as Judge Wineberg took notice of Marty's lips moving.

"Detective Harris? Was my client ever convicted or tried for the murder of Dominika Slovovice?" Spuds asked.

"No," Harris said.

"In fact, some other woman was found guilty and sent to prison for her murder?" Spuds asked.

"That is correct. She died in prison," Harris said.

"Thank you for clarifying that for us. In your investigation of the murder of Fabrizio Giacomelli, did you find a piece of torn clothing at the scene of the crime?" Spuds asked as he stepped towards the prosecution table and picked up the bagged evidence.

"Yes, my partner found it," Harris replied.

"Is this the piece of torn clothing?" Spuds said as he held up the evidence for everyone to see.

"Yes," Harris said.

"Where was it found exactly?" Spuds asked.

"On the roof door jamb about two feet high attached to a protruding nail," Harris said.

"And this piece of evidence, which by the way I'd like to introduce as evidence 'g,' was it examined by forensics and found to have hair fibers on it that were inconsistent with my client's DNA?" Spuds asked.

"That is correct," Harris responded.

"And did you find any articles of clothing that would have matched this piece of evidence during your investigation of my client's hotel room?" Spuds asked.

"No," Harris said.

"Could it then be possible as the actual murderer fled the crime scene via the roof door in haste, they scraped along the nail on the door jamb, which tore off this piece of fabric?" Spuds asked as he held up the bagged evidence.

"Objection. Speculation," Koontz said.

"Overruled," the judge replied.

"Did forensics do a DNA testing of the hair fibers found on the fabric?" Spuds asked.

"Yes," Harris answered.

"Did you make a match with anyone?" Spuds asked.

"There was no one in the system that matched the DNA," Harris said.

"So, in theory, it's possible that there is someone out there who is the killer of Fabrizio Giacomelli other than Marty Remy?" Spuds asked.

"It's possible, but not highly probable," Harris said.

"Is that because you were prejudiced from the outset in your investigation of my client since she eluded your grasp thirteen years ago?" Spuds asked ardently.

"Argumentative. Besides, her record was sealed," Koontz stated.

"Touché, counselor. Sustained," the judge said.

"I have no more questions for the witness," Spuds said, knowing that he had established the tone of the defense and laid the groundwork for reasonable doubt based on the piece of clothing that was brought into evidence.

"Re-direct, Mr. Koontz?" the judge asked.

"Not at this time, Your Honor," Koontz replied.

"Thank you, Detective Harris. You may leave the stand," Judge Wineberg said graciously. "Next witness?"

Koontz called the Chief Medical Examiner for the City of San Francisco as his next witness. After his questioning, which passed without much fanfare between Koontz and Spuds, Spuds had only one question for the ME. "Were Marty Remy's fingerprints found on the murder weapon—the chef knife?"

To which the ME answered, "No."

"That's all," Spuds said. Judge Wineberg then called for a twenty-minute recess.

Chapter Twenty-One

During the recess, Spuds conferred with Marty in a private room as a guard stood outside the door. "That went pretty well, didn't it?" Marty asked.

"Not well enough, because the way it looks, you are still the primary suspect. Do you have any inclination who the killer might be? Does anyone you know have it out for you?"

Of course, Marty knew it was Michelle who had killed Fab. She was sure that if Michelle had any idea Marty might be there, she wouldn't have killed him then. *Certainly, the psycho would have committed the murder some other time*, Marty thought.

At that moment both Didier and Sookie made their presence known. "Marty, Marty, your Hunky Dory friend was in front of Fabrizio's house that night. He saw Michelle," Didier said excitedly. "Tell him. Tell your lawyer."

"I don't know who might have killed Fab. But that night I went over to his place, I think I saw the club owner out front in his car. Maybe he saw Michelle. I mean, whoever it was that came out the alley," Marty said.

"Who's Michelle?" Spuds asked in surprise.

"Um, I misspoke. She's someone who works for me. I was just thinking about my store," Marty said.

"Oh, okay. Why didn't you tell me this before? This can change everything for you. We'll have to get him to testify," Spuds said.

"Yes. We have to," Marty said as she watched Didier and Sookie encourage her.

"Marty, are you all right? I noticed during the hearing you were sort of talking to yourself. And now you look like you're distracted by something," Spuds inquired.

"I'm fine. You know, this is all pretty overwhelming," Marty said.

"Are you sure? Maybe you need to start taking your meds again?" Spuds asked.

"I don't need them," Marty said emphatically.

"Way to go, *mon cherie*," Sookie crooned.

"And I didn't have sex with the club owner. Make sure he testifies to that effect, because they'll think I had no feelings for Fab," Marty said.

"You're right," Spuds said and then the door opened, and it was the guard.

Outside the courtroom, Spuds met with Linda, his co-counsel. "I want you to get a summons for the Hunky Dory owner to appear in court. But first, find out if he was in front of Giacomelli's house the night of the killing. And if he saw another person come from the back alley," Spuds said.

"What? She just recollected something?" his co-counsel asked.

"You know how trials can go, expect the unexpected. Like finding hidden treasure," Spuds said with a grin. "I also want to find out about some woman named Michelle who works for Marty. She mentioned her name inadvertently. Get our private investigator to handle that. Right away."

"Freudian slip?" the co-counsel asked rhetorically.

"Yeah," Spuds said with a nod. "Something funny about that."

Linda drove over to the Hunky Dory Club expecting to be in and out after serving the summons to Tom Roberts, the owner. But a small sign on the front door read: Floating 'Round My Tin Can. Be Back In A Few Weeks—Tom. *Great,* she said to herself. She rang the doorbell to the

188

upstairs apartment, hoping he would still be on the property. But there was no answer. She did a quick search on her cell phone for Tom's cell phone using a paid service that provides such information. She called the number provided. No answer. She also sent him a text. And no response.

She then contacted an associate who did "private consulting" on IT matters locating individuals through their personal electronic devices via a GPS locator. Of course, everything comes with a price. Marty would be billed accordingly. Tom Roberts was at the San Francisco County Courthouse, precisely where Marty's hearing was being held. Linda headed straight back to the hearing with a photo of Tom on her cell phone.

She quietly entered the courtroom, which was in session, and discreetly looked around. No one in the courtroom matched Tom's photo. She rang his cell phone with ears on alert. But heard not a sound except for the DA's voice questioning the man who saw Marty come out of the back alley behind Fab's house. Linda made her way to the counsel table and took her seat next to Spuds. She leaned into his ear and told him that Tom Roberts was in the courtroom, but he must be incognito because she couldn't recognize him.

"My apologies for the interruption, Your Honor, but I'd like to ask for a recess. Something has come up with a potential witness," Spuds said, interrupting Koontz.

"Rather abrupt. It's about time for a lunch break. Everyone be back in court in ninety minutes," the judge said.

"Thank you, Your Honor," Spuds said politely.

The courtroom began to empty out. "Marty, can you recognize the club owner? He's probably in disguise. But don't point," Spuds whispered in Marty's ear.

Marty turned her head towards the galley. "I'm not sure," she said. A taller man with curly blond hair and glasses dressed in khaki casual wear looked back toward Marty as he exited. "That's him. The guy with the glasses," she said urgently.

Linda quickly got up from the table and rushed towards the exit. Outside the courtroom, she chased after Roberts. When she caught up to him, she said, "Tom Roberts, you are compelled to appear in court." He turned around toward her as if he had been caught with his hand in the cookie jar. She handed him the summons. "You two didn't have sexual relations, did you?" Linda asked.

Tom lowered his eyes as if shamed and said, "No."

"You were in front of the house that night. Did you see anyone else leave through the back alley?" Linda asked.

"I did. She was wearing black sweats with a hood. I didn't see her face, though," Roberts said almost reluctantly.

"You did. That's good. Are you willing to testify to that?" Linda asked.

"If I have to?" Roberts asked.

"It would greatly help our client's defense," Linda said. "Of course, we would be prepared to remunerate you for your testimony."

"That won't be necessary. When will I have to appear?" he asked.

"In a few days. Maybe three," she said. "But why didn't you come forward before and why the costume?" Linda asked with interest.

"I wasn't sure if she did it or not. And maybe the other woman I saw was her partner. There is a reason why we have prisons," Roberts said.

"True. You're intrigued by her?" Linda asked.

"Yes. She's like Cleopatra and Lady Godiva and Salome. All in one. She's the most exotic woman I've ever met," Roberts said an aching voice. "She's as hot as Scotch bonnets."

"I got it. But if you want her attention, just show up and help us win her case. Because if not, she'll be in prison for a very long time. Long enough to turn her into an old hag," Linda said.

"Can't have that. But what about this other woman? Do you know who she might be?" Tom asked.

"Don't know. I have to go. I'll see you in a couple of days. And by the way, get rid of the get-up," Linda said and then stepped away. She immediately called the second private investigator on her call list to keep an eye on Tom Roberts, aka Major Tom.

After lunch at the hearing and after Koontz questioned the man who saw Marty come out the alley, Spuds decided not to question him. He saw what he saw, and he didn't want to reaffirm to the jury that the man saw Marty. The woman with the man testified next, and Spuds had passed on questioning her. The cab driver was then called to the witness stand. His testimony would be a setup for introducing Tom Roberts during the defense portion of the trial. Tom Roberts' testimony about seeing the other woman wearing black sweats would link the black swatch of clothing found on the door jamb.

The black swatch of clothing and Tom Roberts' testimony were now the crux of Spuds' defense of Marty. But Spuds was well aware that Koontz had several witnesses lined up who would make statements about Marty that would put her in a bad light. Especially Paul Cooz, whom he knew from the chef murders down in Los Feliz. As much as he would argue against Cooz's relationship to those murder cases, he was unaware of Cooz's current investigation of Marty over the deaths relating to Tina St. Clair and Misty Simms.

On the last day of the prosecutor's case against Marty, Dr. Bollinger was called to the stand as the first witness. He was sworn in by Judge Wineberg and then asked by Koontz, "Please state and spell your name?"

"Paul Bollinger. P.A.U.L. B.O.L.L.I.N.G.E.R.," he said.

"What is your current occupation?" Koontz asked.

"I'm a sex therapist in Carmel, California," Bollinger replied.

"Oh, Christ!" Marty yelled out.

"Mr. Florez, please have your client refrain from making verbal comments," the judge said. "Please continue," she said to Koontz.

"What was your previous occupation before you became a sex therapist?" Koontz asked.

"I was a psychologist for sixteen years," Bollinger stated.

"What is your educational background?" Koontz asked.

"My undergraduate work was done at Cleveland University. And then I received a PhD in Clinical Psychology at Golden State University—Fresno in 2002," Bollinger said.

"You recently ran a clinic in Santa Barbara. Is that correct?" Koontz asked.

"I was a partner in a mental therapy clinic for six years in Santa Barbara," Bollinger replied.

"Is that where you met the defendant, Marty Remy?" Koontz asked.

"Objection. Doctor/patient privileged information," Spuds said.

"I'll allow it. Overruled," the judge said. "Please answer the question, Doctor."

"Yes," he said.

"What was the nature of her visits, without going into specifics?" Koontz inquired. Spuds was about to object when the judge held up a finger towards him, to which he acquiesced.

"Ms. Remy had an arrangement with her ex-husband where she was required to be tested for certain medications she was taking. I had to verify she was actually taking them on a regular basis," Bollinger said.

"Was she taking them on a regular basis?" Koontz asked.

"Not as prescribed. She started to reduce her dosage," Bollinger replied.

"Had her mood changed?" Koontz asked.

"Objection," Spuds said sternly.

"Sustained," the judge said. "Keep it tight, Mr. Koontz, we need to protect the defendant's rights."

"Did you refer Marty Remy to any other mental health clinician after you left?" Koontz asked.

"She had stopped coming into the clinic two months prior to my leaving the practice," Bollinger said.

"So she violated the arrangement she had with her ex-husband?" Koonz asked.

"Objection. Relevance," Spuds said.

"Sustained. Counselor, you need to wrap it up with your witness," the judge said firmly.

"I'm done with the witness. Thank you, Dr. Bollinger, for your testimony," Koontz said, taking his seat.

"Your witness," Judge Wineberg said to Spuds as she hand-gestured towards Bollinger.

"Good morning, Dr. Bollinger," Spuds said. "Is the reason my client stopped taking her medication that it made her feel inept?" Spuds asked. "That she lacked clarity?"

"You could say that," Bollinger replied as he looked over at Marty who was in his direct view. As much as he wanted to elaborate on why she felt inept out of retribution towards Marty, he knew that it would mean trouble for him. He could lose his license to practice in the state. Most likely go to jail for his indiscretions. Best leave well enough alone. Besides, doctor/patient confidentiality was on his side in not having to answer privileged information regarding Marty's mental state.

"Thank you, Dr. Bollinger. No more questions," Spuds said.

"Redirect," the judge said to prosecution.

Koontz gave Marty a hard stare as he stood up and approached the witness chair and then stopped and looked at the jury as if the cat was out of the bag. "Dr. Bollinger, can you elaborate on how Marty Remy felt inept? That she lacked clarity?" Koontz asked as he turned towards the witness.

"She…" Bollinger said without finishing the statement.

"She, what?" Koontz asked in a hostile way.

"She said she had a low libido," Bollinger said.

"Objection. That's privileged information between doctor and patient," Spuds said.

"Overruled. You opened that door," the judge said.

"Your Honor? It's still privileged information that can bias the jury against my client," Spuds pleaded.

"Let's see where this goes. I'm assuming you have a conclusion, Counselor?" Judge Wineberg asked of Koontz.

"I do. But may I treat the witness as hostile?" Koontz asked.

"I think you already have. But go right ahead," the judge said.

"So you prescribed her something that would help her with that?" Koontz asked.

"Yes," Bollinger replied reluctantly.

"And not only did you supply her with a remedy, you took advantage of her situation by engaging in sexual intercourse with her? Didn't you?" Koontz demanded.

Spuds immediately turned to Marty in dismay. Marty just shrugged her shoulders.

"I think I need to speak with an attorney," Bollinger said with a distraught face.

"You are. Answer the question," Koontz pressed on.

"Ah, yes," Bollinger said with hesitation.

"And not only did she have sex with you, she had sex with a man by the name of Gallagher Simms whom she knocked over a cliff in Santa Barbara. Was this a result of her being off her medication and on some sex pill?" Koontz asked.

Everybody in the courtroom was either stunned by the questioning or in awe of what was going to happen next. Spuds was in a state of mental paralysis as he tried to grasp the reality of what he was hearing.

"I heard about that," Bollinger said sheepishly. "The pills had that effect on her."

"Your Honor. What's the relevance of this questioning?" Spuds objected vociferously.

"It all goes to the state of mind Marty Remy was in leading up to and during the murder of Fabrizio Giacomelli. That she killed him in a sexually charged mental state," Koontz said.

"I assume you can back these accusations with witness testimony, Counselor?" the judge asked.

"Yes, I can," Koontz said as if he had just won the Tour de France and was ready to go again.

"Your Honor, I need to confer with my client. I ask for a recess?" Spuds said almost dejectedly.

"Court's in recess for twenty minutes," the judge said.

Inside the conference room, Spuds asked Marty, "What the fuck was that all about?"

Marty stood silent. Spuds then raised his eyebrows, expecting a response. "He blackmailed me into having sex with him. And yes, I needed something for my dead twat because of the meds I was on. Okay? You satisfied," Marty said in an aggravated tone.

"What about this Gallagher Simms fellow? What happened?" Spuds asked.

"We were about to have sex and he got clumsy and fell off the cliff," Marty said as she was hand gesturing the occurrence.

"Is Gallagher Simms going to testify against you?" Spuds asked.

"No chance. He likes me too much."

"As long as you're giving him sex?"

"That's not fair, Spuds. You don't know what it was like to be on those meds. I needed something," Marty said in defense of her honor.

"Were you taking them that night at Fabrizio's?" Spuds asked.

"You know I didn't do it. But, no, I had stopped taking them back in Santa Barbara. I wanted to clean out my system of all drugs," Marty said.

"Are there going to be any other surprises that I should be aware of?"

"I don't know. But one of my employees was found dead in a wine tank. And Gallagher's wife was killed by a shark," Marty said innocently.

"Are you fucking kidding me, Marty?!" Spuds clamored rhetorically with eyes wide open.

"I was a suspect in her death."

"I think you need a new lawyer. Maybe a whole team of twelve, just to get out of this one."

"You still are going to be my lawyer?" Marty asked.

"Yes. We have Tom Roberts, no matter what," Spuds said.

Linda rushed into the room. "Roberts has disappeared," she said urgently.

"To where?" Spuds asked.

"Outer space. The P.I. lost him," Linda said.

"We have a few days. Hopefully, he finds him. But what about our other guy?"

"He's down in Santa Barbara working on the one gal, Michelle," Linda said.

Marty's stomach turned inside out when she heard the name Michelle. Although if Michelle were implicated in the murder, the prosecution could say that they conspired to kill Fab.

"Get him up here. We need to have Roberts found. Marty, are you hiding anything with this Michelle? Could she have murdered Fabrizio?" Spuds asked.

"No. Why?" Marty asked.

"Did you tell her about him? That you had fallen in love with Fabrizio?" Spuds asked. "She could have been highly jealous, and you weren't aware of it."

"I did say something, but she's been in Santa Barbara working at the store," Marty said.

"Marty, this could mean life in prison. If you know of something, speak up," Spuds said.

"We did fool around. A little," Marty said.

"You had sex together?" Spuds asked. Marty replied with a nod.

The guard then came in and escorted Marty out of the room. "Forget it, have our guy in Santa Barbara get into Michelle's place to see if he can find a ripped pair of black sweatpants. And some hair samples," Spuds said. "We need that exculpatory evidence to get her acquitted." Spuds then left the room. Linda immediately got on her cell phone.

Inside the courtroom, Bollinger was about to take his seat on the stand. "Your Honor, I'm done with the witness. And we call Paul Cooz to the stand."

"Dr. Bollinger, we thank you for your testimony today. I'd recommend you seek counsel. It'd be in your best interest."

Cooz stepped towards the stand, and the judge swore him in.

"Mr. Cooz, I want to thank you for appearing in court today," Bollinger said. Cooz nodded. "Can you spell your full name and tell us where you live?"

"Paul, P.A.U.L., Cooz, C.O.O.Z. I live in Laurel Canyon in Los Angeles," Cooz responded.

"What's your current occupation?" Bollinger asked.

"I'm a private investigator," Cooz said.

"What was your previous occupation and for how long?"

"I was a homicide detective with the Los Feliz Police Department for twenty years. And a patrolman for six."

"During your time as a detective, did you encounter the defendant, Marty Remy?" Koontz asked.

"Yes, several years ago during the investigation of the chef murders in connection with the Ultimate Chef Challenge Show. She was one of our prime suspects in the murders."

"Objection. This is inflammatory. My client was never tried in those murders and was completely exonerated of all charges," Spuds professed.

"Your Honor, I'm trying to establish *modus operandi*—method of operation. Besides, my colleague knows he was the state attorney general at the time when he exonerated Marty Remy," Koontz said.

"Sustained. Please continue," the judge said.

"In your current occupation, as a private investigator, is Marty Remy a suspect in the apparent murder of one of her employees?" Koontz asked.

The courtroom went deadly silent as they anticipated the answer from Cooz.

"Tina St. Clair, an employee of Marty Remy, was found dead in a wine tank at her family vineyard in Santa Barbara County. She was apparently murdered. Marty Remy was questioned by the Santa Barbara County Sheriff's Department. And I was present since I was hired by them to investigate the murder," Cooz said.

"This is highly prejudicial, Your Honor. She has not been charged with any crime related to this apparent murder," Spuds said, knowing Marty was getting baked in the jury's opinion of her.

"Overruled," Judge Wineberg said.

"Your Honor?" Spuds pleaded.

"Jury, can you hear me?" Some nodded. Others agreed with a 'yes.' "Mr. Florez, you might want to have your ears checked?" the judge said. Spuds grinned in humility.

"What evidence do you have that implicates the defendant in the murder of Tina St. Clair?" Koontz asked.

"I have a piece of broken taillight found at the scene of the crime that comes from the same make and model of vehicle as that driven by Marty Remy," Cooz said.

Knowing that the taillight evidence was somewhat flimsy since it could not be ascertained conclusively that it came from Marty's vehicle, Koontz asked, "Other than the piece of evidence, what drew you towards the defendant as a suspect?"

"Other than the chef's murders," Cooz said.

"Objection," Spuds said as he interrupted Cooz's testimony.

"Be careful, Mr. Cooz, you could be held in contempt," the judged warned him. "You may continue."

"As I had Marty under surveillance, she was visited by Dr. Bollinger at her residence. That same night she was visited by a Santa Barbara police officer who was wearing civilian clothes. I just felt that all this was peculiar behavior. That she was manipulating them in some way to cover her tracks in the murder of Tina St. Clair," Cooz said.

"This is all speculation. Your Honor, what he said should be stricken from the record," Spuds said fervently.

"You're right. Jury disregard the last statements by the witness. Counselor, this sounds like some fishing expedition. You need to have a conclusion," the judge said.

"Was the deceased a lesbian?" Koontz asked.

"Yes," Cooz answered.

"Is the defendant bi-sexual?" Koontz asked.

"Relevance?" Spuds objected.

"I'm trying to establish if the defendant and the deceased were involved romantically, therefore providing a motive for the murder," Koontz said.

"I'll allow it," the judge said.

"Yes, Marty Remy is bi-sexual. She and Dominika Slovice, the dominatrix, were lovers. And she had sexually propositioned a woman I was dating," Cooz said as Marty proceeded to interrupt him.

"I never made a pass at Evie Ann!" Marty yelled out, feeling the mounting pressure.

"Ms. Remy, you need to restrain yourself or you'll have to answer to me," the judge said. "Counselor, let's close this witness out."

"I'm done with him. All yours, Spuds," Koontz said as he took his seat.

"Sometime around the middle of April, three years ago when you were on your honeymoon in Maui, did you not break into Marty Remy's perfume store?"

"No," Cooz said.

"You know you're under oath. I don't know if breaking and entering is a crime in Hawaii, but here in California, it is. You could lose your license as a private investigator. Would you like to change your answer?" Spuds asked.

"No."

"You were actually stalking Marty Remy. You were sore because your prime suspect got off. And now you're seeking retribution. Isn't that the case?" Spuds said, laying into Cooz.

"Objection, badgering the witness," Koontz said.

"Overruled," the judge replied.

"No, I'm not looking for revenge. She killed Fabrizio Giacomelli, like she killed Tina St. Clair, like she killed Dominika Slovovice, and like she killed Chef Bubba Arnet…" Cooz said going all out and risking a contempt of court charge and possibly losing his private investigator's license as a result. He wanted Marty in the worse way.

"Honestly, Mr. Cooz. You're in contempt of court. That just cost you a thousand dollars," the judge said tersely. "Unless you would like to spend time in a jail cell? The jury, completely disregard the last statement by the witness."

"I'm done with him," Spuds said.

"Bailiff, please escort Mr. Cooz out of the courtroom so he can pay his fine," the judge said. "I think it's time for lunch. All this excitement has made me hungry. Be back in an hour," she said as she looked at her watch.

Marty was brought to the conference room, so she could have her lunch while a guard stood by. As she ate her chicken Caesar salad and fresh fruit cup, Al Capone appeared across the table from Marty. "Hello, Marty, you enjoyin' your lunch?" Al Capone asked. Marty just nodded. "You should be havin' a nice Delmonico steak and a potato. Hell, you're not paying for it. So, you know where your star man is?" he asked.

Marty mouthed, "No."

"Why you so quiet?" he asked. Marty stuck her thumb out toward the guard. "Ah, he's just a low-level bull. Word is, your guy's in Roswell. I was there once. They got some spicy broads down there." Marty mocked him by shaking her head back and forth as she ate her salad with vigor. She was trying to ignore him because she didn't want the guard to get wind that she was talking to a ghost.

"How come you're not in Alcatraz?" Marty whispered through the side of her mouth when the guard popped his head out of the conference room door.

"I'm on furlough. I come and I go. But you need to get your mouth-piece to get him back up here, so you don't wind up on the Rock. You follow what I'm saying?" Al asked Marty who just made a face as if she had already lost her trial and was headed for a lifetime of imprisonment. "Okay, don't worry, doll face, I'll send some of my boys down there. You keep your chin up." Marty gave a conciliatory smile at Al Capone. "That's my girl," he said as he gave her a smile of his own.

"We call John Abruzzo to the stand," Koontz called out. John stood up and stepped towards the bench. Marty looked over at him. Their eyes met as he passed her table. He had that look as if to say, 'When does it ever end with you?' She knew he was angry at her. John was sworn in and he took his seat.

"Please state your name and spell it for us?" Koontz asked John.

"John Abruzzo. J.O.H.N. A.B.R.U.Z.Z.O.," he said.

"What is your relationship to the defendant, Marty Remy?" Koontz asked.

"I'm her ex-husband," John said.

"Do you have any children?" Koontz asked.

"Yes, a son named Jackie."

"When did you two get a divorce?"

"About two years ago."

"Do you have an arrangement for custody of Jackie?" Koontz asked.

"Yes."

"Can you explain what the arrangement entails?" Koontz asked.

"As part of the custody agreement, a therapist is supposed to verify that she is taking her medications on a regular basis," John said.

"Why such a condition?"

"She suffered emotional and mental trauma as a result of having been abducted while in France several years ago. She had been abused sexually and was drugged during her captivity," John said.

"Did she suffer from schizophrenia as a result of her ordeal?" Koontz asked.

"Objection. That would be privileged information between my client and her doctor," Spuds said.

"I'm attempting to establish the theory that she was emotionally unbalanced during the murder of Fabrizio Giacomelli," Koontz replied.

"Overruled. Mr. Abruzzo, please restrict your answer to a 'yes' or 'no,' " the judge said. "Mr. Koontz, I'll have to limit your line of questioning beyond that extent. Please answer the question, Mr. Abruzzo."

"Yes, she suffered from schizophrenia," John said.

"Was your ex-wife's captor a woman with whom she engaged in sexual activity?" Koontz asked.

"Objection. Relevance?" Spuds asked the judge.

"That's okay. I'll withdraw the question," Koontz said.

"Slip of the tongue, Counselor?" the judge rhetorically asked Koontz.

"Where did you meet your wife?" Koontz asked.

"She applied for work on the Ultimate Chef Challenge Show I produced, and I hired her as my personal assistant."

"That's the show where three of the chefs were murdered during the time your ex-wife worked for you?" Koontz asked.

"Your Honor, that's highly inflammatory," Spuds objected.

"Establishing a fact, Your Honor," Koontz pleaded.

"One of the chefs was murdered by the ex-wife of the witness. One of the other chefs mistakenly ate poison mushrooms and the other chef went missing during a hunting trip. Get your facts straight," Spuds said to Koontz.

"Terrible luck," the judge quietly said as she leaned towards John. "He's right, though. But Mr. Florez, if anyone is going to chastise someone in this courtroom, it's going to be me. Would you like to re-phrase the question, Mr. Koontz?" the judge asked.

"I'll withdraw that one, Your Honor," he replied. "When the Los Feliz Police went to pick up the defendant, your personal assistant, had she disappeared from your production facility?"

"She wasn't there at the time," John answered.

"Where did she go? Wasn't she missing for a week?"

"She was at a monastery in the San Gabriel Mountains," John replied.

"Disguised as a monk?"

"I suppose? I don't know."

"You don't know? You two got married after her sudden disappearance. You two didn't talk about it?" Koontz asked.

"Asked and answered," Spuds said.

"The defendant was still a suspect after she left the monastery and was in the hospital after she suffered a car crash?" Koontz asked.

"Yes," John said.

"That's when she was exonerated by my colleague on all charges by some magical twist of fate where photos appeared out of nowhere of your first ex-wife and Chef Bubba Arnet engaged in explicit sex at his restaurant the night he was murdered?" Koontz asked.

"Yes," John said awkwardly.

"Your Honor, where are we going with this?" Spuds pleaded.

"I'm finished with my questioning," Koontz said. "But I wonder who took those photos?" Koontz asked as he took his seat.

"I did. Raveneitzkya was up to no good," Marty whispered into Spuds' ear as he was about to stand from his seat. Spuds brushed Marty's arm and gave her a reassuring glance as he stood.

"Mr. Abruzzo, did you fall in love with your son's nanny during the time your wife was seeking treatment for her condition as a result of the abduction in France?" Spuds asked.

"She was there. I sought her comfort," John replied.

"You eventually married her?"

"Yes," John said. "Marty had become distant and unavailable."

"Prior to your divorce from Marty, you had her sign the custody agreement while she was still seeking treatment. Did she express reservations about taking the medications that were prescribed to her? Because they were too harsh for her? Because she was more into holistic healing?" Spuds asked.

"The holistic approach wasn't working," John answered.

"Did you feel that way because you were impatient? Because you were eager to divorce her so you could marry your son's nanny?"

John paused for a moment as he stared at Marty. "I loved Marty, but she proved difficult, especially after she came back from France a different woman. She had fallen in love with a ghost. The dominatrix, Dominika Slovovice," he said suddenly. The courtroom went deadly quiet. John looked over at Marty whose eyes began to well up. She knew that he spoke the truth.

"I'm sorry, John," Marty said. Judge Wineberg was caught up in the emotion of the moment and allowed Marty to have her peace.

"Why don't we take a recess?" the judge suggested.

Chapter Twenty-Two

Jim Smoot, Spud's private investigator, a slightly built man, opened Michelle's apartment door with a master key, looked down the first-floor corridor and stepped inside. He made his way through the living into her bedroom. He picked up a scent of tangerine as he browsed the room. He picked up a photo of her that was perched on a bureau and then another one of Marty. He quickly rifled through the bureau looking for anything that was of black cotton. He then went through her closet.

He stepped into the bathroom, picked up a hairbrush, slipped it into a resealable plastic bag and pulled on the brush for some hair samples and then replaced the brush and sealed the bag. He rummaged through a clothes hamper that was half full of undies and a bra and some other articles of clothing. At the bottom of the pile of clothing, he found a black cotton hoodie. He pulled it out and inspected it. On the left sleeve was a hole about a quarter-inch square. He rummaged further and found a matching pair of black sweatpants.

As Jim Smoot slipped back into the living room and was about to leave the apartment, he felt something heavy hit his head and was knocked out cold. Michelle had used a bottle of Silver Eddy Pinot Noir to knock him out. When she had heard the front door open, she hid in the kitchen closet. When she peeked out and saw him leaving with the clothing, she picked up the wine and sneaked up behind him. She quickly taped his mouth shut as well as his wrists, ankles, and legs.

Michelle left her apartment for about an hour. When she came back, she carted a large trunk on a dolly. Jim Smoot was awake and had managed to squirm his way towards the door, which prevented her from opening it fully. She shimmied her way in and then dragged Jim Smoot by the legs away from the door, wheeled the trunk inside and closed the door. She "shushed" him, picked up the wine bottle again and whacked him on the head. This time the bottle broke, and the wine and glass splattered. Smoot was out cold with a mix of bloody red wine and glass shards dripping from his head.

Michelle waited till well after dark, close to 11:00 p.m., before she lifted the trunk and shimmied it on the dolly. She peeked outside her door and wheeled Jim Smoot down the corridor and out the rear entrance of the apartments where her truck was parked. She flipped open the bed of the truck, leaned the trunk on the tailgate and heaved the trunk onto the bed—exerting herself and grunting. She placed the dolly on the bed, closed the tailgate and drove north along the coast.

When she arrived at the Jalama Beach County Park, a multi-usage recreational campground, she shut her lights, drove slowly through the parking lot and made her way onto the beach with her truck. She crept along the sand several miles north to where it was remote. She parked the truck, got out and looked around.

Michelle then pulled out a dirt shovel from the truck and began to dig a hole in the sand four feet wide by five feet long and six feet deep. She climbed up onto the bed of the truck and pushed the trunk onto the sand. She jumped onto the sand and heaved the trunk into the hole. The trunk landed cockeyed about a foot above the surface of the sand. She proceeded to dig along the edge of the trunk to submerge it. She then replaced the sand she dug out of the hole over the trunk.

Michelle grabbed a bucket from the truck, filled it with sea water and poured it over the buried trunk. She then filled any holes that the water made in the sand with dry sand. She repeated the process until she felt satisfied that the trunk would not be exposed over time by the movement of the surf. She got back in her truck and slowly drove southward the way she came. When she reached the coastal road, she drove several miles and then tossed her black hoodie and pants out the window, free of any remorse.

Spuds' primary private investigator, Harry Brandt, tracked down Tom Roberts in Roswell, New Mexico, where he was attending a UFO festival. Brandt entered the convention center with a photo of Tom Roberts in hand. It was quite the odd environment with all types of costumes worn by the convention-goers. Brandt thought it resembled an Ed Wood movie set and worried he'd never find Roberts among the mix. Then he recognized him, albeit with dyed reddish-orange hair, ice blue eyeshade, a metallic looking sweater with large gold epaulets and matching pants. Brandt approached Roberts, who was in the midst of entertaining similarly dressed young women. "Tom Roberts?" Brandt asked.

"It's Major Tom," Roberts said as the girls giggled. "What can I do for you?"

"This has to do with you appearing at Marty Remy's trial," Brandt said as he handed him a summons.

"What's this?" Roberts asked.

"It's a summons."

"Girls, can I hook-up with you later?" Roberts said. One of the girls smiled at Tom with eager wantonness as they stepped away. "When do I have to appear?" he asked.

"Tomorrow. But we'll make it worth your while," Brandt said as he handed him an envelope loaded with five thousand dollars in one-hundred-dollar bills. Roberts thumbed through the cash with eyes wide open.

"You saw another woman that night. Right? We need you to testify stating so. If you do, there's another five thousand in it for you," Brandt said.

"Okay. But how did you know I was there?"

"We just do," Brandt said. "I have a plane ticket for you. If you don't mind, I'd like to accompany you to where you are staying and then we can go to the airport together."

"I'm assuming you'll be with me on the way back to San Francisco?" Roberts asked.

"Yes."

"I think my testimony is worth more than ten grand in light of her situation," Roberts said.

"What's your price?" Brandt asked.

"Fifty thousand."

"Okay," Brandt said after a slight pause.

"You mind if I say goodbye to my friends?" Roberts asked.

"Sure. But, when we get to your hotel room, can you change into some regular clothes?"

"Not your gig, hah? So, how is she?" Roberts asked.

"Marty Remy? She needs your help. That's how she is doing."

Back at the court before it was in session, Linda rushed in and headed straight to the defense table where Marty and Spuds were seated. "Smoot's gone missing. Last time I heard from him was two days ago," Linda said anxiously as she leaned in toward Spuds.

"Fuck," Spuds responded in frustration. "Marty, who the hell is this Michelle girl? What is she capable of?" Spuds asked in a serious tone.

"I don't know," Marty said as she stared into Spuds' eyes. She was just as baffled as he was. But she knew Michelle was capable of what she herself was capable of. *They were a lot alike*, Marty realized.

"Well, at least we have your spaceman, but, I'm going to have you testify. You're going to tell them exactly what happened. This will corroborate his testimony. And hopefully, the jury will believe it all. Okay, Marty?" Spuds said.

"Yes, I want to tell my side of the story. That fucking little bitch, Michelle. I was falling in love with Fabrizio and she took that away from me," Marty said, finally opening up emotionally to all that happened.

"You let it out. But I don't know how we can claim that it was her without her clothing and DNA," Spuds objected.

"We get a warrant," Linda interjected.

"Is there enough probable cause? That's the question," Spuds said.

"No, I'll take care of her. Just get me on the stand," Marty said.

Judge Wineberg then entered the courtroom. "Please rise, the Superior Court of California—County of San Francisco is now in session," the court clerk called out.

"Defense, your first witness?" the judge asked of Spuds.

"We call Tom Roberts to the stand," Spuds said.

Roberts took the stand and after he was sworn in, Spuds asked, "Please state your name and spell it for us?"

"Tom, T.O.M. Roberts, R.O.B.E.R.T.S.," he replied.

"Do you own a business here in town?" Spuds asked.

"Yes, the Hunky Dory Club. It's a small nightclub on Geary Street," Roberts replied.

"Is this where you met the defendant, Marty Remy, for the first time on January twelfth of this year?" Spuds asked.

"Yes," Roberts answered.

"Tell us what transpired that night between you and Marty Remy," Spuds asked.

"She came in around 11:00 that evening. She ordered a drink. She asked if she could look around. In the basement, particularly. The club was a former business, and she was curious, I suppose," Roberts said.

"You're referring to the dominatrix who conducted business there?" Spuds asked.

"Yes," Roberts said.

"What happened after she looked around?"

"I closed the club for the night, and we went upstairs to share some drinks and talk."

"Did you two get involved sexually?" Spuds asked.

"No. I had given her a kiss, but she seemed uninterested. And then she suddenly decided to leave," Roberts replied.

"After she left, did you follow her to Fabrizio Giacomelli's residence on Pfeiffer Street?"

"Yes. She had taken a cab. I drove in my car. But I didn't know who lived there."

"Why did you follow her?"

"I was taken by her. I was hoping maybe I could get to see her again," Roberts said.

"Where were you parked?"

"Across the street from the house," Roberts replied.

"Were you in a position to see the alley leading to the side street off of Pfeiffer?"

"Yes."

"Now, when Marty Remy got out of the cab, did she go to the front door of Fabrizio Giacomelli's residence?" Spuds asked.

"Yes, she rung the bell and waited," Roberts said.

"What happened next?"

"Marty looked like she was texting on her cell phone and that's when I saw someone come from the back alley and trot up the side street," Roberts said.

"What was that person wearing?"

"A dark hoodie and sweatpants."

"What did Marty do after she apparently had used her cell phone to text someone?"

"She walked up the side street towards the back alley," Roberts said.

"What happened then?" Spuds asked.

"I waited about another ten minutes and saw Marty reappear on the side street."

"Was there anyone else on the side street at that time?"

"Yes, a couple who were out walking their dog," Roberts replied.

"Did you follow Marty again?" Spuds asked.

"Yes, to the Regency down in the Embarcadero. And then I went back home."

"When you saw Marty reappear on the side street, did she look like she had killed someone?"

"No."

"Objection. Calls for speculation," Koontz said.

"Sustained. Strike the last response. Any more questions?" the judge asked.

"Not for now," Spuds said and then took his seat.

"Mr. Roberts, were you paid for your testimony today?" Koontz asked.

"No," Roberts replied tersely.

"Hmm. What's your vision?" Koontz asked.

"Perfect. 20/20."

"How would you say the lighting was on the side street by the deceased's home where you saw this phantom person wearing a dark hoodie?" Koontz asked as Spuds was about to object but held back.

"There's actually a streetlamp right where the back alley and the side street intersect. So, I was able to see fairly clearly. Albeit it was at night," Roberts replied.

"Were you stalking the defendant that night?" Koontz asked.

"No, not that I would consider," Roberts replied in embarrassment.

"Then what were you doing? Were you hoping that the defendant would jump in your car, and you would have wild sex?" Koontz said with a grin.

"Your Honor?" Spuds objected.

"Mr. Koontz, you know better. Rephrase, please," the judge said.

Koontz stood there and rubbed his chin in contemplation. "It just seems highly coincidental that you were right outside Fabrizio Giacomelli's home where his murder was being committed," Koontz stated.

"Question?" Spuds asked.

"Are you an intuitive?" Koontz asked sarcastically.

"Badgering the witness," Spuds declared.

"Sustained," the judge said. "Looks like you're running out of questions, Counselor."

Koontz took his seat.

"I thought so," the judge said. "Mr. Florez, do you want to call your next witness, or would you like to recess?"

"Yes, we call Marty Remy to the stand," Spuds said.

The courtroom was attentive and eager for her testimony. The jury watched carefully as Marty, dressed in a dark blue Armand dress suit, took the stand and was sworn in.

"Please state your name for the record," Spuds asked.

"Marty Remy."

"Did you kill Fabrizio Giacomelli?" he asked.

"No," Marty replied assuredly.

"Why is that?" Spuds asked.

"It wasn't me. I was falling in love with him," Marty said.

"Where did you two meet?" Spuds asked.

"At his restaurant," Marty replied and then looked over towards the gallery where Sookie, who waved at Marty, Chef Bubba Arnet, Al

Capone, Robert Morris, and the two Anglin brothers appeared, as well as Didier who was totally naked and high stepping across the courtroom like a Russian soldier. Marty burst out in laughter because she knew Didier was being a clown, and it was working.

"Ms. Remy, is there something you would like to share with us?" the judge asked.

"Ah, no. It's nothing. My apologies," Marty said as she tried to curtail herself. But when Didier bent over and spread his butt cheeks towards the judge, Marty lost all control and howled with laughter. The judge threw a stare of annoyance at Spuds, silently questioning Marty's behavior.

"You need to get control of her," the judge said to Spuds.

"I'm sorry, Your Honor. I have the ability to see the dead, and, well, there's a naked man standing in front of you," Marty said as the gallery was in complete chatter mode.

"Is that right? And what is he doing?" the judge asked in a concerned voice, yet she had an air of condescension about her.

"He's being obscene. Didier, go cook something," Marty said as she let out a chuckle.

"Your Honor. May we have a recess? My client is obviously under a lot of pressure," Spuds pleaded.

"In light of what I have seen and heard in the last several days and this latest incident, I'm ordering that your client go through a complete psychological evaluation. I have serious concerns about her mental well-being," the judge stated.

"Your Honor, I'm completely sane. Believe it or not, Al Capone and the Anglin brothers are here in court. And so is Chef Bubba Arnet and Sookie," Marty said.

"The *stage*," Didier quipped.

"I'm a chef, just like you," Sookie quibbled back.

"Court will be in recess, and we will reconvene in a week after your client's evaluation," the judge said to Spuds as she motioned for him and

Koontz to come toward her. When they both stood in front of her, she leaned over with her hand on her microphone and said succinctly, "Spuds, this better not be a ploy for some late-game insanity defense?"

"I don't know what it is," he returned as he looked Marty in the eyes. She just shrugged her shoulders.

The judge waved the two counselors away as she began to exit the courtroom. "She looked like Angela Jordan up there. What a performance," Koontz said to Spuds as they stepped towards their respective tables. Spuds took a seat, put a hand on his head in frustrated contemplation while the courtroom emptied.

"What is she doing?" Linda asked.

"I have no fucking idea," he said. "Maybe she is crazy?"

"Maybe?" Linda responded sarcastically. "Are you thinking about changing her plea?"

"Let's see what happens with her evaluation," he said. "Still no word from Smoot?"

"No. But do you want to send Brandt there?" Linda asked.

"This is starting to get macabre—as if we stepped into Dante's *Inferno*. She's obviously the killer. But we'll have to contact the Santa Barbara Police and let them know about Smoot's disappearance. And let's hold off on Brandt. I wouldn't want to be responsible for another death."

"What if Marty and Michelle conspired?" Linda asked.

"I don't want to think about that," Spuds replied.

"But you have?" Linda asked.

"Yeah, but Marty is too smart to have exposed herself by taking the cab. We're here to defend her, not prosecute her, Linda," Spuds said. "I'm really concerned about her."

"That she's actually schizophrenic?" Linda asked.

"That and a lifetime in prison," Spuds replied. "That would be hell."

"Imagine what is going inside her head?" Linda said rhetorically.

Chapter Twenty-Three

Marty was escorted into the therapist's office by a guard. He uncuffed her. She then took a seat, and he left the room. Dr. Jenna Brown, a clinical psychiatrist by training, smiled at Marty and said, "Marty, my name is Dr. Brown. Do you know why you are here?"

"To see if I'm crazy or not," Marty replied as a torrential downpour pelted the outside of the medical building.

"That's good. You have a sense of humor. But what a storm we are having," the doctor stated.

"Perfect day to be on the porch in a comfortable chair reading something good," Marty replied.

"Who do you prefer?" Dr. Brown asked.

"Peter Mayle of late," Marty said.

"*A Good Year*," the doctor responded. Marty nodded with a smile of affirmation.

"Marty, you're obviously not having the greatest of years with being on trial. But we have to determine your psychological profile as ordered by Judge Wineberg. I promise you I'll try to make this as painless as possible. Okay?" the doctor remarked to allay any concerns. Marty returned a curt half-smile. "You were treated before for emotional trauma as a result of being abducted?" Dr. Brown asked.

"Yes," Marty said. "In Hawaii several years ago at Alala Holistic."

"Can you give me the specifics that brought you to the clinic?"

"I was very depressed and going through withdrawal from opium," Marty said.

"You had been drugged by your captors?" Dr. Brown asked.

"Yes."

"What other symptoms were you experiencing while you were under treatment?" the doctor asked.

"I encountered Dominika. She was the dominatrix with whom I had my first same-sex affair and who was subsequently murdered," Marty said.

"Did this affair last long?" the doctor probed.

"It was a one-time thing."

"Do you enjoy the sex?"

Marty paused to think about the question and questioned the purpose of the query. "She turned my world upside down in an instant. It was the first time I ever had been with a woman. And she was so exotic," Marty spoke softly.

"Did you have something to do with her death?" the doctor asked.

"No. I had dreamt about her from time to time. But she appeared to me when I was held captive. And then she started to visit with me during the time I was at Alala," Marty said.

"Did she appear real to you?"

"No. She was more of a spirit. But I could feel her presence," Marty said. "And then when I was transferred to a more traditional clinic and put on stronger meds, she stopped appearing."

"But you began to see other spirits later on?" the doctor asked.

"Yes, when I started taking *Amoros*—a sex drug. While I began to wean off my meds, several people who I had known and who had died started showing up," Marty said.

"You had cogent conversations with them?"

"Yes. And for some reason, I was compelled to go to Alcatraz, and I met Al Capone there. He spoke to me. That's when I questioned my own sanity. I decided to go see a clairvoyant who told me I had the same ability."

"As a clairvoyant?"

"Yes. I didn't believe it at first, but after I was introduced to Frank Morris and the Anglin Brothers by Al Capone, men whom I never heard about, I researched who they were. I was amazed that they looked exactly like who I saw," Marty said.

"Maybe you read a book or saw some Alcatraz documentary on them, and you just forgot, and their images were triggered by something?" the doctor probed.

"Unlikely. Big Al, Al Capone, told me that Tom Roberts, one of the witnesses at trial who went missing, was in Roswell, New Mexico. How would I know that unless I actually communicated with his spirit?"

"So, you believe that you can communicate and see these entities?" Dr. Brown asked.

"Absolutely," Marty said emphatically.

"Are there any in the room with us now?" the doctor asked.

"No," Marty said.

"How do they appear?"

"At random. They just appear. Maybe it's subconscious? But they appear and they're real, as spirits," Marty said.

"Are you cognizant that you are on trial for murdering Fabrizio Giacomelli?" the doctor asked, switching tack.

"Yes, of course," Marty replied.

"Have you seen his spirit since his death?"

"No, I have not," Marty said solemnly.

"Did you have anything to do with his death?"

"No. Not directly. It was someone I know who killed him," Marty said.

"How do you know this?"

"I was told by Didier. He's a spirit," Marty said. "He was in the courtroom yesterday," Marty said with a feigned chuckle to hide the pain she felt about Fabrizio. "He's a real character. He was my cousin's boyfriend who was torched by a kitchen fire. He was a chef," Marty said.

"Did you have something to do with his death?" Dr. Brown asked.

"No. There was a gas leak in his kitchen, and he lit a cigarette. And poof, he went up in flames. He couldn't smell the gas because the night before I had kicked him in the nose," Marty said.

"But maybe indirectly you did have something to do with his death?" the doctor probed.

"Never thought of it that way. The night before we were at a chef banquet. I was sitting at the table with him, my cousin and two other women, Sookie and Lorraine. Didier was being sexist, and one thing led to another. Sookie jumped across the table towards Didier and happened to bring me down with her and him. While we were on the ground in a tussle, Didier looked up my dress, and I reacted by shoving my shoe into his nose. So, indirectly, maybe I had something to do with his death because he couldn't smell the gas," Marty said.

"Accidents do happen," the doctor said placatingly. "So, his spirit comes to you? Is he ever angry towards you?"

"No, not at all. He's very entertaining. Especially when he's together with Sookie," Marty said.

"Would you say that these spirits keep you company, or they entertain you in some way?"

"Sometimes and sometimes they annoy me. Especially if I'm taking a shower. I want to be left alone."

"I suppose that would be inappropriate," the doctor stated. "Marty, would you like something to drink? Water or tea?"

"You have green tea?"

Dr. Brown got up poured hot water into some tea cups from a dispenser, dropped two tea bags into the cups and brought them over to a small coffee table next to Marty. The doctor then stepped toward the door, opened it and said to the guard, "Please don't disturb us for an hour. It's very important since it deals with hypnosis." She then closed the door and locked it. She shut the lights off and closed the window shutters, so the room was almost completely dark except for a light that emanated from a small side room. "Did you want some honey for your tea, Marty?" the doctor asked.

"Sure," Marty said in a soft voice. Dr. Brown brought over a squeeze bottle of honey and dropped some into Marty's cup. She put the bottle back and stepped toward the back of Marty's chair.

"Marty, what I would like to do is have you lie down on the couch. It's a gentle relaxation approach so I can probe a little deeper into your condition. Are you okay with that?" the doctor asked. "But please drink your tea first."

Marty knew what Doctor Brown was inferring when she said 'probe' and 'gentle relaxation,' especially after the way she had scanned Marty's body with her *probing* eyes during the session. *Whatever it takes,* she whispered to herself and said, "Sure. Whatever you think can help."

Marty and the doctor quickly sipped their tea in silence. Marty stood up and stepped towards the couch. The doctor shadowed her, extended her hand and eased Marty's dress off her shoulder. "I think it works best with your dress off." Marty acquiesced and slipped out of her dress. The doctor proceeded to caress Marty's shoulders and gently kiss her neck. Marty shuddered, turned towards the doctor and kissed her on the lips. The doctor unhooked Marty's bra as they tenderly caressed each other's lips.

The doctor cupped Marty's breast with one hand and slowly kissed her way towards her areola. Marty moaned softly for effect. The doctor slipped out of her own dress and undid her bra, exposing plump breasts, which Marty paid attention with her tongue as she rubbed the doctor's vagina through her lace panties. The doctor reciprocated by rubbing

Marty's clitoris. As they continued to fondle each other, Marty felt the doctor's heaving breasts against hers and a moist flow from her vagina.

The doctor then eased Marty's panties off while brushing her hand on Marty's firm rear end. The doctor let out a deep moan of delight. She then eased Marty down on the couch in a sitting position, knelt on the floor in front of her and proceeded to indulge in Marty's pussy. Marty moaned softly, partly out of sensation and partly for effect. As Marty gave in to the doctor's whim and desires, she realized how a prostitute must feel while servicing some John—trapped in a world where she was forced into role-playing. It was called survival. She had been in worse situations.

Spuds Florez, the opposing counsel, and Dr. Brown met with Judge Wineberg inside her chambers to review Dr. Brown's psychological assessment of Marty.

"All's I want to know is, is my client schizophrenic?" Spuds asked the doctor.

"Looking for an insanity plea, Spuds? It's a little late for that," Koontz said sarcastically.

"Mr. Koontz, you mind taking off the boxing gloves? Dr. Brown, what are your findings?" the judge asked.

"Marty Remy is not schizophrenic. She suffers from what we call delusional psychosis where she believes that she is clairvoyant. That she can speak and engage with dead spirits," the doctor stated. "Such as Al Capone, Frank Morris and people that she has encountered previously."

"It's like a carnival freak show," Koontz muttered underneath his breath to his co-counsel.

The judge then threw him a stare. "Is she cogent enough to continue to stand trial?" the judge asked.

Randy Shamlian

"Yes, she is. But if this condition is not properly treated with anti-psychotics and therapy, her condition could worsen. I certainly could provide the treatment for her, which I highly recommend since I have had sessions with her," Dr. Brown recommended.

"I'm going to leave it up to Ms. Remy and her counsel whether she wants to seek therapy or not. But in the meantime, when she gets back on the stand, I want her to try to ignore her friends that have crossed over to the other side," the judge said to Spuds.

"I understand," Spuds said with a nod.

"Good. Dr. Brown, I thank you for your services. Now let's see this trial come to a speedy end," Judge Wineberg said.

"Marty, Dr. Brown said you were fine to continue with the trial. But she wants to see you as a patient. Thinks you're delusional," Spuds said to Marty.

"If anyone is delusional, it's her," Marty said with a smirk. "You can believe it or not, I am clairvoyant. How do you think I knew where Tom Roberts was? And how did I know about Michelle?"

"You're no ordinary woman. I'll give you that," Spuds said.

Linda rushed into the courtroom straight toward the defense table. "You won't believe this. The storm we just had exposed a buried trunk on a beach just north of Santa Barbara. And whose body did they find inside? Smoot's. The Santa Barbara Police have Michelle Sloane in custody," Linda said exasperatedly.

"Sorry, Smoot. But we just got our buried treasure," Spuds said as he stepped towards Koontz. "The Santa Barbara Police just found my P.I. dead in some trunk that was buried in the sand. They have a woman in custody whom he was surveilling pertinent to this case. I guarantee the hair sample taken from the clothing that was found at the Fabrizio Giacomelli crime scene will match hers," Spuds said.

222

"What's her motive?" Koontz asked.

"She works for my client. What else? Obsession. I believe Marty can fill you in on that," Spuds said.

"What if they conspired?" Koontz asked.

"She was in love with the guy. It's this other woman, Michelle Sloane. I'm telling you," Spuds pleaded. "The DNA will match and put her at the crime scene."

"It's flimsy," Koontz said.

"You didn't hear it from me. But my P.I. was looking in her apartment for the clothing she wore at the time of the murder. She must have caught him in the act," Spuds said.

"Alright. Let's talk to the judge for an adjournment. That DNA better match or I'll bury your client," Koontz said emphatically as he stepped towards the court clerk. Spuds looked over at Marty and Linda and nodded as he followed Koontz.

Chapter Twenty-Four

Marty was back at her wine store. She was emotionally exhausted from the trial, but she had to get back into it and right the ship that she had been away from for the past several months. Although her father took care of business while she was gone, the volume of business had diminished dramatically due to the gravitas of her trial. Her graffiti-smirched store sign that read: Remy Killer Wine and Spirits didn't help any, either. *Should she continue the business or sell the store and seek out a new venture?* she questioned herself. She decided to build the business back up the best she could and sell it. Since she did not want to waste the opportunity of winning the wine challenge, she thought about becoming a wine broker for high-end wines.

Several employees had quit as a result of her trouble and especially after the arrest of Michelle. Marty felt it best to keep the staff lean and just fill in herself where needed. The financial strain of the trial had put a dent in her savings, so she felt it be best to be prudent till she sold the store. She had the old nightclub building, which she could use as storage and offices for the wine brokerage business. Maybe even lease office space so she could generate cash-flow as she built up the wine broker-age. *She had options,* she speculated. But she was happy to be free from the clutches of the prison system and swore that she would keep it that way.

While she was taking inventory of imported French wines in front of the store, Paul Cooz just happened to drop by for a visit. Marty looked over at him as he approached her. "What is that you want, Cooz?" she asked in an annoyed tone.

"I just wanted to congratulate you on your good fortune. I'm always amazed at your luck," he said.

"What does luck have to do with it? They have their killer," Marty said as she continued to take inventory.

"Yeah, but there's the business of Tina, your other former employee who was killed," Cooz said.

"Unless you're here to buy some wine, I'd suggest you leave. Or would you prefer to deal with my attorney?" Marty suggested.

"You mean Spuds Florez? You two are like a cabal. How many times is he going to assist you in skirting the law? Sooner or later your luck will run out. And when it does, I'll be there," Cooz said.

"Do you mind? I have too much to do to have to deal with your fantasies. I think that's what this is all about. You have some infatuation with me," Marty said as she handed him a bottle of wine. "Here, take this. It's on me. No hard feelings."

Cooz took the bottle and read the label. "Mas de Cadenet Rosé. Nice," he read out loud.

"Goes well with fish. Have a good day," she said.

Cooz placed the bottle on the shelf in front of him and said, "Thanks, but I'll be in touch." And then he stepped away, leaving Marty aggravated and in need of a glass of wine. She grabbed the bottle of Mas de Cadenet and made her way to her office, poured herself a glass and drifted off to Provence.

Later that evening after she closed shop for the day, Marty decided to get a long-overdue massage. As she disrobed, she felt the ease of the massage room envelop her. She lay on the massage table face down and took in some deep breaths. As she lay there, she heard a voice say, "Hey, Marty, you're a bitch!"

"Who's that?" she inquired as she looked up from the table. It was Misty, who was shredded, with pieces of her flesh missing. "Oh, God," she said exasperatedly.

"Where was he when you threw me in the ocean to be bait for the sharks?" Misty said angrily.

"It would have happened sooner or later. Swimming around the water like some minnow waiting to be eaten," Marty said jokingly.

"Maybe you're right. You going to see Gallagher? I think he likes you," Misty said.

"I don't think he's my type—ya know, a surfer dude," Marty said mockingly.

"You're not going to find anyone more loyal," Misty said.

"That's admirable. I'll go see him. On a friendly basis," Marty said and then the massage therapist entered the room.

"Any areas that you would like me to work on?" the massage therapist asked as she ran her hands over Marty's back.

"Yeah, her pussy," Misty said.

Marty let out a laugh and then replied, "My upper neck. I've been under a lot of stress lately."

When Marty arrived at her condo, she carried a bottle of St. Clair Pinot Noir that Tina's mother had brought to the store and left with her father. It was her way of saying that she didn't believe Marty had anything to do with her daughter's murder. At least that's what Marty's father presumed. As Marty relished the wine, she thought of Tina and how much she missed and liked her. She was saddened how Tina had slipped. *The things you wished had happened differently, but that was an accident. Plain and simple.* What happened with Misty was a matter of survival. *She would have met her demise, sooner or later, anyway.*

Marty laughed at what Misty had said about her pussy. At least, she didn't have to deal with angry spirits. *Delusional, hah?* Marty thought about what Dr. Brown had said about her. But she didn't state that she was schizophrenic. Letting the doctor have her way with her worked its magic. They both got what they wanted. Yet after all that happened, there was no more Fabrizio. *He knew how to work my pussy like no other man could,* Marty thought as tears ran down her face.

After a second glass of wine, Marty took her clothes off, slipped into bed and fell fast asleep. She quickly began to dream of Fabrizio and the first night they were together. Her dream turned into a nightmare as she saw him being stabbed to death by Michelle. She tossed and turned and sweated profusely. She then heard a voice call out from the deep. "Marty. Wake up, Marty." A voice that she knew well spoke to her. Marty opened her eyes. Through her blurry vision, she saw Fabrizio at the edge of the bed.

"Fabrizio, what are you doing here?" Marty asked groggily.

"I've missed you," he said. Marty pulled the sheets to the side. Fabrizio entered the bed, and they began to make passionate love.

When Marty awoke the next day, Fabrizio was gone, yet she was totally naked. She questioned herself if she had been dreaming about Fabrizio, yet it felt real to her. She got up and took a shower, all the while feeling Fabrizio's presence. She realized that carrying on sexually with a spirit couldn't be a good thing. She needed to preserve a clear state of mind, keep the spirits at a certain distance so as not to confuse reality with a realm that, although not imaginary, could confuse her perception of the everyday world.

After the shower, Marty got dressed for the day at work and stepped into the kitchen. Didier and Sookie were sitting at the kitchen table drinking coffee and eating croissants. "Good morning, Marty," Didier said with a full mouth.

"Great. Good morning, you two," Marty said as she made some coffee.

"Good to have you back, Marty," Sookie swooned.

"Oh yes, it's good to be back," Marty said. "How come you're not over in Nice somewhere? Like maybe visiting with Lorraine?"

"She wouldn't understand," Sookie replied. "She doesn't have the frame of mind."

"Too self-obsessed," Marty said.

"Mmm, but what a pair of breasts she has," Didier said as he gesticulated.

"*Cachon!*" Sookie yelled out

"He's right. She does have some big boobs," Marty offered up.

"You would know. You two were lovers," Sookie objected.

"To be a fly on the wall for that," Didier fantasized.

"Your penis should have gone up in flames," Sookie said, which prompted Marty to laugh.

"Don't laugh, it did," Didier said sadly. "Especially with the rubber stuck to it."

"Oww, that had to hurt," Marty said as she winced just thinking about how that must have felt for Didier.

"It happened so fast, ya know, like poof," Didier replied.

"Before I go, I have a question. Why is it that you two are always paired up when you visit with me?" Marty asked.

"I know, because we remind you of the *Cote d'Azur*. Why else?" Sookie said.

"You're right. I really wanted to set up my perfume business there. I love the place," she said. "I'll see you guys later," Marty said walking toward the front door.

"I worry about her," Didier said.

"Me too," Sookie replied.

Marty wasted no time with her new venture. She called an architect to design her new offices, setting an appointment for later that day. In the meantime, she decided to call Michelle Sloane's father to not only settle affairs about Michelle but speak to him about the wine collection she had heard about through his daughter. She found his number on Michelle's employment application. "Sloane Investments, how can I help you?" the receptionist answered.

"This is Marty Remy, could I speak to Mr. Sloane, please," Marty said.

The receptionist paused a moment and then responded, "I'll see if he is in."

After about a minute, Mr. Sloane picked up the phone. "Yes, what is it I can do for you? I'm awfully busy," he asked almost reluctantly.

"I'm sorry about your daughter. Actually, I am not since she killed someone close to me and I was locked up because of her," Marty said.

"Well, she's in jail now. And if it matters, I apologize for the troubles you had to go through."

"I appreciate that, Mr. Sloane. But I'm calling about your wine collection. I would be curious in seeing what you have and maybe you would be interested in parting with some of your vintages. Maybe we could meet over dinner?"

"I don't think it's such a good time," Sloane said.

"Are you paying for Michelle's trials?"

"What does that have to do with anything?" he asked bitterly.

"I'm sure it's costing you plenty. As it cost me during my trial," Marty responded.

"Well, you are right about that."

"It's only wine," Marty said, attempting to reach his sensibilities.

"So you say."

"Just look at it as a goodwill gesture considering what I had to go through," Marty said.

"Well, I guess I could do that," Sloane replied.

"Good, how about 7:00 tonight at Yum Yum's?"

"Fine," he said and hung up.

Marty observed a professionally dressed man approach the table where she was seated. He looked stressed. "Ms. Remy? Henry Sloane," he said as he stuck his hand out for Marty to shake.

Marty shook it while smiling curtly. "Thank you for coming," she said. "You look like you could use a drink."

Sloane took a seat opposite her and replied, "Yes, a few."

"How is she?" Marty asked as she waved over a server.

"You know she's not well—mentally, that is," he said with a distant look as if his mind was elsewhere. The server stopped by the table. "What are you drinking?" Sloane asked Marty.

"A Brenny Walsh Pinot," she replied.

"I'll have the same. Bring a whole bottle," Sloane said to the server. "Ms. Remy…" he said when Marty interrupted him.

"Call me Marty."

"Marty, I just want to say I'm sorry about what happened to you. I feel responsible because I know I should have done more for Michelle. She had difficulties growing up, but this latest with murdering two people. I had no idea she was capable of that," he said in embarrassment.

"The mind is an intricate machine. It's prone to malfunction. I've had my own difficulties," Marty said. "Sort of runs in the family."

"I see," he replied. "So, you understand?"

"In more ways than you can imagine," Marty said.

"Are you okay?"

"I'll be okay. The best catharsis is to keep busy. Keep your mind occupied with what you're passionate about and try not to focus on too many problems. At least for me, that works," Marty said.

"We share a passion," he said as the server came by with the bottle of Pinot. The server showcased the bottle, opened it and poured a taster. "That's fine, you can fill the glass," Sloane said to the server.

"I'm eager to see your wine cellar," Marty said as she and Sloane lifted their wine glasses. "*Salut*."

"Cheers," Sloane said half-heartedly. "My collection is pretty impressive."

"How many bottles?" Marty asked.

"The question is, what's its total value?" Sloane replied. "Marty, I work with several brokers worldwide who have impeccable reputations. You're a relative newcomer. I normally wouldn't work with someone like you. No slight intended, but I do feel like I owe you."

"I fully understand."

"I'm not guaranteeing anything, but I'm willing to move a portion of my collection. If you can broker the right price, then we can do business," Sloane said. "There's a lot of shady characters out there. And nothing moves without funds that are secure and in place."

"Do you ever make deals strictly in cash?"

"From time to time, but I don't personally get my hands dirty. Too risky," Sloane said. "Why the question of cash?"

"Just in case I have buyers who want to transact in paper," Marty replied.

"Do you have your own security?" Sloane asked. "Because if you don't, I do."

"That's good to know."

"Nice choice of wine by the way," Sloane said.

"One of my favorites," Marty said as Sloane took a good glance at Marty, not only sizing her up, but noticing how attractive she was. Marty, in turn, got a sense that she was dealing with a sophisticated and savvy man.

***

Marty followed Sloane to his estate that was nestled in the hills above Santa Barbara. Short of a security guard, the two-acre compound was secured by high walls and a remote gate. Marty parked in front of the Spanish Revival home that was split on various levels and had views of the Pacific Ocean and the coast. The sun was just setting, and Marty got a glimpse of the sprawling vista. Sloane had parked his car in the garage and appeared moments later. "So, what do you think?" he asked.

"I'm in awe. It's incredible," she responded gleefully.

"Caught the sunset just in time," he said as they walked through a courtyard that was brightly colored with an array of rose-looking camellias, violet-bright anemones, milk-white Arum lilies and the lemon-yellow daffodils.

"You must have a wife?" Marty asked.

"No. Just a very good gardener," he responded as he keyed in numbers on an alarm system keypad. He unlocked the door. "My wife's been gone for a couple of years now."

"Why would she leave this?" Marty asked as they entered the foyer.

"She's in an institution."

"I'm so sorry. I didn't mean to imply anything."

"Don't worry, Marty. You didn't know," Sloane said. "I think that's where Michelle gets it from."

"That's where I get it from. My mother," Marty said with a hint of sarcasm.

"You seem pretty normal," Sloane said as they stepped towards a hallway that spiraled downward to a lower level.

"What's normal?" Marty said rhetorically. "This is awesome. When was it built?"

"1926," Sloane replied as they stepped towards a polished steel door with a windowpane that was situated at eye-level. Sloane plugged in some numbers on a keypad that unlocked the door to his wine cellar, which was temperature and humidity controlled. "After you," he said to Marty. They stepped inside a massive cellar. Wooden racking covered the walls. Each slot held a bottle of wine that was perched so you could read the label. In the center was a long island that had cabinets on either side. "On the left side is Old World. On the right is New World."

"Now I know how Columbus must have felt when he landed on Hispaniola," Marty said. "Wow!"

"This is the largest private collection in the Western Hemisphere. Few people have visited this cellar. So, I guess, consider yourself lucky," Sloane said proudly.

"It's an honor," Marty said. "Oh, my God, how many Richebourgs do you have? You have a Romanee-Conti Grand Cru Pinot Noir 1983?" Marty cried out as she read the wine label.

"Several," Sloane said as he took in Marty's excitement while she continued to browse the cellar like a child in a candy store for the first time. Sloane pulled a 1998 Domaine Jean Grivot Richebourg off a rack, placed it on the island, pulled out two wine glasses and an opener and proceeded to open the wine. He let it breathe some before pouring the wine in the glasses as Marty enthusiastically pranced her way through the cellar. Sloane grabbed the wine glasses, stepped toward Marty and handed her one.

Marty gazed into Sloane's eyes. Sloane was immediately taken by her sparkling cobalt-blue eyes. He could have kissed her then and there, but he let her sniff the wine first. "Berries, cherry liqueur, white pepper and Asian five spice. Wonderful." She then sipped, swirled and gurgled. "Um, leather, earth and truffle."

"Maybe I should have let it breathe some more?" Sloane said.

"Yes, I agree. But it's still a fabulous wine."

"I just wanted to celebrate our new friendship. Considering the circumstances."

Marty felt the flush from the wine. But maybe it was the empathy mixed with a certain loneliness coming from Henry. She approached him and kissed him on the lips.

"What was that for?" he asked softly.

"I felt like I needed to do that," Marty said. Sloane returned the kiss as he pressed his body against hers. He quickly removed her panties and caressed her gluteal cleft. Marty moaned hot breath in his ear as she lay back on the island. Sloane undid his pants and underwear and slid his penis inside her. Marty panted as Sloane motioned back and forth with closed eyes. He was so excited that he didn't hear his daughter sneak up behind him. She cold cocked him on the head, knocking him out right on top of Marty.

"I can't believe it. Fucking my father," Michelle cried out as Sloane fell to the ground.

Marty was startled at the sound of Michelle's voice. "What are you doing?"

"Oh God, I want to kill you both. But I love you too much," Michelle said as she approached Marty, wanting to kiss her. Marty swiftly moved to the side, avoiding the contact with Michelle.

"What are you doing? I escaped for you," Michelle moaned.

"You're fucking insane, Michelle," Marty said as she pulled up her undies and then bent down towards Sloane to check on his condition. "You could have killed him."

"He'll live," Michelle said flippantly.

"They'll catch you. Sooner or later, they'll catch you," Marty said.

"No, they won't. Because you and I are going to Costa Rica," Michelle said.

"Like hell we are. You are so delusional right now. You have no clue. It costs money to live down there," Marty said.

"My father has plenty of money in his safe."

"How are you going to get there? They'll be looking for you everywhere. And besides, how did you break out of jail? No, that's okay. You definitely tricked some female guard into thinking you loved her."

"You know me well," Michelle said with a smirk.

"I'm sure she'll be paying the price," Marty said.

"Help me get him up. I need him to get into his safe," Michelle said as she bent down to lift Sloane up. "Were you enjoying yourself?" Michelle angrily asked as she and Marty lifted Sloane up. The man was slowly coming to.

"I don't owe you anything. You made my life a living hell. Besides, you killed the one man I truly loved," Marty said with Sloane between her and Michelle.

"You just loved his cock. I'm surprised, though, that you would, given the way you made love to me," Michelle said.

"It was the Amoros."

"You could have fooled me," Michelle said. "Hey, Dad, we need to get into your safe."

Sloane looked at his daughter with blurry eyes. "Michelle, what are you doing here?" he asked groggily.

"I need some money."

"I only have about ten thousand. Most of it's in Catalina," he said.

"Catalina?! I don't have time to go there. Why?" Michelle cried out. "Fuck it, we're going to Catalina."

"I'm not going," Marty said sternly.

"I have this gun. You're going," Michelle said. "Grab some of those bottles. We're going to make this a party." Michelle pointed the gun at the bottles.

"Michelle, what are you doing this for?" Sloane asked.

"The other option would be to spend a lifetime in jail. You have to ask?" Michelle said. "Let's go."

The three entered Sloane's master bedroom. "Open it up. Please, Dad," Michelle said, imploring her father.

"Why did you have to hit me? I've always been there for you," Sloane whined.

"I'm sorry, it's just that you were fucking my girlfriend," Michelle responded.

"I'm not your girlfriend!" Marty yelled.

"Oh, yes you are," Michelle said with raised eyebrows as she held up the gun.

Sloane opened his floor safe that was near the foot of his bed and pulled out a bundle of bills. He held it up to Michelle. "This is all that's here."

"What happened to the rest of it?" she asked.

"I used it to pay for the attorneys you desperately needed," Sloane said.

"You know I love you. If you don't mind, can you step in the bathroom? I have to take care of some business," Michelle said as her father complied and shut the door behind him. "Take your panties off," Michelle said to Marty as she took off the jeans and t-shirt she was wearing. Marty complied with Michelle's request. She had no other option without risking being shot, knowing how crazy Michelle had turned out to be. "That's a good girl. Now lie down on the bed. And spread your legs."

"You didn't get any in jail?" Marty asked sarcastically.

"Yeah, I was chased down by some gimpy dyke who had it out for you," Michelle said as she mounted Marty and began to tribble her with her vagina. Michelle moaned, "I missed you so much."

"I didn't," Marty said.

"Why do you have to spoil it?" Michelle asked as she began to climax. "Oh, oh, oh," she cooed. "Why did you have to ruin my life?" Michelle complained as she quickly got off Marty and began to put on her clothes. "Get yourself dressed."

After Michelle had Marty gather some food supplies, she, Marty and Sloane drove to the marina where Sloane's eighty-foot Nor-Tech power yacht was docked. They boarded the yacht. Sloane primed the engine and prepared the craft for the hundred-mile trek to Catalina. "Michelle, you know my security will figure out where we are," Sloane said.

"By sunrise, I'll be gone," Michelle replied.

"In this? The Coast Guard will have you before you get past San Diego."

"I have another plan," she said.

"What's that?" Sloane asked.

"Come on, Dad. I'm your daughter. Give me some credit," she replied. Her plan was to get into Mexico and lay low, traveling through its interior while heading south toward Central America and Costa Rica.

After twenty minutes, they finally hoisted off. At a top speed of sixty miles an hour, it took them almost two hours to reach Catalina Island where Sloane had a private dock that led to a small bungalow on the south side of the island near Avalon. The Catalina Casino, which reminded Marty of a squat Coit Tower in San Francisco with its art deco design, was in their sights as they neared Avalon. It was brightly lit. Marty forgot her troubles with Michelle for a brief moment, enjoying the ocean breeze and Catalina's famous landmark. They continued in a northerly direction along the coastline until they reached the private dock.

Inside the bungalow, Sloane opened a false wall in one of the back rooms where an old, black-painted combination safe had a gold Wells

Fargo & Co. Bank est. 1857 legend inscribed on its door. He dialed the combination and opened the door. He quickly pulled out a 9mm Smith and Wesson pistol and pointed it at Michelle. "Alright, put it down, Michelle," he said firmly. Michelle shot at him. She hit him in the shoulder, throwing him back against the safe. "Christ," he said as he winced in pain.

"Drop it or I'll shoot you again," she barked at him. Marty looked on in horror. Sloane complied, and then picked up the pistol. "Move," she said to him and grabbed a briefcase. She opened it, holding it against her knee, looked at the cash, and then shut it. "We're out of here," Michelle said grimly.

"What are you going to do with your father? He needs a doctor," Marty asked with concern for Sloane.

"You have bandages and peroxide?" Michelle asked her father.

"There's a first-aid kit in the kitchen," he said.

"Marty, go get it," Michelle said. "Let's go, Dad," Michelle commanded, gesturing with the gun. They stepped in the living room. Marty went into the kitchen.

"Where is it?" Marty called out.

"In the cabinet by the refrigerator," Sloane said, throwing his voice towards Marty.

"Hurry up," Michelle barked at Marty. When Marty didn't return, Michelle stepped towards the kitchen while holding the gun on her father. She saw the back door open, and Marty gone. "Fuck!" she yelled out. Michelle grabbed the briefcase, a flashlight from a kitchen drawer and ran out the back door after her.

It was pitch black outside. "Where the fuck is she?!" she called out in the dark while scanning the bushes with the flashlight. She followed a path that ran along the beach. Michelle flashed the light on the path. She followed footprints that she assumed were Marty's. Marty hid behind a boulder not more than twenty yards away. When Michelle got to the boulder, she flashed the light at it. Marty ran into the bushes. Michelle shot at her. Marty tripped and fell over a ledge that ran down to the beach. She hit her head against rocks and was out cold.

Marty was escorted by a prison guard onto the ramp that led to cell block D at Alcatraz Prison. "Well, hello, doll face. I knew I'd be seeing you sometime soon," Al Capone said with a smirk.

Marty stepped towards his cell and hand-motioned him to come closer. She then whispered in his ear as smooth as a well-aged rye whiskey, "I've already planned my escape off the Rock."

Big Al raised his eyebrows as if to say, *I'm impressed, but I'd like to see you pull that one off.*

Marty winked back at him. Escorted by the prison guard, she continued down the cell block, shuffling her feet with a distinct rattling of the leg irons.

"Get up, Marty," Michelle said as she pulled at Marty's dress. Marty looked up at Michelle in a haze. "Get up, we have to go," Michelle said as she assisted Marty to her feet. Marty wiped the sand from the side of her face that was moist with fresh blood. They climbed back up the ridge towards the path and then back towards the bungalow.

"What about your father?" Marty asked dazedly as she stumbled toward the speed boat.

"He'll be fine," Michelle said as they stepped onto the boat, started it up and left the dock.

Chapter Twenty-Five

Michelle docked the speedboat at a Marina in Rosarita, Mexico, under rainy skies. She knew that her father's security probably had a bead on her whereabouts knowing that the speedboat and the briefcase had a GPS finder. So, she and Marty headed to the nearest bodega and purchased some tortas to eat and a carry bag. She filled the carry bag with the cash and quickly got rid of the briefcase. She and Marty then hopped a bus heading south.

"How long you think this is going to last? I'm sure the Mexican authorities will get word about you. We also don't have any passports. And as soon as I get a chance, I'll be gone," Marty said as Michelle devoured a beef torta.

"These are really good. You should try one," Michelle said, oblivious to what Marty had just said.

"Are you even here? Hello, earth to Michelle," Marty quipped.

"Don't worry; we have cash. We'll buy some passports. What's the problem?" Michelle finally responded to Marty's concerns.

"You have a major flaw in your thinking. I know a woman in France who was just like you. She's serving a twenty-five-year sentence in some dank prison cell," Marty said.

"I read about her. She was your lover," Michelle said excitedly.

"It was by force. Just like you're doing now. As if I'm some *thing* that you can possess. And what makes you think I would ever be with you after what you have done?" Marty questioned Michelle angrily. A Mexican peasant woman with her young daughter sitting across from Marty and Michelle kept looking over at them.

Michelle turned to the lady and asked angrily, "*Curioso?*" And then back to Marty, "Like you're some nun who is as pure as the driven snow? Come on, Marty. I know what you were up to in Los Feliz with those chefs. I followed the stories in the news. Didn't that detective Cooz quit the police force because they arrested some other woman and let you go?" Michelle asked fervently.

"Raveneiztkya. She was a bad woman," Marty responded as the rain turned into a torrential downpour.

"So, what are you saying? That it was actually you?" Michelle asked.

"Let's put it this way. There are people out there who deserve to die. They do terrible things. Unlike Fabrizio whose only crime was being innocent. You didn't have to kill him," Marty said sadly.

"I was upset that you had fallen in love with him," Michelle responded.

"I think that you were spoiled rotten as a child. When you don't get what you want, you lash out," Marty said. "That's not a pretty attribute."

"Nobody's perfect in this world," Michelle said humbly. The road became very muddy with the heavy rains. The bus driver didn't slow down considering the conditions of the road, even when the road veered to the right where conditions got very slippery. When a car lost control in the other lane, heading north, it veered toward the bus. The bus driver tried to avoid the car by steering to the right, but he didn't have enough room, lost control and went straight down a ravine, which caused the bus to tip over its side. The occupants, their baggage, drinks, and belongings tumbled about. By the time the bus stopped moving, the occupants of the bus were moaning in pain. The bus smoked from the engine and the rain continued to pour.

Marty gingerly crawled towards Michelle, who was not moving. Her head was limp and to the side. Blood poured slightly from her nose and eye sockets. Marty called out to her and then checked her pulse. There was none. She caressed Michelle's head and looked for life, but it was gone. Marty attempted CPR, although she was battered and bruised, but got no response from Michelle. The world around Marty stopped as she tried to revive Michelle. She was unsuccessful. Michelle was dead. Marty assisted the woman and her child out the back door of the bus. Above on the street, several people watched as another came down the ravine to help. Marty tried to assist others. Some were unconscious. A few were dead. Others she was able to help. She grabbed the carry bag of money and crawled out of the bus.

Marty assisted those needing help up the ravine. Traffic had stopped, but not the rain. It poured even harder. Marty grabbed a bundle of hundreds and gave it to the woman and her child who sat next to them. The woman hugged Marty, partly out of grief and partly out of gratitude. After about a half an hour of waiting in the downpour, the local police and emergency services arrived. Marty was taken to an Ensenada clinic where she was checked out for any concussion, bone breaks and internal damage to her body. She was then released after they bandaged her bruised arm and head. She called Sloane to advise him of his daughter's death. He was somber, yet stern. She made the arrangements for Michelle's body to be returned to Santa Barbara. That she would do, she told Sloane, for which he was grateful.

Marty needed a drink after what she had been through, so she took a cab and was taken to one of the beach resorts where she sat at the bar and had one of their house margaritas made with tequila, Gran Marnier and fresh lime juice. Marty was delighted with the cocktail and began to feel at ease for the first time since her ordeal in San Francisco. "Looks like you're a little banged up," the bartender said as she leaned over the bar towards Marty.

"Yeah, just a little. Bus accident," Marty replied with a hint of sadness in her voice.

The bartender, who was an American woman with an earthy sun-shiny quality, Marty felt, grew friendly with her as she mixed Marty another margarita. "Well, this should help," the bartender said as she placed another drink in front of Marty. What Marty didn't realize was that the bartender spiked that drink and the third one with a barbiturate after getting a peek at the cash inside the travel bag Marty was carrying when Marty paid the bar tab.

When Marty stood up after deciding to go back to the speedboat, which was how she was going to travel back to Santa Barbara, she quickly realized how very inebriated she was and sat back down on the bar stool. "Maybe you had one too many?" the bartender asked.

"Woo, I think so," Marty replied and thought it best that she spend the night at the resort. "I think I'll get a room," Marty slurred as she cautiously stood up and wobbled. The bartender quickly made her way from behind the bar and assisted Marty towards the front desk. The bartender veered Marty down a short hallway to an exit where Marty was placed into an older Dodge van with the bag of cash. The van sped away. The bartender went back inside to continue her duties.

"Are you a cab driver? I didn't order a cab," Marty said, sounding like a drunken sailor. "Let me out," she called to the driver who had long, sun-bleached blond hair. He turned toward her and placed a pair of handcuffs around her wrists.

"Don't worry. Just sit back and everything will be alright," he said as he drove.

"Don't worry? I've just been kidnapped," Marty said sarcastically. "She drugged me, didn't she?" Marty asked, knowing exactly what had happened. She had gotten sloppy with the money.

"Do me a favor. Just stop talking," the driver said.

"Is that what you do down here, scam people out of their money?" Marty asked in a slurred voice.

The driver "shushed" Marty as she slowly fell out while leaning over onto the back seat of the van.

After a twenty-minute drive outside of the city, the van drove down a dirt road towards an unfinished A-frame house. The driver parked the van, pulled Marty and the money bag out, slung the passed-out Marty over his shoulder and entered the house. He stepped down some stairs towards the basement and lay Marty on a cot in a caged room. He stepped outside the room and locked the door with a chain and key lock.

Marty fell into a deep sleep. She found herself in the bus she and Michelle had been in. Around her were the passengers, zombie-like, crawling towards her and pawing at her. Michelle, who was dead, opened her eyes suddenly, which startled Marty. She began to squirm away, feeling anxiety as she twitched in her sleep. She pulled herself out of the bus. It was dark outside, and she was surrounded by a canopy of foliage. Night noises of whooping birds and growling mountain lions invaded her senses. Tree limbs shook in front of her, whisking against her face. She heard footsteps approach and then she began to run through the brush.

Marty woke to two men speaking Spanish and a flashlight probing into her eyes. "*Muy bonita. Demasiado Viejo aunque,*" a Mexican man said.

"Are you sure, man?" the long-haired blond man asked.

"*Chikas,*" the Mexican replied.

"Okay," the other man said in disappointment and then they ascended the stairs.

Later, in the middle of the night, Marty was dragged out of the caged room by the blond-haired man and brought back in the van. "Where are you taking me?" she asked in a more cogent voice than earlier.

"Don't worry. You'll be fine," the bartender spoke from the passenger seat.

"So, the money wasn't enough? You were going to sell me off?" Marty asked indignantly.

Neither the blond-haired man nor the bartender said anything.

"You know what they call that? Greed," Marty said.

The bartender leaned back toward Marty and slapped her in the face. "Now, shut up or we'll find someone who will pay for you."

Marty rubbed the side of her face. "Oh, and by the way. You say anything to anybody about us, we will hunt you down and they'll never see you again. Do you understand?"

Twenty minutes later, the van pulled off to the side of a dark and desolate road. "Give me your hands," the bartender barked at Marty, who complied. The bartender unlocked Marty's handcuffs, got out of the van and pulled Marty outside. The bartender stepped back inside the van, and they sped away, leaving a trail of dust behind them.

Marty stood there, still a little groggy, and pondered her next move. She plodded down the darkened road with not a car in sight for at least an hour. She then noticed house lights in the distance and steered her way towards them. But before she could reach the house, the van pulled up beside her, the bartender got out and shoved Marty inside.

"You change your mind?" Marty angrily asked.

"Yeah, greed got the better of us," the bartender replied. "But we know who you are."

"Who's that?" Marty smartly replied.

"Seems like you're a bit of a celebrity. But what's more important is that you have more than the two hundred thousand you had on you," the bartender said.

"That was stolen money that I was returning," Marty stated.

"Likely story," the bartender responded.

"I guess you didn't read the news. The woman who murdered the man I was accused of murdering broke out of jail, abducted me and stole the money I had on me from her father."

"So what were you doing in Mexico?" the bartender asked.

Randy Shamlian

"Michelle, this woman, had some fantasy that I was in love with her. She had me at gunpoint. We were in a bus crash, and she died."

"Lucky for you," the bartender said.

"Not so. Now you have me. So, you're looking for a payout in return for me?"

"Exactly," the bartender said.

"I don't have much. The trial in San Francisco tapped me out," Marty said.

"I told you it would be a waste of time coming back for her," the blond-haired man interjected. "We should let her go."

"Brian, just shut up. She has money or has access to money," the bartender said.

"You should listen to your man. Besides, you wouldn't want to get caught for your other activities. You know, trafficking in humans. That's why you abducted me," Marty stated.

The bartender whaled off and smacked Marty in the face. "Shut up! You're too smart for your own good." She hit Marty several more times.

"Stop it. Leave her alone," the blond-haired man called out.

"Are you taking a liking to her?" the bartender asked angrily.

"We have the money. Just let her go," the blond-haired man said.

Between the resistance she got from her boyfriend and the reality of what Marty said, the bartender realized that Marty was more trouble than she was worth, even if they could somehow get a ransom for her. She heard in her head the line her mother used to say, *A bird in the hand is worth two in the bush,* picked up a can of dog food that was on the floor next to her and smashed it across Marty's head. Marty keeled over on the side of the seat with blood trickling from the side of her temple.

"What the hell did you do that for?" the blond-haired man asked as he pulled over to the side of the road and looked back at Marty. "She better not be dead."

The bartender opened the side of the van, dragged Marty outside and then kicked her in the belly. "Bitch," she yelled and got back in the van. "Drive!" she commanded her boyfriend. Just then the bartender's cell phone rang. She picked it from the console, looked at who was calling and answered it. "Yes?" she asked eagerly and then paused. "Yes, we have her," she responded to the question from the other end. She paused again to listen to the caller. "Right away. We'll be there in less than an hour," the bartender said firmly and ended the call. "Turn around. It was Rosa Rita. She wants the bitch." The van then made a sharp U-turn.

About the Author

Randy Shamlian wrote a culinary memoir, *A Slice of Apple Pie*, that is often times tongue-in-cheek about his life growing up in New Jersey and California and his exposure to a variety of cultural foods, which influenced his career choices as a baker, pastry chef and business owner. He explores his life choices that he made with an occasional blunder, yet it was baking that was his muse to which he created a wholesale cake company, won several apple pie contests and was a pastry chef for one of America's premier chefs.

He is a graduate of the University of Massachusetts at Amherst where his interest in screenwriting took hold after writing "Lincoln Shivered," a "what if" story about Abraham Lincoln and that fated night at the Ford's Theater. Shamlian went on to develop the screenwriting craft while honing his ability to create intriguing stories, characters with depth and fluid dialogue, which lead him into novel writing. His first novel, *Deadly Recipe*, is a dark fiction story with a humorous bent that was originally flushed out from a screenplay. It is easy to say that Shamlian has a knack for sinister prose. A trilogy is in the works.

Now Available!

IVAN BLAKE'S

THE MORTSAFEMAN TRILOGY
BOOKS 1 - 2

For more information
visit: www.SpeakingVolumes.us

Now Available!

CHRIS JORDAN'S

RANDALL SHANE
SUSPENSE / THRILLERS

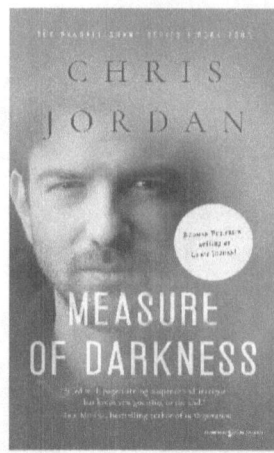 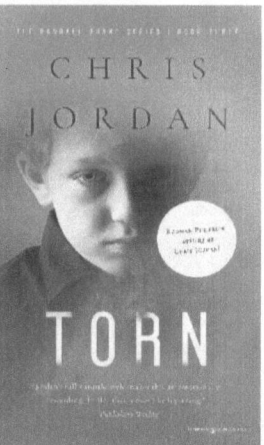

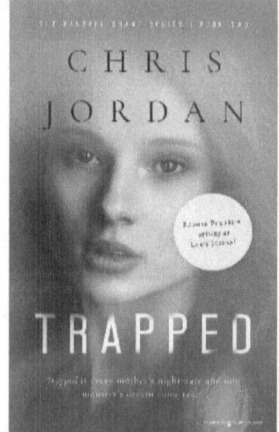 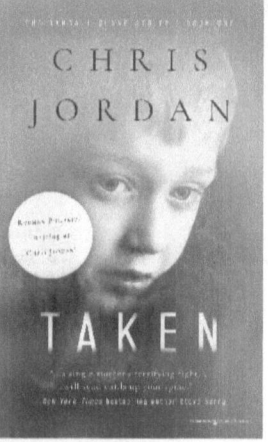

For more information
visit: www.SpeakingVolumes.us

www.ingramcontent.com/pod-product-compliance
Lightning Source LLC
Chambersburg PA
CBHW030500260626
47157CB00014B/1105